If I Die Today

If I Die Today

N. L. Collier

Copyright © 2021 N. L. Collier
The moral right of the author has been asserted.

Apart from any fair dealing for the purposes of research or private study, or criticism or review, as permitted under the Copyright, Designs and Patents Act 1988, this publication may only be reproduced, stored or transmitted, in any form or by any means, with the prior permission in writing of the publishers, or in the case of reprographic reproduction in accordance with the terms of licences issued by the Copyright Licensing Agency. Enquiries concerning reproduction outside those terms should be sent to the publishers.

This is a work of fiction. Names, characters, businesses, places, events and incidents are either the products of the author's imagination or used in a fictitious manner. Any resemblance to actual persons, living or dead, or actual events is purely coincidental.

Matador
9 Priory Business Park,
Wistow Road, Kibworth Beauchamp,
Leicestershire. LE8 0RX
Tel: 0116 279 2299
Email: books@troubador.co.uk
Web: www.troubador.co.uk/matador
Twitter: @matadorbooks

ISBN 978 1800464 001

British Library Cataloguing in Publication Data.
A catalogue record for this book is available from the British Library.

Printed and bound in Great Britain by 4edge Limited
Typeset in 11.5pt Aldine401 BT by Troubador Publishing Ltd, Leicester, UK

Matador is an imprint of Troubador Publishing Ltd

„Und sterbe ich noch heute
So bin ich morgen tot
Dann begraben mich die Leute
Um's Morgenrot."

"And if I die today, then
Tomorrow I'll be dead
And they'll put me in the grave, when
The dawn turns red."

(Drei Lilien, Deutsches Soldatenlied)   *(Three Lilies, German soldiers' song)*

„Wer durch dies Schlammfeld voll Sterben und Schreien gewatet, wer in diesen Nächten gezittert, der hatte die letzten Grenzpfähle des Lebens passiert und trug nachher tief in sich die dumpfe Erinnerung an irgendeinen Raum, der sich zwischen Tod und Leben oder jenseits beider befinden mag…" Werner Beumelburg, Douaumont, Oldenburg i.D., Berlin 1924, s. 127

"He who had waded through this field of mud full of dying and screaming, who had shivered in these nights, had passed the last border-posts of life, and afterwards carried deep within himself the dull memory of some place that may be found between death and life, or beyond both…" Werner Beumelburg, Douaumont, Oldenburg i.D., Berlin 1924, p. 127 (my translation)

Den Gefallenen von Verdun
To the fallen of Verdun

Author's note: Verdun 1916

The battle raged for 303 days, from the first German attack on 21st February to the end of the last French attack on 18th December 1916, at a cost of approximately 303,000 dead Germans and Frenchmen, and a further 380,000 wounded. The exact figures have never been established.

The Germans never reached the city of Verdun; they moved the front line a few kilometres south, reaching their furthest point of advance on 1st August. The Battle of the Somme had begun on 1st July, and its demands caused German attacks at Verdun to cease. On 18th August, the French began retaking the lost ground, and by 18th December, they had recovered almost all of it.

During much of the battle, the front line hardly moved. Repeated intense fighting in the same small area of ground created a landscape of horror, referred to by both sides as Hell (*die Hölle*, *l'enfer*). The dead lay unburied and decaying, dismembered over and over by shellfire. Evacuating the wounded was extremely difficult, as is reflected in the high death toll (the usual ratio of dead to wounded is 1:3, rather than the 1:1.25 at Verdun). Men in the front line were tormented by freezing cold, or by heat and burning thirst, quite apart from the constant shelling and bitter combat.

After the war, the ground was too polluted, and too full of unexploded munitions, for the pre-war population to return. Today it is a site of memory, whose scarred ground still holds the dead.

Among the German troops assembled for the initial assault was the elite Brandenburg Corps, comprised of the finest regiments of the Prussian Army, their men well trained, aggressive and battle-hardened. In its two deployments at Verdun, the Corps suffered such heavy casualties that it was never the same again.

Max Schelling's Verdun 1916

January: Hirson, France, training for the battle

6th February: Train to Luxembourg, march to Loison, north of Verdun

9th–11th February: Camp near Loison

11th February: Front line south of Azannes

12th February: Planned first day of the battle, but bad weather causes postponement until the next day

13th February: Weather still bad

14th–20th February: Weather continues to be bad. Max's Company marches back to rear area, then back to the front line on 20th February

21st February: First day of the battle, massive artillery bombardment. Initial infantry assault at 5pm (German time)

21st–23rd February: Fighting in Herbebois

24th–25th February: In reserve in the Herbebois ravine and in the Caurières Wood

25th–26th February: In the village of Ornes

27th–28th February: Up to Fort Douaumont and back through the Hassoule Ravine

29th Feb–3rd March: In reserve in the Brûle Ravine

3rd–6th March: In the front line at the Eastern Turret, Fort Douaumont

6th–9th March: In reserve in the Caurières Wood

9th–10th March: In the Zig-Zag Trench, waiting to attack the village of Vaux

10th–12th March: Fighting in the village of Vaux

13th March: Regiment pulled out, sent to Alsace

20th April–5th May: Regiment returns to Verdun, in camp

5th–10th May: Fighting in the Casemate Ravine and the British Ravine

10th–22nd May: In reserve in the Brûle Ravine

23rd–29th May: Fighting in the Caillette Wood

29th May–13th June: In reserve near Azannes

By the Same Author

The Flowers of the Grass:
Home Before the Leaves Fall
Below Us the Front
Him or You
Glory is Bought with Blood
To the Great Army

I

'And if I die today, then tomorrow I'll be dead, And they'll put me in the grave, when the dawn turns red...'

Max Schelling woke with a jolt. The song and the boots echoed in the silent bedroom as the grey figures marched through the wall, every man loaded up with pack and rifle.

Shit. But at least this time they were just marching… That was on our way up, before the first time in.

There was just enough light to see the hands of the clock. 4am.

That's that, then. Won't get back to sleep now.

He started to get out of bed, as carefully as he could.

"Another bad dream?" asked Frieda quietly.

"Sorry, darling. Go back to sleep."

"I wish it didn't bother you so much."

"So do I."

He leaned over and kissed her, and she put her arms around him and pulled him close.

"You don't have to get up, you know," she said. *I wish they didn't have to come into our bedroom. But then I suppose they go everywhere he is.*

They're just inside his head – aren't they?

"Put the light on if you like," she said.

Max switched on the bedside lamp. The room was empty apart from the two of them, and they both breathed out quietly.

"I hope I didn't wake the boys," he said.

"You didn't shout this time."

It scares them so much, she thought, but couldn't say. *It's not his fault.*

"Maybe they'll understand when they're older," she added.

"I hope they never have to."

"So do I. Oh, so do I. The thought of my little boys…"

His arms tightened around her. "Don't worry, my love."

But I do. There's always another war…

Peter looked at his father over breakfast. "Papa."

"Yes?"

"Why do you have bad dreams?"

Max sighed. "Everyone has bad dreams. It's just something that happens."

"Is it the war?"

He sighed again. *Tell him the truth – or some of it.*

"Yes."

"You were very brave."

Max smiled. "Who told you that?"

"Grandpa. And I've seen your medals."

"Ah."

He gave Frieda a sharp look, and she shook her head.

No, I didn't think you'd do that, he thought.

"Peter," he began, and realised that there were no words.

The boy looked at him, waiting.

"I did what had to be done. I was no braver than anyone else."

"So why did you get medals?"

Because I was still alive…

"Life isn't fair, Peter. Sometimes a group of men do something brave, but there's only one medal and the officer gets it. Now I'd better get to work."

Frieda went to the door with him.

"I'm sorry, darling," she said. "I'll have a word with Papa. I don't know what he was thinking."

He kissed her. "Don't bother – it's too late. And he won't listen anyway."

She laughed. "No, you're right."

I know exactly what the old bastard was thinking, Max thought as he left the house. *He was trying to explain why I'm odd.*

He didn't want Frieda to marry me – though to be fair that was after Verdun, and I was obviously damaged in both mind and body. Quite apart from the lack of a 'von'.

But he could hardly forbid his daughter to marry a 'wounded hero' – and she'd have married me anyway, no matter what he'd said.

No one tells Frieda what to do. Tough little thing she is, earned my respect many times over. Still does.

As he walked to the office the men started singing again, and their boots rang in time with his feet.

*

Fucking hell, how much further is it? Surely Strecker will order ten minutes' rest soon?

God, this is a gloomy song – but then most of them are.

"When the dawn turns red, the dawn turns red, then will I buried be, And my sweetheart in her bed all alone will be…"

"COMPANY, HALT! Ten minutes' rest, boys."

"At long fucking last," mutters Lorenz.

"Get the weight off my bloody feet for a bit," says Dachwitz.

"And the monkey off my back," Tiemann says.

The men sit down beside the road.

As Lorenz lights a fag he sings, half under his breath, "And my sweetheart in her bed all alone will be—"

"No, she bloody won't!" says Dachwitz. "Cos we'll all go and look after her, won't we, boys!"

"You bet!" Berger agrees. "Keep her nice and warm."

"Stop her getting lonely," says Tiemann.

"No you won't," Lorenz retorts. "Cos guess what? It'll be me wot gets home, and you wot the Frenchies do for!"

*

"Morning, Schelling."

Morning? Already? And where the – oh. Potsdam. How…?

Max shook his head slowly, and the street and his colleague came fully into focus.

"Morning, Kurowski."

He barely registered what Kurowski said to him.

Is it my imagination or am I getting worse? The past is just as real as the present, and sometimes I don't know which is which.

When is it ever going to get any better?

He seated himself at his desk, unaware of the look that Horstmann and Kurowski exchanged.

"*Good morning, Schelling,*" Horstmann repeated.

Max looked up. "Oh – good morning, Horstmann."

Thought I'd said that – or maybe that was Scheumann I spoke to…

His post was on his desk. The first letter he opened contained a vivid account of the fighting for Fort Vaux.

The room disappeared, and he saw the men climbing the steep hill under fire, saw them fall…

A gust banged the office door shut, and he started violently and almost dived under the desk.

The other two pretended not to notice.

Not his fault, thought Kurowski. *I have days like that too.*

"Bit fresh in here," Horstmann said, and got up and closed the window. *Didn't do much for me either*, he thought. *Right bunch of messed-up bastards we are.*

Maybe Frieda was right about this job, Max thought as he read on. *But the story has to be told, and accurately. That's the best way to honour the dead – to record the battles, the war, so they can never be forgotten.*

Maybe I shouldn't be working on the volumes about Verdun, though...

Most of the other veterans are just like me anyway. Kurowski stares into space, and so does Müller, and Horstmann has that tic in his eye.

'Vicious hand-to-hand fighting...' read the Hauptmann's memoir.

Max smiled to himself. *Is there any other sort?*

*

Jump into the shell-hole.
    Stick the nearest Frenchie.
    Knife goes in up to the hilt.
    Pull it out. Shower of blood.
    He staggers, goes down.
    Stadler clubs his mate.
    More blood. Brains.
    Screams. Shouts—

*

"Schelling. *Schelling.*"
What?

Horstmann was looking at him with concern. "Have you got a light?" he repeated patiently.

*

The rain's pouring down, running off my helmet and the tent quarter round my shoulders. *How can the sky hold so much water?*

"May I ask for a light, sir?"

Axel smiles at the formality, and lights our cigarettes—

*

"Schelling," Horstmann said firmly, but his colleague was staring blankly into space.

Having a bad day, he thought. *Not that I can comment.*

Horstmann tried again. "My bloody lighter's run out."

"Oh – sorry, Horstmann. Miles away again."

"Yes, I realised."

Max got his lighter out of his pocket and passed it to Horstmann, and then decided to have a cigarette himself.

"Nice lighter, that." Horstmann wasn't sure whether he should have commented. *Hope it doesn't set him off again. You never know what's going to do it.*

"One of the other snipers made it for me – he made them for all of us. Until he bought it, that is."

"Would have been a bit difficult to make them afterwards!"

Max laughed. "Maybe in that special corner of Hell that's reserved for snipers!"

"Glad you realise where you all belong!"

I'm glad I've got this job, Max thought. *The others understand and don't ask stupid questions. I'm not sure I could manage among civilians.*

*

A couple of evenings later, he got home to find his father-in-law in the living room with Frieda.

"Ah, Max…" Herr von Erhart said awkwardly, "I – er – I owe you an apology."

"Why's that?"

"I didn't realise I wasn't supposed to show Peter your medals." Max stiffened.

"You see, I…" his father-in-law continued, "do forgive me, I'm going to say this completely wrong… but I just wanted to…"

To find some value in your lame, half-mad son-in-law who has no prospects beyond a temporary job at the Imperial Archives?

Max only just stopped himself saying it.

"He mentioned you'd been having nightmares…"

Max lit a cigarette, willing himself to be patient.

"And I wanted him to know that there's a reason why you are – as you are."

Half-mad. Max bit his tongue hard.

"What I mean is that everything has its price," Herr von Erhart continued. "I told him that you'd been very brave indeed, and that when men have to do things like that, they – well, they're affected. He said he's seen your scars."

"Yes, they both have." Max managed a short laugh. "You know what small boys are like – they were fascinated."

"I said there are other scars which don't show."

Did you now? And who the fuck asked you to put in your ten Marks' worth?

"And he said he understands."

Can anyone understand who wasn't there? Let alone a little kid?

"Well, that's cleared that up," Max said. "Are you staying to dinner?"

"If I'm invited."

"Of course you are." He tried to put some warmth into his voice. "You're always invited, you know that."

"Thank you."

Frieda gave Max a grateful look, and he smiled at her.

Your father might be an awkward, interfering old bastard, but you wouldn't be here without him, so I'll let him off. And he must be lonely since your mother died.

The boys adore their grandpa, and it's good for them to have someone a bit more... sane in their lives. Especially with my parents having moved to the coast.

"He's very proud of you," Frieda said to Max later.

He looked at her in surprise. "Bollocks."

"No, really – he is. He told me he's glad I married you."

"That's a change of heart!"

"Yes. He said that in the War Ministry they had no idea how things really were – all the reports from the Front were so sanitised, and so he couldn't understand why you'd been so..."

Max smiled. "Bonkers?"

"*No. Of course not.* But he thought you were overreacting, until he started to hear more about it – Verdun, that is."

"From whom?"

"Someone showed him the draft of the book about Douaumont – you know, the first volume of the Official History that you're working on."

"Ah... Have you read it?"

"Yes."

Max lit a cigarette. "And what do you think?" he asked slowly.

"I think it's a miracle anyone came out alive."

You're not wrong there... And that is quite enough about that fucking place for one evening, or I'll have another bad night.

"Shall we go to the country for the weekend?" he suggested.

"Oh, yes – that would be lovely! We can go to that hotel by the lake again – it's so beautiful there."

"And we can hire a boat and go out on the water."

That's a much nicer thing to think about before going to bed – but he lay awake, unable to sleep as the war filled his head, wondering whether anything really made any difference.

Frieda's an angel, putting up with me… Hope she doesn't get fed up…

She was a very long way from being fed up with Max.

There has to be some way of helping him to start to – not get over it, I don't think he'll ever get that far – but come to terms with it, she thought. *I love him so much and I want to help him. I just don't know where to start.*

How do you get back, once you've 'passed the last border-posts of life', as it says in that book about Douaumont?

Maybe he hasn't.

Maybe he never will, she didn't want to think.

There must be something that would work…

"Darling," she said one night, as they got ready for bed, "I've been thinking."

He looked at her and raised an eyebrow. "And what, my love, have you been thinking?"

He wrapped his arms around her and pulled her naked body against his. *Lovely arse you've got… and such beautiful soft skin…*

She giggled softly, holding him tight. "Not what you're thinking!"

"And why not…?"

Some time later he asked, "So what were you thinking?"

There was a pause and then she said, slowly and rather awkwardly, "Would it help if you went back?"

I'm glad you said that after we made love.

"Er – I don't…"

"Why not think about it?"

"If there's one place on Earth I never want to see again, it's fucking Verdun."

He'd spoken more vehemently than he'd intended.

"Sorry, darling. I didn't mean it to sound like that."

She kissed him. "I know."

It was three months before he felt like discussing it, three months just like the eight years that had gone before.

Almost every night he was at Verdun – in the woods, or the trench whose name he still couldn't say, or the village.

The dead were as real as his own family.

I'm scaring the boys, he thought after he'd woken screaming yet again.

Ernst was crying in the next room, and Frieda hurried to comfort him.

Max curled up, pulled the quilt over his head, and lay shaking. *I could fucking well cry too.*

Please don't suggest again that I go back, he thought as she got back into bed – *and yet, maybe I should try it.*

I'm scared of what might happen. I don't want to end up in an asylum…

But maybe I'm heading for one anyway.

*

A week later, he managed to say, "Darling, I've been thinking about what you said about – about going back – and… well, it's worth a try, isn't it?"

She looked at him. *What do I say? It could tip him right over the edge, and then what will I do?*

"Would you like me to come with you?" she asked.

No. That's the last thing – though maybe you'd help me stay sane. It'll be just me and the ghosts otherwise.

"I'm not sure…"

"What about the boys?" she said.

The boys are not going to that terrible place. Not until they're a lot older. "They could stay with your father, or my parents."

"Maybe they should see what war is."

"They are far too young," he said firmly. "And I'd have to try to explain what happened."

You will if I come with you, she thought, *but we can discuss that later.*

"Why don't you ask Oberst Geissler when you get in today?" she said.

"Yes, I think I will."

Get it done as soon as the boss arrives, he thought on his way to the office. *Before I have time to change my mind.*

"Excellent idea," Geissler said. "You could have a look at Fort Vaux while you're there, make sure our account matches up with the ground. People's memories are sometimes a bit out."

I wish mine were.

"And – er – were you thinking – are you going back to where your regiment was deployed?"

Nicely put. "Yes, sir."

Geissler looked at him gravely, and then nodded. "That would be most useful."

"What did the boss want?" Kurowski asked.

"I wanted to see him – I'm going back. To Verdun."

There was a long pause.

Horstmann looked at Max very steadily.

"Are you sure that's a good idea?" he asked, his eye twitching.

"Don't know. Only one way to find out."

Horstmann raised his eyebrows, and went back to writing.

"Anyone going with you?" Kurowski asked.

"In case I have a funny turn?" Max said.

Kurowski and Horstmann exchanged glances.

Oh. I see. I must be even more bonkers than I realised. Though neither of you is quite right.

"Don't know yet. Frieda, perhaps."

But in the evening, he said, "Darling, I think you should stay here and look after the boys. It might be too unsettling for them if we both go away."

She tried not to show her relief, but he saw. *That's settled, then.*

"When are you going?" she asked.

"As soon as I can make the arrangements – Geissler wants me to do some work, so with a bit of luck the Archives will help with the cost."

"How long will you be?"

"I don't know yet."

"Will you telephone me? In the evenings?"

"If I can."

Several times during the next week he wanted to change his mind, but it was too late. Geissler had begun making the arrangements, and once the Colonel started something, he got it finished as fast as he could.

"Well, Schelling – I've booked your hotel, starting from next Tuesday. The reservation's open-ended."

"Thank you, sir."

That's that, then, Max thought. *Can't back out of it now. Probably just as well.*

Frieda struggled to hide her misgivings.

It's all my idea, she thought. *If it all goes wrong then it's my fault.*

"Are you quite sure you don't want me to come with you?"

"No, darling." He saw the look in her eyes. "It'll be fine. *I'll* be fine."

And who am I trying to convince?

I'll miss you, my love, he thought as he boarded the train. *And the boys.*

He said goodbye to them as cheerfully as he could.

It's going to be so strange being without them all. And maybe I shouldn't be going at all. God knows what it's going to stir up.

When I get back, I'll treat them to a holiday.

He laughed. '*When I get back from Verdun*' – *that's a sentence none of us could ever say. I never expected to come back, not after the first deployment, and part of me never really has.*

II

The hotel was rather shabby, on the outside anyway, but it was near the station.

Geissler's obviously gone for the cheap option, but then there isn't much money now. God alone knows what the war cost, and now we have to pay the Allies as well, being as we lost and they think we started it.

I wish I did know who fucking started it. I'd shoot the bugger myself.

His right leg grumbled slightly as he walked down the street.

Too much sitting. Never likes it.

Maybe a room in our old rear area would have been better, but this way at least one of us made it to Verdun.

The proprietor was friendly and welcoming, until he heard the German accent.

The smile left his face.

Yes, I know. I expect you'll tell me there's a mistake with the booking.

The man gave Max a key.

"First floor," he said curtly.

"Thanks."

The room was starkly simple. There was a double bed with a thin mattress, and the walls were plain white. A large window looked west.

Max smiled. Not so different from the barracks – and Geissler clearly reckoned that a dry bed was all an old Front swine really needed.

And he's right – it's a bloody sight better than the accommodation I had last time I was here. And no one's going to try to kill me this time, and I don't have to kill anyone either.

He unpacked and went downstairs.

"Where can I hire a horse?"

"At the station."

Again there was a slight frown at Max's accent.

The man thought for a moment, looked up at Max's broad shoulders and then at the horses.

"You can have this one, Prince."

He indicated a big coal-black gelding, who laid his ears flat against his head as the stable owner approached him.

The price was rather high, and the man wanted payment in advance.

Probably your attempt at reparations. I'd do the same in your place.

"Nine tomorrow," Max said.

"Agreed."

Might as well go for a walk, being as I've made it here. Ease my leg out as well.

The wartime damage was being repaired, and the city was rather pleasant in the afternoon sun. He walked beside the river for a while, then found a bar and had a beer.

'I'll stand you champagne in Verdun!' Axel said clearly.

Max started, and almost looked round.

I wonder where you are now. With the Great Army, of course, but is your body really in that grave?

'Does it matter?'

No, but I'd like to pay my respects.

'You're here, aren't you?'

There was a sudden chatter of voices, and Axel was gone.

Max gazed at the bar, trying to dispel the feeling of unreality, and saw a telephone kiosk in a corner.

Oh, good – I can phone Frieda.

"You want a call to where?" asked the operator, although he'd spoken clearly.

"Potsdam."

"I'm sorry, but that's not possible."

No, it wouldn't be.

He went to the post office and sent a cable instead. 'In Verdun can't phone love you M'

And that's it. Still better than waiting weeks for a letter, though.

He stared at the river for a while, feeling flat and lonely, and then wandered slowly back through the city.

Better get some food. Might lift my spirits a bit.

He ordered steak and chips in a bistro. Again there was a slight frown at his accent.

Not as bad as I thought it would be, though…

But when he got into bed and turned the light off, a voice said, 'Filthy Boche. You came here to kill us.'

Oh, bloody wonderful.

Guilty as charged, he replied flippantly, but the voice wasn't satisfied with that.

'Filthy Boche,' it said again, with some vehemence.

You killed a lot of our blokes as well. And no one chooses where he gets sent.

Silence. The resentment and hostility were still there.

This is going to be real fun, having to put up with you every night.

No reply.

Frenchie officer, I expect, probably stayed here on his way up… Not out, or he wouldn't still be here.

Sleep was elusive, and when it did come he was in the Zig-Zag Trench with the shells slamming in—

He woke with a start, soaked in sweat, and lay awake, too afraid to go back to sleep.

Finally daylight crept through the curtains. *Thank fuck for that.*

There were fresh croissants for breakfast, still warm. Max ate two with strawberry jam, wishing there were rye bread and cheese – but at least the coffee was good and strong.

The French officer sneered at him when he went back upstairs.

"See you later," Max said, as he left the room. *Wish I didn't have to...*

The sun was shining, and it was a relief to get into the fresh air. His leg eased out as he walked to the stables.

Prince flattened his ears against his skull again at the sight of his owner, then shook his head and skittered as Max tried to mount.

I've played this game before, Max thought. *Many times.*

He paused, then swung himself swiftly into the saddle. The horse danced with indignation, but in vain.

"Right," Max said. "Let's get going."

Better get the work at Fort Vaux done first, being as the Archives are helping with the cost.

He smiled wryly. *That old Prussian sense of duty – it never leaves you.*

Now I need to take the Avenue de Douaumont – how appropriate...

And there are the Meuse Heights, rising above the town.

So many of my comrades lie up there... And what's waiting for me now?

Shut up and get on with it.

As they left the town behind, Prince tossed his head and started skittering again. He was quite a handful.

I get the picture – give the unruly bastard to the fucking Boche. Maybe he'll fall off and break his fucking neck.

I've been riding unruly bastards since I was a kid. You can gallop up the bloody hill.

He gave Prince his head, and the gelding thundered up the dirt road, hooves and mane and tail flying.

Max felt the wind and the warm sun on his face and, for a moment, was actually happy.

Prince started to slow, and Max urged him on. A few minutes later, he let the horse drop to a trot, and then a walk.

There was no more skittering.

That's better. You just needed a good run.

"Fun, wasn't it?" he said, and stroked the sleek black neck. One ear swivelled round to listen, then both ears pointed forward again.

Did me good, too. That's the best I've felt for quite a while.
Better enjoy it while it lasts…

They took the turning for Fort Vaux and carried on through a wasteland of craters, up to the battered strongpoint. The concrete and stone façade was deeply scarred, the ditch half-full of debris.

Amazing what high explosive can do, especially by the ton…

Max looked round for somewhere to leave Prince, but there was no water anywhere.

That was why the Frenchies had to surrender – they ran out of water in the Fort.

I'll have to leave him by the pond in the valley. And that's far too near the bloody village.

They went back to the main road, and then down the hill to the north of the Fort. The sides of the valley closed in, dimming the light. *Pretend the village isn't in the bottom…*

The road turned round the spur of the hill – and Max's breath caught in his throat.

In front of him was the ruined village of Vaux: shapeless heaps of rubble, here and there a wall still standing, empty windows leering at him.

Jesus fucking Christ.

Cold ran down his back.

Of all the fucking places to see first.

The dead called.

"Not yet." It sounded like an excuse. "I have to go up to the Fort."

'When?'

"Soon…"

If I can do it at all.

The village seemed to shimmer slightly. Prince skittered.

"Easy, boy." *So it's not just me.*

I don't think I should have come…

Get on with it. No one's going to try to kill you, are they? Not like back then.

He tore his eyes from the ruins, and coaxed Prince the short distance to the pond and the narrow path beside it.

I was never here, but I've read enough about it. This was the Path of Death. All the reinforcements, all the supplies for our fellows fighting for the Fort had to be carried across it, and everyone on the way out had to go the same way.

And of course the Frenchies knew that, and it was constantly under shellfire.

How many men died here…?

Hope the water's fit to drink now. It doesn't smell, anyway.

"You'll be all right here, won't you?" he said as he tied Prince up and unsaddled him.

The horse looked at him uncertainly, one ear twitching to and fro.

Not sure what to make of me, are you? Or maybe it's this place.

Max turned his back to the pond, and set off straight uphill.

How easy it is to do this now, and how nearly impossible it was then. Even when our boys had taken the Fort, it was still a bloody slog to push the front line any further.

The slope was steep, and his leg started aching and made him pause a couple of times. Finally, he crossed the cratered moonscape to the top of the Fort, and turned round.

The Hardaumont Ridge was bare opposite, sloping steeply down into the ravine where the village lay. Even through the scrub that had sprung up he could see the line of the Zig-Zag Trench on the hillside.

Fuck me. We were on a platter for the guns here and along this ridge. It's a fucking miracle we weren't wiped out.

And there's Douaumont, looming over everything. For all the boys in the 24th banged on about it, it's just as well they did take the fucking place.

So many of our boys must still be over there, and in the village down below.

Such a fucking waste…

He sighed, and got out the drafts from the Archives and the old maps.

Relating the eyewitness accounts to the ground was more than a bit difficult – the later shelling had all but obliterated the trenches shown on the maps, and he had to walk some areas several times.

Even so, there were a few places where the man's account was clearly out, and a few more that raised questions, and Max made careful notes.

I don't want to have to come up here again…

By the time he'd finished work, the shadows were lengthening. He walked back down into the valley, almost missing his footing several times.

The light was very dim in the bottom. He shivered, and told himself that it was getting chilly.

Prince seemed pleased to see him, and pushed his muzzle into Max's hand.

I'm making one friend here, anyway.

Suddenly Prince stiffened, staring over Max's shoulder into the ruins, his eyes wide.

"What is it, boy?"

The atmosphere had thickened, and Max had a strong feeling of being watched.

"Let's get home," he said as steadily as he could.

Prince was shivering and trying to back away.

When I untie you, you'll bolt, and I'll have a bloody long walk back to Verdun…

A whirring noise, accompanied by a light, swift crunching—

Man and horse both started. Max turned quickly.

A cyclist, belting down the dirt road, crouched low, his hands on the drops.

Racer, Max thought.

The spell had been broken. He turned back to Prince.

"Let's go." *And please behave yourself.*

Prince skittered slightly as Max mounted, one ear flicking to and fro uneasily, and as they started up out of the gloom he shied and cantered sideways.

"Steady, boy. Steady."

After a couple of minutes, Max gave the gelding his head again, and they galloped up to the top of the hill.

Thank God we're away from there. I'm not looking forward to going into that bloody village, not one bit.

Prince trotted quietly back into town, but as they neared the stable he started playing up, and his ears went halfway back.

"What's the matter, boy? Don't you want to go home? Haven't you had enough of me for one day?"

He almost had to persuade the horse to turn into the yard.

Not what you expect at all. Quite the opposite, in fact.

The stable owner appeared from the tack room, and Prince's ears went back flat.

You really don't like him, do you?

The man seemed almost disappointed to see them.

"How was he?" he asked.

"Lovely," Max said. "Goes very well indeed."

That was clearly not the expected answer.

"Same time tomorrow, then," Max said, and gave Prince a friendly slap on the shoulder.

As he left the yard, he felt a pair of liquid brown eyes gazing at his back.

Must bring you a treat in the morning...

He had a coffee, and then went back to his room to finish work.

The brooding presence was there, but Max ignored it as he wrote up his notes.

That walk really was worth doing. Must make this as clear as possible, so we can write a good, accurate account.

'Pleased with yourself, are you?' asked the voice.

Oh, shut up.

In the middle of the night he sat up suddenly, shaking, his heart pounding.

He switched the light on, and the stinking black face disappeared.

Was that the man who slept in this room?

Or just one of the many up there on the battlefield?

Either way, sleep was over.

I am so fucking sick of this. It's eight years now since I fought here, and the bloody place won't leave me alone.

God knows the Somme was bad enough, but this place...

Maybe it's because of the dead, unburied and churned up and dismembered over and over, until we were all covered in putrid filth... Filth that had once been our friends and comrades.

Or because we knew that our chances of making it out were next to nil.

Whatever it is, I don't know how long I can keep going. It's not right for Frieda, putting up with my nightmares and seeing things. The boys are getting older and...

He stopped himself.

If I carry on thinking like that, I'll end by shooting myself. Maybe that would be best.

'We didn't die for you to shoot yourself,' Axel said.

True. And I wouldn't be able to look any of you in the eye.

Better carry on then... Wonder how it's going to feel, seeing those places again.

I'm not sure I can do this, he thought again.

Shut up and get on with it.

Over breakfast, he put a couple of sugar lumps in his jacket pocket.

Buying affection, Max.

Prince nuzzled his pocket.

"You are such a tart," Max murmured into one black ear. "A lump of sugar and you're anyone's. Or is it just that I get you away from your owner?"

Prince stood quietly for him to mount, and trotted obediently out of town.

"You don't care about me being a filthy Boche, do you?" Max said. "Shall we gallop up the hill again?"

He gave the horse his head, and the gelding charged up the hill until he started to snort, then shook his head as he slowed to a walk.

Max slapped the gleaming neck affectionately, and Prince snorted again.

I'll take the road past the villages to Azannes. Start at the beginning...

Or maybe it's because it was such a fucking catastrophe, because so many good men died for nothing. That's what's so hard to take – that we lost that battle and, in the end, the war.

And look what a fucking shambles we're in now.

It's not as if we didn't try. We trained so hard for Verdun, all those weeks rehearsing in the trenches we'd dug in the woods near Hirson. In sections, platoons, companies – until we had the really big exercise.

That was the day the General came to watch the manoeuvres – and by God, they went well.

*

12th January 1916, woods near Hirson, France

My Sections take the 'enemy' positions as planned and we consolidate our hold on them.

"Bloody well done, boys."

"That'll show those fucking Frenchies," Tiemann says with a grin.

"If it goes like that," says Stadler.

No plan survives… but it's not the time to say that.

"Keep up the hard work and it just might," I say instead.

The rest of the Platoon's done a good job too.

"Well done, boys," says Leutnant Messner.

"Good effort," says Oberleutnant Strecker. "But…"

His dissection of the Company's performance is merciless and accurate.

How the fuck did he see all that? Surely we were out of sight part of the time. He's like fucking Argus with the thousand eyes.

"I thought it went pretty well," Officer Cadet Jahnke grumbles as we march back to the huts.

"That's why he's the Company Commander and you've not got your epaulettes yet," Messner points out. "We need to know what went wrong, don't we?"

"Oh, yes, sir."

And Jahnke won't have epaulettes for quite a while, if at all. Just like a puppy, all enthusiasm and no sense. Probably get killed in no time flat.

"Right, boys – parade in an hour," says Strecker.

"Jesus, that's going to take a bit of doing," mutters Lorenz.

*

And it did, Max thought.

We were all filthy – but we were the elite of the finest army in Europe, and no man would be anything less than immaculate on parade.

Immaculate was the word, all right. Fucking nigh perfect.

*

The band strikes up 'Wir präsentieren', and the General and his entourage begin the inspection.

We're it, the best there is. The battering ram of the Brandenburg Corps, hard as fucking steel, forged in months of fighting.

We've bashed the crap out of everyone so far, and we're going to do it again.

With men like these you could walk on water. Fucking privilege to be one of them, let alone to lead them.

And I can see His Excellency thinking exactly the same. There's even a hint of approval in that granite face.

We won't let you down. You'll be even prouder of us after the battle.

We'll break through, then it'll be on to Paris and victory. Then we'll parade through the Brandenburg Gate and then we can go home.

Our blood-red colours catch the breeze as we wait to move.

Wonder which march we'll get – 'The Glory of Prussia' or 'Prinz Friedrich Karl'?

'The Glory of Prussia'.

Let's hope the buggers don't start singing – though the General probably wouldn't mind.

Nice, boys – beautifully in step.

We're almost at the first marker. In a couple of seconds, it'll be "Eyes right!" and the parade march.

Messner's order rings out over the music, and the sound of the boots changes in unison.

Beautiful. Bloody beautiful.

My eyes meet the General's again, and I can see the pride in his face.

Wonder if he recognised me. There was a slight crease at his eye corners.

*

Max sighed. Nearly all those men are dead. Only a handful of us survived the war.

Good bloke, the General, not like some of them – and that's not me being biased because we're related.

I heard what he really thought of the Verdun battle plan after I got whacked at the Somme. Frieda and I went to visit him, and he let rip in fine style, called Falkenhayn all the names under the sun.

"Complete waste of our finest troops. I told him at the time it wouldn't work, but the pig-headed bastard wouldn't listen…"

Not that it mattered in the end.

We were already fucked by the time Verdun started – it's so easy to see now.

The reserves the General wanted couldn't be deployed here, because there weren't enough men.

It was as simple as that.

We should have made peace in autumn '14. Friedrich would

still have fallen but Axel would be alive, and so many of the fine men I knew.

Max sighed again.

There's no point thinking like that. The dead are dead.

And I wouldn't be quite as fucked up as I am now... But then, maybe I wouldn't have married Frieda.

Quite a girl, my Frieda... feels very strange being away from her.

Prince trotted past the road to Fort Vaux, and down into the valley.

The direct route across the battlefield would have been much quicker – it was only a few kilometres from Verdun to Azannes – but it was a mass of craters, stuffed with unexploded munitions, and there were signs warning visitors to stay on the roads, and not to touch anything they found.

Of course – thousands of people must come here, looking for the men they lost or, like me, trying to pick up the pieces they left behind.

When I left here, I thought at first that it was only my blood that I'd left. And then I started to realise that there's more to it than that.

The atmosphere became oppressive as the sides of the valley closed in. Prince skittered.

"Easy, boy. It's all right."

I wish I didn't have to come through here. This road must go right through the village...

Just before the ruins, the road turned and ran parallel to the old village street. Max shivered, unable to tear his eyes from the heaps of stone, almost seeing the ghosts.

Prince stopped dead, and Max could feel him shivering as well.

Someone was watching from the ruins, watching and waiting.

Prince started to back away.

"Easy, boy. It's all right," Max said again, hoping the horse would understand his tone.

But it's not all right, he thought. *Why the fuck did I come here?*

Don't be a stupid bastard. Just get on with it. No one's going to shell you or shoot at you, are they?

It just feels so…

If anywhere deserves to be haunted it's this bloody place. It was fucking slaughter, and not just us but all the poor bastards before and after.

I'll have to go there, but another day. I'll try to keep it all in chronological order.

"I haven't forgotten, boys. Just a couple of days…" *I'm not really putting it off.*

He coaxed Prince forward. The horse moved reluctantly at first, then broke into a brisk canter.

Max didn't try to slow him down.

The terrain opened out again, and the feeling of darkness lifted as the light grew.

It's as if the violence still resonates. How many thousands of men died in that valley…?

He turned Prince towards Azannes with relief.

III

The feeling of relief was short-lived. To Max's left the terrain rose, scarred and with a haze of scrub.

Only a few fields right beside the road were cultivated, and a few hundred metres beyond them was the ruined village, now slightly hidden in the folds of the land.

Max shuddered again. The warm sun failed to dispel the chill that went through him.

Keep going and don't think.

How often did I say that to myself?

They carried on, the road rising and falling gently. The surface was uneven, the old shell-holes crudely filled, and Prince picked his way carefully.

A signpost: 'Bezonvaux. Destroyed village'.

Ah, Bezonvaux…

Quite a few memories there.

'Ornes. Destroyed village'.

And there too. That's where we were when I heard – but that's for later.

He sighed, the sadness and loss almost unbearable.

You can't change it, Max. And maybe the dead are better off…

Aren't they going to rebuild the villages? Maybe it's too dangerous, with all the unexploded stuff. And maybe it's all too poisoned. Corpses, gas, explosives… not the playground you'd want for your children.

Here's Gremilly, not destroyed. This was the eastern limit of the battlefield.

The next road was somewhat better, and Prince trotted along briskly.

Azannes-et-Soumazannes. Not destroyed either. Just rather damaged.

Now I really am behind our lines. It was plain Azannes then, and Soumazannes was the hamlet in the bottom of the valley. Not that there was much left of it.

It's so quiet now – there's hardly anyone about. Then it was always full of soldiers, the streets jammed with traffic.

Men on their way up to the front line, loaded with equipment and cursing the weight. Men coming back down, cold, hungry, bone-weary and almost asleep on their feet. Men covered in blood, stumbling or being carried to the main dressing station. Trucks full of supplies, ambulances…

I've never known how I got here that day – I do know I nearly didn't make it…

Keep it chronological, Max, as far as you can.

He left Prince in Azannes, on the grass near the church, and set off along the dirt road towards the old front line.

We came up here before it all started… So long ago, now.

In a minute, I'll be able to see across the valley, to the wood on the hill.

Such high hopes we all had. We really believed we could do it. And then that wood – Jesus, that fucking wood.

Herbebois. Another name I can't say.

It's going to be very strange seeing it again – it was bad enough seeing the village. I wonder how much of it is still there.

I'm not sure I should be doing this – it's going to bring it all back and I don't know if I can deal with it.

He stopped.

What if I lose my mind completely?

Too late to worry about that.

No one's going to try to kill you. The war's over.

As he left the village behind, the road climbed steadily along the ridge, and the ground fell gently away on the left.

The day was getting warm, the sun high in a cloudless sky.

Such a contrast – it was a fine day when it all finally started, but so fucking cold. For all I grew up in rural Brandenburg, for all my time in the trenches in winter, I swear I've never been so cold in my life as I was here.

A buzzard circled overhead, and the small birds sang. *That's another contrast – it's so peaceful. You could almost imagine none of it happened.*

But there was the wood – the shattered, blasted wood on the crest beyond the valley to the south.

Max stopped and stared at it. The cold nausea was so powerful that for a moment he thought he would lose his breakfast.

The wood held his gaze as if nothing else existed.

If I had to choose the place where I was the most frightened, this would be very high on the list.

God alone knows how I survived.

He shook himself, got to his feet and carried on up the path.

I don't remember sitting down...

That was too disturbing.

This side of the valley looks almost normal, except for the shell-holes – and here's concrete, must be the remains of our old positions.

The terrain had opened out on his right, and he could see down the hill on that side as well.

That's where our Stollen were, tunnels dug deep into the shelter of the reverse slope.

Max turned right off the road and walked down beside the field. There was more concrete, and dark holes going into the hillside.

Well, bugger me – the Stollen are still here.

This is where we waited for the big show to start.

And waited. And waited.
And all it did was piss down with rain.

*

14th February 1916, front line near Azannes

"Fucking hell, I've never been so bloody wet," says Lorenz.

"We'll be swimming to Verdun at this rate," Degenhardt agrees.

'In the event of bad weather, the battle will take place indoors!' someone's written on the wall.

"'Bout sums it up," grouses Tiemann.

"I'm sick to death of fucking waiting," says Berger. "It was supposed to be two days ago, and they just keep saying, might be tomorrow, boys."

"You wouldn't want to go in without the artillery, would you?" Jahnke says. "And they can't start the bombardment until the weather clears."

"Yes, Officer Cadet, sir, we know that," Gefreiter Weidner answers. "We're all just sick of sitting in this fucking tunnel."

"We just want to get on with it," adds Tiemann.

Amen to that. It's fucking nerve-shredding, this sitting around thinking every day that it might be tomorrow, and then hearing again that it isn't.

We were only meant to be here one night. We're crammed in like sardines, and the tunnel's bloody cold. Water drips from the ceiling and runs down the walls, and the bottom's shin-deep in it. It's a fucking miserable place to be stuck, even without the thought of what's ahead of us.

Better keep them busy.

"Kit inspection, boys."

Not that I'll find anything wrong – this lot won't let their rifles get rusty.

Everything's in order.

Every man's coat is sopping wet, but there isn't anything that can be done about it.

If the weather turns cold, we'll all fucking freeze.

Time for some fresh air. It's getting a bit bloody rank in here.

It's still raining. Wrap my tent quarter tighter round myself. Water runs off my helmet and drips onto my shoulders.

How can it keep going like this? Surely the clouds must run out at some point.

Squelching footsteps.

A very familiar voice says, "Evening."

Axel's standing beside me.

Smile. "May I ask for a light, sir?"

Axel smiles back, barely seen. "Of course, Sergeant Major."

He gets both cigarettes lit in spite of the rain, the flame bright.

Then it goes out, and the only light's from the sporadic shelling and the odd flare.

"Bloody long way from playing soldiers as kids," says Axel.

"That's for sure!" *And we've got the scars to prove it…*

You've done bloody well, Axel. Officer Cadet at the start of the war, Leutnant and Battalion Adjutant now.

"Gneist wanted a word with the Company Commanders," says Axel. "It won't be happening tomorrow either, as you've probably guessed."

He uses the familiar 'du' – no one else is in earshot.

"Yes, I had… Everyone's getting pissed off."

"Waiting's always shit."

"And it's fucking wet, even in the Stollen… How's your leg?" I ask, saying 'du' as well.

"Pretty good. Doesn't like the weather much. What about you?"

"I'm fine. All healed up."

Long way from the barracks as well. I hope he's telling the truth about his leg – though with his job it shouldn't matter too much.

"Ah, Paetow, there you are," says an older voice.

Heels together and salute.

There's just enough light for me to recognise the Battalion Commander.

"Feldwebel Schelling, isn't it?" Gneist asks.

Well done – especially in this poor light.

"Yes, sir."

"How are the men?"

"Fed up with waiting, sir – want to get on with it."

"Don't we all. Paetow, time we were off. Oberstleutnant Jagenow wants to see us at ten sharp."

"Yes, sir."

Gneist looks from Axel to me, peering at us in the dimness. "Do I see a resemblance?"

"Yes, sir," Axel says. "We're first cousins."

"Ah, right… Well, carry on, Schelling."

"Sir."

*

Almost without realising it, Max had carried on up the road. It ran along the old German front line as it had then, and stretches of trench were still there.

He sat down again in the sun, and stared across the valley to what remained of the wood, seeing only the trench in the rain and the darkness.

This was the last place I saw him.

Axel was one of those people that I'd always known. He was just a few months older than me, and we grew up together. We were more like brothers than cousins.

He'd only ever wanted to be a soldier, not like me. And he was bloody good at it.

It was so good, finally, to be serving together, even with the difference in rank. That's what I intended when I volunteered – to serve with my cousins, even though they were officer cadets and I a mere war volunteer.

But there were too many volunteers and we got sent to the new regiment instead, and into action in Flanders after a few weeks of cobbled-together training.

I've never known how I survived that, either...

*

30th October 1914, near Diksmuide, Ypres, Belgium

There's the church tower. Bixschoote. Only about five hundred metres away.

Five hundred metres over flat ground, with fuck all cover apart from hedges and ditches. We're well aware now that the enemy is hidden, that we are all too visible.

The 'Company' consists of what remains of the First Battalion, led by Leutnant Hirsch, the only remaining officer.

"Five minutes, boys," says Sergeant Rogge.

Wonder how many of us will be alive this evening.

Two weeks we've been here, thrown in too soon and hopelessly out of our depth. Most of us have gone.

This is probably the last place I'll ever see.

"Go."

Go to die...

Get out of the ditch – or try to.

The mud holds my boots like glue.

Pull my feet out somehow.

Stagger forwards.

They're not shooting.

The next ditch is a hundred metres away.

They're still not shooting.

Right foot sinks in. Stuck.
Fuck!
Pull harder.
Left foot's stuck.
Jesus fucking Christ!
Pull harder.
Right foot comes free, then the left.
Plod on.
Fifty metres…
Forty…
The air cracks and sings.
Men fall ahead of me, beside me.
The rest of us hit the furrows—

*

By some miracle I came through intact, Max thought.

It was spring '15 before I got my transfer. By then, Friedrich was dead.

I was put into the Seventh Company while Axel was in the Sixth, and we hardly saw each other. Then I got that splinter across my stomach in the July, so I didn't go to Serbia. He got whacked in the leg there, and we were in the barracks at the same time for a couple of weeks before coming to France, to train for Verdun.

Max lit another cigarette.

*

15th February 1916, front line near Azannes

"Right, boys," says Leutnant Messner. "It's off for a few days."
A murmur runs through the Stollen.

"Yes, I know. But you'll be pleased to hear that we're going back to Billy, where at least we'll be in huts and – hopefully – a bit drier than here."

"Did he say Billy, Sarge?" says Tiemann.

"That's right," Kropp replies.

"But that's God knows how far!" Lorenz protests.

"Ten kilometres from Azannes," I say. *And over that fucking bridge...*

"Oh, fuck me!" says Degenhardt. "Lugging all this stuff here was enough – and now we've got to lug it all back again."

"Through all that fucking mud as well," grumbles Berger. "And then back here again when the show's finally on."

"Stop us getting out of shape, won't it?" says Sergeant Kropp. "And it might stop any more of you getting the shits."

It's fucking insanitary in the Stollen. Food goes mouldy overnight and water gets a strange taste. Add in the stress of waiting, and it's not surprising blokes are getting sick.

It is a fucking long way to Billy, though. And the Frenchies are shelling more and more.

"Makes you wonder if they've guessed what's up," Kropp says to me as we tramp through the woods.

"Let's hope not..."

"That bridge could be fun."

Best not thought about, like so much else.

The only way into Billy from Azannes is over the bridge – and the Frenchies know it and have guns trained on it.

"We'll just have to hope everyone keeps moving."

"Down to you and me, that, isn't it?" Kropp replies with a grin.

It is not a good feeling arriving back in Billy – everyone's knackered and pissed off, and we all know we'll be going back to Azannes and the front line in a few days. We'd all rather get on with it.

I suppose we should be grateful for the stay of execution, but it's impossible to relax.

No one knows how much longer he'll live – but then, no one ever does. In peacetime, we all assume that we'll be here next year, and we make plans…

That was the first thing I learnt, back in October '14 – how transient life really is.

I've been on borrowed time ever since.

The men are losing fitness, and there's very little we can do about it. And there's bugger all to keep their minds off waiting.

"You know what's really strange?" Kropp says to me.

"What?"

"There was room for us when we got back here. You'd think it would be full of reserves."

"Maybe they moved them all back."

"Yeah. Must have done."

*

Finally the weather broke, Max thought, gazing at the wood but not seeing it.

And here we were, back in the freezing wet Stollen, having slogged back along the 'road' through the mud that was shin-deep in places. At least all our boys made it over the bridge.

The morning of 21st February was clear, bright, and fucking cold – a real crisp winter's day. And we came out of the tunnels and stood in the trench up here, watching the biggest bombardment there'd ever been.

Shell after shell slammed into the French positions in the wood, every calibre imaginable. The racket was unbelievable as the shells roared and whined overhead, and exploded with massive force. Branches and even whole trees flew into the air, in a storm of fire and smoke.

You could almost feel sorry for the Frenchies – but at the time all we could think was that the more of them the artillery did for, the fewer would be left to kill us.

Nice theory that turned out to be.

*

21st February 1916, front line near Azannes

At four, the bombardment steps up to drumfire, the rolling thunderous detonations merging into a gigantic cacophony. I can barely hear myself think.

Leutnant Chrobak's Platoon gets ready. The sun, already dimmed by the clouds of smoke, is starting to slip behind the hills.

At five, the bombardment lifts to the French rear.

Chrobak and his boys quietly climb the ladders, make their way through the gaps in the wire and set off down the hill.

Bloody long way. Nearly a kilometre over open ground with no cover – but the French front line should be full of the dead and dying.

There won't be any resistance.

"Wish we were going in first," Tiemann grumbles to a murmur of agreement.

"Yeah," says Degenhardt. "They'll get all the fucking glory."

"There'll be plenty for us to do," says Kropp.

Just as the words leave his mouth, a French machine gun fires. And another.

What – how in God's name is anyone still alive?

"Fuck me!" says Berger.

"How the fuck did anyone survive?" Lorenz demands.

Chrobak's Platoon and those from the other companies disappear from sight in the undulating ground. *I hope it's as dead to the Frenchies as it is to us…*

We barely breathe.

This is not what was supposed to happen.

The fuckers must be in fortified positions, and those could be real bastards to take.

No plan survives first contact…

Our boys reappear going up the hill, under fire from the French artillery, and from machine guns in the wood and in the Knochgraben, the trench to the right. It runs parallel to our line of advance, and is clearly full of live Frenchies.

"Aren't the 24th supposed to take that trench?" Kropp says to me.

"It'll take time, won't it?"

They'll have to fight their way along it – but the last thing our boys need is flanking fire.

Even in the fading light we can see grey forms on the ground. Some lie still, some writhe, others try to crawl or drag themselves back up the hill.

I fucking hate seeing that.

You'd think I'd have got used to it – but seeing blokes get smashed up, especially fine, strong fellows like ours, always gets to me.

And I hope it always will.

Those still on their feet disappear into the wood. The crackle of rifle fire, the clatter of machine guns, and the explosions of grenades are loud when the shelling abates, the darkening wood lit by flashes and the long jets from the flamethrowers.

The French artillery starts up, shelling the trenches and the valley sporadically.

"Makes you want to get stuck in as well," says Lorenz.

"Yeah," says Degenhardt. "Boys need our help."

And all we can do is fucking well watch and wait…

But they're likely to want us before too long. Be careful what you wish for, Degenhardt – at this rate, there'll be plenty of glory to go round.

And there was, Max thought with a sigh. *More than enough.*

I wonder how you measure glory. Decorations, blood? Forts captured, ground taken? Victory?

Or holding firm in a desperate position without hope of relief, until your last breath, and not yielding a metre?

Glory and honour, concepts as old as mankind.

He sat staring into space.

What makes men fight? What made us go through our wire and on to meet the enemy, when we all knew what fighting is and that we might well die?

IV

We were so pissed off at not going in first. You'd think we'd have had more sense, but Degenhardt had spoken for us all – we wanted our share of the glory.

*

21st February 1916, front line near Azannes

Axel waves to me and squeezes his way along the crowded trench.

"I've just told Oberleutnant Strecker," he says. "You're going in at six – the rest of the Seventh, and the Sixth as well."

"Bloody marvellous!"

"Thought you'd be pleased to hear that!" 'Du', regardless of the men around. "So – may you be shot in the neck and stomach!"

Just like the fucking theatre. And in truth, don't we all have to put on an act when we know what we're going off to do?

Laugh. Axel embraces me.

"I'll stand you champagne in Verdun!" he says.

"I'll hold you to that!" 'Du', not 'Herr Leutnant'.

That gets us a few looks, but the boys know better than to push their luck.

The fighting in the wood is intensifying, and the Frenchies are lobbing over more and more shells.

We look at each other, suddenly serious.

"I'd best get back," Axel says.

"See you when it's over."

I hope I do. I hope I make it – it's a bloody long way over open ground, down the hill and up the other side, under increasingly heavy fire. And it'll be fun when we get there…

*

Funny, isn't it? Max thought. *In spite of being up to my eyeballs in the shit, I was the one who came through, and he got killed – and I left Verdun not knowing where he lay.*

We were told much later that he'd been found and buried. I've always wondered how much of him is in that grave. It's probably just a few bones with his tag, and they might not even be his. I'll pay my respects, anyway, just in case.

*

There are real clouds now, lit by the setting sun, and a few flakes of snow in the air.

Ten to six.

I've done this more times than I can count. My hands are steady, I feel quite calm and I want to get stuck in – and yet my mouth's as dry as dust and my heart's beating fast.

Driving my blood through my veins… where I'd rather like it to stay.

Just time for a fag.

Nine minutes to… Eight… Eight…

I swear my watch has stopped.

These last minutes always spin themselves into eternity.

They really might be my last minutes…

We all have to die, and it's better to die for something. If I fall, it will be for Prussia, for Brandenburg, my beautiful, beloved homeland.

Always, just before we go in, this silent, private dedication of my life.

Wonder what the others are thinking.

Degenhardt is joking with Berger, Stadler's smoking, Kropp looks very thoughtful. Weidner is a long way away.

All their eyes are resolute.

Everyone's ready.

Good blokes.

"Go."

Up the ladders and through the wire in the fading light.

Funny how my nerves always disappear…

Near me someone starts to sing 'The Glory of Prussia': "And when our Regiment was young…"

And in a flash we all join in.

That's the spirit, boys – sing the regimental song…

Fuck me but it's a long way down here.

The Frenchies' 'Good evening' whistles and sings past my ears.

Men fall on our right.

Just keep missing me, you bastards.

Strecker's out in front, that bloody walking stick in his hand.

Fucking idiot.

When I was a sniper, I'd have shot you straight off. Let's hope the Frenchie snipers are asleep.

More 'Bonsoir!' from the Frenchies.

"Friedrich Karl, the General, taught his—"

Start to run. No more breath to sing.

We're *still* not at the fucking bottom.

Shells, bullets – Jesus—

A man goes down in front of me, and another.

Screams, cries of "Medics!"

"*Keep moving, boys!*"

Bachmann rolls face up at my feet. He looks more surprised than hurt.

Hopefully it's only minor and he'll get picked up soon.

*

Max turned round, and looked back up the hill.

Why the fuck did they do that to us – send us in across so much open ground, and so late in the day? It's a fucking miracle any of us got there at all. And the French snipers must have been asleep, because Strecker made it to the wood, without even dropping that fucking stick of his.

I was grateful for that stick, though – but that was much later.

Suppose I'd better keep to the paths this time, even if it's not quite where we went.

His leg started to ache as he walked up the hill.

Bloody thing – but I should be grateful. If I hadn't got whacked at the Somme, I wouldn't have survived that, or the rest of the fucking war.

Am I really glad I survived? Wouldn't it have been better to get killed here at the beginning of this, like Axel, when we really believed victory was possible?

*

21st February 1916, No Man's Land

Shit but it's steep. Can't run – have to plod.

The bloody machine guns – fucking hell, I'll be shot any moment—

Scream of shell.

Hit the ground.

Blinding deafening crash brain reeling. Fountain of earth, clods hit my back.

Hope it is only clods, not red-hot sharp shards.

Screams.

"MEDICS!"

Get up.

"*Come on, boys!*"

Let's get into the fucking wood.

Climb as fast as I can heart pounding sweat pouring…

Into the wood.

Into gloom – except when the explosions and jets of flame give us glimpses of the inferno.

Here's the French front line, trenches shelled to pieces, sandbags, beams, wattle fencing, bodies everywhere.

Half an arm.

Most of a torso.

Stinking guts.

A flattened head.

A body smashed into a tree.

Sharp smell of blood. Litres and litres of it, soaking into everything.

Men mutilated and groaning.

A hand clutches at my leg. A bearded, contorted face looks up.

"Aide-moi!"

"Sorry, mate."

Shake him off.

German bodies as well, and wounded. The Frenchies didn't give up easily.

The fight for the second line is ahead up the slope. The flashing darkness is alive with gunfire and explosions and shouts and cries.

It's impossible to make sense of it.

The Frenchies are there somewhere, behind the confusion of fallen trees and broken branches.

Move cautiously forwards, well spread out.

Messner beckons to me.

"Schelling."

"Sir?"

"Take a patrol forward and to our left. See if you can find the French."

"Sir."

Degenhardt, Tiemann and Lorenz come with me.

Creep forward, rifle in hand…

Quiet, stealthy.

Forwards, forwards, the others close behind.

Loud crack of breaking branch.

Blinding flash air parts by my head ear-splitting bang hit the ground.

Fuck me.

Feel the left side of my head. Seems intact, but it's wet.

Lick my hand.

Sweat not blood.

Thank fuck for that.

Well, now I know where the Frenchies are.

Squirm on my stomach to the other three.

"You all right?" Degenhardt whispers in my ear.

"Yes. All of you?"

"Yes, Sergeant Major."

We wriggle some way back.

Unhook a grenade, unscrew the cap and pull the string, lob it towards the Frenchie.

Lie flat.

Pause.

FLASH BANG.

Hope that got him.

"Back."

Wriggle away.

The other side of a splintered tree, we get to our knees.

Nothing happens. Stand up.

"Sorry, Sergeant Major," Tiemann whispers.

Oh, it was you who trod on the branch. Cheers.

It's pitch-dark. There are branches lying everywhere. It wasn't his fault.

"Forget it."

*

Fuck me, but that was a close call, Max thought. *No crack-thump, but flash bullet past my head and bang, all in the same fraction of a second. He can't have been more than five metres away.*

Just as well it was so bloody dark.

Don't suppose he liked the grenade much – that's if it landed anywhere near him.

Max carried on up the hill.

Oh.

This was the 24th's cemetery.

The graves have gone, and the bloody Frenchies have taken most of the stone walls. The obelisk could do with a clean. Wonder if anyone will bother now.

And where have they taken the bodies? Wrong, that, moving men when they've been laid to rest. Hope they did it properly...

Max bowed to the dead, but with rather mixed feelings.

Bloody glory boys, the 24th were – always banging on about taking Fort bloody Douaumont, but I can't count the number of times we had to go forward without them.

Never bloody ready.

And if they'd taken the Knochgraben at the start as they were supposed to, a lot of our boys would have lived a bit longer.

Maybe one of those machine guns got Axel.
No point thinking about that.

He turned left and carried on along the track, the wrecked wood on his right.

And not only the wood, but trenches, shell-holes and the remains of blockhouses.

This was the French front line, he thought suddenly. *Looks a bit different now.*

There was a pile of unexploded shells beside the track.

Nice job someone's got, clearing those away. Wonder how often they go off – and how many more there are lying about. Better take the warnings seriously, then.

Next to the shells was a pile of splintered timber. A group of men in overalls came towards him carrying more wood, deposited it, and went back the way they'd come.

That's another dodgy job, cutting the ruined trees down with all the explosives lying around.

About fifty metres further on, there was another pile.

Bones.

Jesus. There's a femur… and a few more… hands… a lot of ribs. Part of a skull, a piece of pelvis, another hand. Intact rib cages still attached to spines, jawbones with teeth. A whole skull, staring blankly.

Tatters of cloth. A German boot with a shin bone sticking out of it.
The whole battlefield must be one huge boneyard.

He took his hat off and bowed his head.

Some of those must belong to our boys. Maybe some are Axel's. What in God's name are they going to do with them?
Maybe there's a mass grave somewhere…
Such a fucking waste.

He sighed and looked away, down the hill.

There, in the bottom of the valley, was the pond and the wreckage of Soumazannes. Beyond them, the ground rose to the old German front line.

This was our sector. Soon I'll be opposite the place where I last saw Axel.

In spite of the warm sun, the path was muddy, and his boots squelched audibly – someone was right behind him, boots squelching slightly out of time with his own.

Max stopped and turned round.

He was alone – and yet not.

Axel.

This must be close to where he was killed.

It's as if he were standing next to me.

He could see his men climbing the hill towards where he stood, with their assault packs and rifles, their helmets without the spikes.

You're still here. Axel, all of you.

I had a Comrade, a better one you won't find…

He turned again and faced the shattered wood.

Time to go back to where we fought.

I don't know if I should be doing this. Apart from my sanity, it would be a bit much to get blown to shreds here after the war.

Frieda and the boys would probably be better off without me.

There were a number of paths, no doubt used by the clear-up teams.

Should be safe enough, he thought, and chose one.

*

21st February 1916, Herbebois

Get back to Messner.

"Frenchies are about fifty metres that way, sir."

"So I heard! All in one piece?"

"Yes, sir."

Five minutes later, the French artillery starts up – 7.5s at first, soon joined by heavies.

The heavy shells aren't meant for us. Not directly, anyway.

They howl over our heads, and explode behind us in a curtain of fire that cuts us off from the rear.

Any hope of hot food, coffee, or supplies of grenades and ammunition gets blown to shreds.

Let's hope the bastards can't keep it up...

They do. It's a truly splendid barrage, but I would rather it were somewhere else.

The 7.5s are dropping into the wood. Horrible fucking things, fire far too bloody fast. No gun should be able to pump out twenty shells a minute.

Make ourselves small in the shell-holes, try to dig in but the ground's frozen solid. Fortunately they're holding back with the 7.5s for fear of shelling their own fellows, or it would be really unpleasant.

The night is fucking freezing, and it keeps on snowing. The sweat of earlier chills my body, and every time I jump into a shell-hole I get soaked. When I get out again, my uniform starts to freeze solid.

My coat's a rigid horseshoe, and I have to break the ice to unroll it. I put it on, and it's so bloody cold that I wonder if I'm better off without it.

Post sentries, and fall asleep in spite of the cold and the noise.

Wake with a jolt. I have never been so fucking frozen. Wiggle my fingers and toes, try to get some circulation into them.

My stomach's so empty it aches.

"What I wouldn't give for a hot meal and a coffee," Kropp says to me.

Hand him my hip flask. He takes a swig and gives it back.

"Thanks."

"Frenchies!" shouts Hoffmann.

"*Sound the alarm!*" Messner yells, and the bugle rings out.

Where the hell—

Shapes. Running towards us in the flashes.
French or German?
Wait.
Wait…
Flash—
Steel helmets.
"FIRE!"
Can't see them clearly, but we send them a wall of lead.
No more running shapes.
Usual cries and calls for help.
No way. Not in the pitch fucking dark, when we can't see who's waiting for us.

Their own will have to help them – which we'll let them do, provided they don't come too close.

Stealthy movements in the undergrowth, sounds of dragging, cry of pain.

Warning shot over their heads.

We're watching you. Don't even think of coming any closer.

At least we're in one piece. The wood echoes with groans, whimpers, and cries for help. It must be agony lying there injured in this cold, with the freezing air biting into raw flesh.

Can't get back to sleep. It's too cold and I'm too fucking hungry. Check on the boys, share a few words and a joke.

They're in good spirits in spite of everything.

"This feather bed's crap!" says Lorenz, gesturing at the snowy shell-hole.

"Be a real one in Verdun," Tiemann replies.

"With a mademoiselle!" says Degenhardt.

"Nah, mate – who'd want your ugly mug!" says Tiemann.

Good blokes. Bloody good blokes. We'll get the job done.

Dawn starts to gleam through the shattered canopy.

"Right, boys," says Messner. "Time to start clearing this wood."

Confer briefly.

Start creeping forward through the maze of fallen branches and thick undergrowth.

CRACKCRACKCRACKCRACKCRACK

Degenhardt drops.

All hit the ground.

Where the fuck did that come from?

*

Max carried on slowly through the remains of the wood, the path threading between the splintered trees.

In front of him the ground rose in a long mound, surrounded by pale lumps of shattered concrete and fragments of blackened branches.

He stopped.

Fuck me. That's the remains of a blockhouse…

*

22nd February 1916, Herbebois

Where the hell are the Frenchies?

Crouch in the undergrowth.

Degenhardt is only about five metres away. Blood is soaking through his tunic.

Berger, his inseparable mate, goes to help him.

A brief, loud rattle. Berger lies beside Degenhardt.

"Stay here, boys."

"Where the fuck did that come from?" Kropp mutters in my ear.

"Fucked if I know."

More of my boys are moving up—

"HALT!"

Another brief, loud burst cracks over our heads.

They hit the ground.

Crawl over to them on my hands and knees.

Schwarz is hit but the others are all right.

"Stay here."

They nod.

There is no sign, anywhere, of the Frenchies.

To our left is a wattle fence, ivy and brambles growing through it.

What's to our right?

"Pieper."

"Sergeant Major?"

"Take two blokes and find out what's over there – but keep low."

They crawl away and disappear.

Messner walks – *walks* – towards us.

"*Get down, sir!*"

He doesn't need telling twice, reaches me on his hands and knees.

"What's the situation?"

Just as I finish telling him, Pieper and the others come back.

"There's a fucking great wall," Pieper says. "About two metres high."

Messner and I look at each other.

Neither of us needs to spell out that we have a fence on one side, a wall on the other, and an alert enemy hidden somewhere in front.

Whatever they're hiding in has survived the bombardment.

Get my binoculars out, but they're broken – must have landed on them at some point.

"Fuck it."

"Mine went the same way," says Messner. "Luckily I've got reinforcements!"

He gets a pair of opera glasses out of his pocket, looks through them for what feels like two hours, then hands them to me with a very eloquent expression.

There's an almighty tangle of undergrowth and broken branches, and the rising sun sends long shafts through the remains of the canopy, lighting the smoke.

I look and look, but I still can't…

A narrow, black, rectangular slit. And another.

There's a fucking blockhouse built into a rise in the ground. And the wall and the fence force anyone approaching it into the line of fire.

Nicely done, Mr Frenchie.

Give Messner his opera glasses back.

"We'll have to go back, find a way round," he whispers. "Take it from behind."

Pass that on to Kropp, crawl as low as I can to the rest of my fellows, tell them.

We need to fetch Degenhardt, Berger and Schwarz.

There's no shortage of volunteers.

"Careful, boys," Kropp says softly.

Stadler looks at him as if to say, Yeah, we had worked that out.

He and Goldenbaum crawl out to Schwarz first.

Schwarz nods, starts wriggling back to us.

Stadler and Goldenbaum reach the other two.

Another rattle. They sink flat.

Fucking hell.

Kropp and I exchange looks.

We don't want to leave anyone behind, but we've got a job to do and we need the boys alive.

Goldenbaum wriggles on his stomach towards Degenhardt.

Reaches him.

Shakes his head.

Wriggles to Berger, beckons to Stadler.

Another rattle as Stadler wriggles towards them.

"For fuck's sake," Kropp says into my ear. "Can't those fucking Frenchies see what they're doing?"

God knows.

They probably want to kill us all.

Goldenbaum and Stadler struggle back with Berger. The Frenchies don't fire again.

Now comes the tricky part.

"Back that way," Messner says.

V

Strecker is coming the other way, and he's not pleased to see us.

We're supposed to be moving forward, not coming back dragging two wounded and reporting one dead.

He's even less pleased with Messner's report.

"You as well."

Kropp and I look at each other.

"We've already lost Leutnant Chrobak to one of those bloody blockhouses," Strecker goes on. "And the other companies have found the damn things as well. So the artillery's going to shell them from eight, and the attack's planned for twelve."

He and Messner confer for a few minutes, then Strecker vanishes into the undergrowth.

Fuck me, but it's bloody cold.

The low, feeble sun has no warmth, and it starts fucking snowing.

It gets right inside you and chills your bones. No one slept last night – you started to nod off, but the cold soon woke you. My coat's warmed up but it's not much help, and I really could do with a pair of long johns. My legs are freezing.

Hope my feet are all right – and everyone else's. If I do a foot inspection they'll have to take their boots off, and that could make things worse.

Food would warm up us, but there isn't any. I'm running on empty. You'd think they could send us a bucket of stew or two.

My stomach rumbles loudly – but it might mean I won't need a shit today. Having a piss is bad enough. I can't undo my buttons with gloves on. My fingers don't like being exposed to the freezing air, and a more vital part of me likes it even less.

Taking my trousers down and baring all will not be pleasant – and being as we have to stay in the shell-holes, it's crap on a spade and throw it out, and hope you don't land on it next time you hit the ground.

Have to laugh. *Here we are, officers and men alike, all shitting on spades and taking the piss if someone misses. Amazing what 'civilised Europeans' can get used to.*

As I'm pondering all that, Messner joins us.

"Right," he says. "As you heard, the artillery's going to shell the blockhouses from eight, then we're going in at twelve. We'll split the Platoon in half, go round that bastard we found earlier and take it from behind."

Vogelsang sniggers.

Messner grins. "And give it a proper shafting. I'll take half to the right, the other side of the wall. Schelling, you're in command of the other half – go to the left, the other side of the fence."

"Yes, sir." *No plan survives… wonder how long the wall and the fence are.*

"And the cookers can't get anywhere near, so the men can have one day's iron rations."

They are unimpressed.

"I'm fucking frozen," mutters Stadler. "And there's not even a mug of coffee."

"Bet the cooks are having nice hot stew," said Lorenz.

"Best beat the Frenchies quick, then," Weidner says. "Then we can have their nice hot food."

Amen to that.

Cold food is better than fuck all, but I'd love a coffee, strong and black and hot…

We've just started eating when the bombardment starts up, and we're a fucking sight nearer to it than we were yesterday.

If we get shorts we're fucked.

I do wish Stadler didn't pray so loudly. He's right next to me and I can hear every word.

Screams off to my left, shout of "Medics!"

Huge splinter flies just over our heads with a nasty whirring sound and crashes into a tree, lopping off a branch.

"Fuck me," Stadler says.

"Don't think the Good Lord wants to hear that!" says Wredow.

"How would you know, you fucking heathen?!"

The bombardment gets heavier. The racket is unbelievable.

Let's just hope they're hitting the fucking blockhouses – and that they miss us…

Try to bury ourselves deeper in the holes as more splinters fly back.

No shorts, boys, please.

The sun creeps higher, filtering through the clouds of acrid smoke.

Twelve cannot come soon enough – I hate this fucking waiting.

Wishing your life away, Max…

At least I'll be warm when we go in.

At ten to twelve we're all ready.

How can time slow like this? Maybe I should try to read that Einstein fellow.

For Prussia, for Brandenburg.

At twelve, the bombardment stops and the bugles ring through the woods, sounding the assault.

'Potato soup potato soup—'

Rise as one, go forward together.

Leave the fence on our right.

It goes on and on. *Surely we've passed the fucking blockhouse.* Here's the end.

Creep round it – and there's the back of the blockhouse, apparently untouched by the bombardment.

Messner and most of his boys are already there.

The door is shut.

Messner bangs on it with his fist and shouts to the Frenchies to surrender.

No response.

Everyone backs away apart from Pioneer Sergeant Schneider.

He places blocks of explosive by the door, lights the fuse, and runs to join the others.

The bang blows the door in.

"Come on, boys!"

Messner's fellows are at the door a few seconds before us.

"Come out!" Messner shouts in French.

A dozen Frenchmen emerge blinking into the light, with their hands up.

"Our Lieutenant is in there, wounded," a corporal says.

Bloch and Schwenck guard them, and we enter the blockhouse cautiously, in case it's a trap.

Our eyes take a few moments to adjust.

The door went right across the room, and rests against the far wall. A rivulet of blood is pouring from beneath it and pooling in a depression in the floor.

Lorenz and Goldenbaum lift the door and recoil visibly.

They let it drop back into place and shake their heads.

Lorenz has been at war since late '14 and he's seen it all, so God knows how mangled the corpse must be.

The French Lieutenant lies against another wall, unconscious. The left side of his face is covered in blood, and so's his shoulder.

"Looks like the corner of the door got him," says Tannwitz. "Quite a mess."

He isn't joking. Cheekbone, upper and lower jaw are all

mashed to red pulp, studded with fragments of bone and teeth, and his eye's gone.

"Won't be charming the mademoiselles any more," Lorenz says.

"If he survives," says Tannwitz.

"His chaps can carry him back," says Messner.

Tannwitz and Lorenz carry him out.

The Frenchies seem surprised, but don't want to show it. Maybe they remember shooting at our blokes, who were trying to help Degenhardt and the others.

Our fellows certainly remember that, and the mood is not friendly. There are mutterings and black looks as they make sure the Frenchies are all disarmed.

The Frenchies pick up their Lieutenant and set off for our rear, as ordered, with one of Messner's boys guarding them.

"Nice souvenir," Tannwitz says, studying the French steel helmet.

"Bloody sight better than our leather ones," Lorenz says.

It is a bit much, really. Only our storm troops have steel helmets. The rest of us are still using the spiked ones from the last century – and they're fuck all use against shell splinters.

*

And of course that was only the first blockhouse, Max thought as he sat down on top of the ruin. *A dozen prisoners and three machine guns wasn't a bad haul, though.*

*

22nd February 1916, Herbebois

"Right," says Messner. "Let's get moving."

Pick our way through the fallen branches and broken trees.

It's such a fucking tangle – can't see far in any direction…

Schwenck drops. A fraction of a second later we hear the 'thump'.

Where the fuck…?

Bloch takes another step, and he too falls to the ground.

Messner holds his hand up. "Halt."

Tannwitz crawls carefully to Schwenck.

We hold our breath.

Let's hope the Frenchies can see the red cross on his armband. Trouble is, we all have white armbands for identification…

Lorenz crawls to Bloch, shakes his head.

Messner and I look at each other.

We make use of his opera glasses again, stare and stare, but see nothing. There's just a jumble of winter vegetation and splintered branches. It all looks the fucking same.

Examine the undergrowth again. Obviously the Frenchies are there somewhere – but where?

Horrible skin-crawling feeling, knowing they're watching us and just waiting for the chance to shoot us, while we can't see them at all.

I suppose that's how the Tommies felt when I was a sniper… Funny how I never felt that about their snipers – maybe I felt less helpless, being as I was doing the same job.

Weidner crawls to Tannwitz and Schwenck. And then back again.

"He'll need carrying."

That means the poor sod's stuck until the stretcher-bearers reach him. Unenviable, that.

"Did you get any direction on that shot?" Messner asks me.

"No, sir."

Weidner is looking very thoughtful.

"Sir," he says to Messner, "as I was crawling back, I noticed a gap in the trees, like a narrow firebreak."

"Show me."

That's fucking stupid.

"Sir – why don't I go instead?"

Messner looks at me. "No, Schelling – I'll go."

I know him too well to argue. He'll die before he puts any of us in more danger than he has to.

Weidner sets off, Messner close behind him.

We hardly dare breathe.

As they crawl back, there's a loud crack-thump.

Thank God they were keeping low.

"Came from that way, Sergeant Major," says Lorenz.

"Thanks."

"Just as Weidner said," says Messner. "There's a gap."

He points in the same direction as Lorenz.

Nicely done again, Mr Frenchie.

It's increasingly clear what we've walked into.

"We'll use that fallen tree as cover," Messner says, "and keep low."

I bring up the rear.

Fürst, right in front of me, is a tall fellow.

"Keep your—"

Shower of wood splinters his helmet and part of his head disappear in an explosion of blood and brains.

Fuck me. Duck right down low.

…head down, I was going to say.

Nasty things, ricochets. He wouldn't have felt it, anyway. Messner won't have to lie in that letter.

Stadler, in front of him, turns round and grimaces at the mess.

"Keep going."

Messner and the others have stopped.

In front of us is a deep belt of barbed wire, completely undamaged, stretching as far as we can see.

"Thought the bombardment was supposed to cut that up," mutters Kropp.

Messner looks at Schneider.

"Sorry, sir," Schneider says. "I can't do anything with that."

"We'll have to go round it."

And what will we meet when we do that?

Kropp's eyes meet mine and he raises an eyebrow, clearly thinking the same as me.

Off to our right we hear the bugles.

'Potato soup potato soup—'

And again, further away.

"Schelling, you take your boys to the left. I'll take mine to the right."

"Sir."

Sit my fellows down.

"Mr Frenchie's a cunning bastard, and all his obstacles direct us into fire from somewhere. Stay low and keep your wits about you. If you see something, tell me at once."

Creep along beside the wire. It goes on and fucking on.

In front of us is a wild tangle of brambles – thorny stems looping over and over each other, just as impenetrable as the wire.

But it's not quite in front. It's slightly to our left, so we have to go right.

"Halt."

Kessler hasn't heard.

"GET DOWN!"

In the same instant a Frenchie machine gun rattles. Kessler dives into the brambles and the Frenchies give him another burst.

He hangs limp in the grasp of the thorns.

The rest look at each other.

*

What... where...?

Max looked around him, wondering where his men had gone and why the wood was so quiet.

He was sitting on the ruins of a blockhouse, a wrecked trench snaking away to both sides.

Shit – better take cover – get into the trench—

Too late. Three men were approaching him. With rifles.

Max reached for his rifle.

It wasn't there. Nor was his pistol.

"Bonjour," one of the men called out cheerfully.

FUCK.

Why don't I have any weapons?

Maybe I'm a prisoner. Maybe I had a bang on the head and can't remember.

Those Frenchie rifles look bloody odd...

He stared at the men and their weapons.

Oh. They're just bits of wood – misshapen, broken branches, charred black.

The men dropped the wood onto the nearest pile, and went back along the path.

Have a fag, Max, and try to work out what's going on...

The Frenchies aren't in uniform, and neither am I. There are no sounds of fighting. And the fellow seemed friendly.

The shattered trees are putting out shoots, and there are young saplings, and green leaves and even flowers.

There's a wedding ring on my right hand – but I married Frieda after we left here.

He thought for a few minutes, and slowly his head cleared.

The war's over.

Not in my head it fucking isn't.

He got up and started to walk further into the wood.

Amazing how nature can recover – you'd think these splintered trunks would be dead, but the roots must still be alive.

Surprising how friendly the fellows were, as well. Maybe they didn't realise I'm a Boche.

Oh – here's a bit more of their second line.

He climbed cautiously down into the battered remains of the trench. Most of its wattle sides had collapsed, and some of the logs that had rested across the top of it had fallen into the bottom.

Fuck me – that's a deep hole. Must be a blockhouse or dugout entrance.

Part of a concrete roof a metre thick was exposed. Beneath it, smooth concrete walls framed a descent into total blackness.

No wonder the bombardment didn't do much to these – that concrete would survive anything except a direct hit.

He peered into the darkness, not wanting to go too near the edge.

I'll bet there are still blokes down there. Who's going to go down to bring them up?

Careful, Max – if the trench floor collapses you'll join them. God knows what you're walking on.

He climbed back out – and stopped dead, rooted to the spot in horror.

In front of him was a dense tangle of brambles, sprouting fresh new leaves.

Fucking evil bloody things…

He shivered as cold ran down his back.

The curving stems seemed to reach out to grasp him with their sharp thorns, to hold on and pull him in…

The wood shimmered, his vision blurring, and he shook himself.

They're just brambles, Max, that's all.

But it wasn't all, and it never would be.

I think I should get out of here and walk back to Azannes.

*

22nd February 1916, Herbebois

Kessler's screaming and writhing in agony.

The brambles tighten their grip on him – the more he writhes, the more deeply embedded he becomes.

Vogelsang crawls out to him but can't free him.

"Rest of you stay here," Messner says.

He's right – we can't risk losing anyone else. We're going to have to fight our way through this fucking wood, and we need all the blokes we can get.

Vogelsang straightens slightly, trying to get a better grip on Kessler.

"GET DOWN!" we shout.

Too late. Vogelsang hangs in the brambles.

Messner crawls to me.

"There's another blockhouse," he says, handing me his opera glasses. "In the trench, there."

He points and I look.

And look – nothing – nothing…

Ah. There.

It's built into a rise, like the last one, but it's quite a bit above us – so there's a fair bit of dead ground right in front of it.

And while the bombardment hasn't touched the fucking thing, it's left plenty of shell-holes.

"How much dead ground d'you reckon there is?" Messner asks me.

"A good twenty metres."

"Shell-hole to shell-hole until we're in the dead ground, then grenades through the apertures."

Messner has echoed my thoughts perfectly.

Kessler has stopped screaming, for now anyway, but no one can get close enough to patch him up.

Take the blockhouse and that problem will solve itself.

So easy to say. It's fucking solid, set into the ground, and full of well-armed Frenchies who don't actually want to die today.

Can't say I disagree with that sentiment – but someone has to die, and I'd prefer it to be them.

Not the time to ask myself what the fuck we're all doing here. The most pointless of pointless questions.

What was it we used to hear the Tommies singing? "We're here because we're here because we're here because we're here…" We joined in once Hoffmann had translated it for us, and everyone laughed, them and us.

All in the same shit together.

Fucking bloody politicians. Give them all a week in the front line and there'd be peace the day after.

VI

22nd February 1916, Herbebois

"So what's the best way to do this?" Messner asks me.

That is a very good question.

"Stealth won't work," I reply. "They're watching us. Covering fire won't bother the fuckers in the blockhouse, but might stop anyone else joining the party."

"Agreed. Your lot forward while my lot cover and so on, then. Unless you've got a better idea?"

"No, sir – I haven't."

"Ten minutes from now."

Crawl on my hands and knees to one group of my fellows, brief them, then go to the others.

All the while I have the nasty feeling that I'll be shot any moment.

Boot on the other foot, you might say.

It takes almost the whole ten minutes to brief them all. At least I don't have long to think.

'Potato soup potato soup—'

Messner's boys open fire at the same instant.

Leap up run like fuck.

Frenchies let loose, cracking whistling metal round my ears tumble into the next hole—

Fire as Messner's boys charge forward.

And so on, just like on the exercise ground except that

they want to kill us. Fair enough, really – they want to get us first.

The last leap takes us into the dead ground.

Now the French machine guns are firing over our heads. They'll have lost sight of us as well.

Most of us have made it this far – but of course the Frenchies know what's coming next.

A grenade flies out of the blockhouse and lands at our feet. In a flash Lorenz picks it up and throws it to the side and we flatten ourselves.

Ear-splitting bang shower of wood and metal.

No damage.

Creep right up to the wall, quiet as mice.

Two more grenades fly out over our heads, explode behind us.

Weidner curses.

Wonder how many of the bloody things they've got.

Pieper, Dachwitz and Tiemann are right beneath one of the slits. Messner's boys are under the other.

Pieper lifts Dachwitz, Tiemann passes him a grenade, and he posts it through the slit like a man delivering a letter.

The bang is shattering even out here.

I do not want to imagine being in a concrete room with a detonation like that bouncing off the walls…

Messner bangs on the door with the butt of his pistol.

"Open up!"

No reply.

Messner looks for Schneider to blow the door, but he's not with us.

We could tie grenades together, but we'll need them later.

Messner bangs again, harder, and the iron door rings.

A grenade rolls out of the slit above Messner's boys.

"GRENADE!"

One picks it up.

Fling ourselves down—

Thunderous crash shower of wood metal something soft liquid—

Sit up slowly, ears ringing.

We're all covered in blood and globs of flesh.

"Right, you bastards," says Tiemann viciously.

"Let's keep our heads," I say.

"Not like poor old Schmidt!" says another of Messner's boys. He points to a head rolling away, still in its helmet.

We all laugh. If you didn't, you'd go mad.

We move a couple of metres away from the wall. Messner and I confer.

Try one more grenade, we agree. If the bastards hold out after that then we'll have to get the flamethrower boys.

"Can you lob one next to the door?" I ask Tiemann.

"Do my best, Sergeant Major."

Another thunderous crash. *Surely the bastards will have had enough?*

But the door remains in place, jammed shut.

Another grenade rolls out and away from us. One of Messner's boys gets a nasty gash in his arm.

How can anyone still be alive in there?

And how are we going to summon the flamethrower crew?

Someone will have to go back the way we came and find them, wherever they might be - and that's going to be fucking dangerous.

"I need a volunteer," Messner says, and explains.

"I'll go," says Lorenz, before anyone else opens his mouth.

There is a brief rattle from the blockhouse as he legs it, but that's all.

Messner bangs on the door again.

"Open up!"

We can hear arguing inside.

"OPEN UP!"

The door starts to open. In a flash every man has his rifle levelled.

It slams shut again in a jabber of voices.

"OPEN UP!!"

More arguing. The door moves again. Pieper barges it with his shoulder, shoves it wide open.

"COME OUT HANDS UP!" Messner shouts.

Out stumble seven Frenchies, in a very sorry state. All are bloodied, and their faces and hair are blackened.

All honour to them.

"Who's in charge?" Messner asks. All their uniforms are filthy and tattered.

"I am. Lieutenant Bertrand."

"Leutnant Messner." He holds out his hand, and the French officer hesitates and then shakes it. "Do you have more casualties inside?"

"Yes."

We make sure the seven men aren't armed.

"You can bring your chaps out," Messner says. "One at a time."

Schorr guards them as they go to and fro. Each time they come out, they're carrying a poor smashed-up bastard. No one wants to look at them.

"Last one?" Messner asks.

"Oui."

Messner and I enter the blockhouse cautiously, pistols in hand.

It stinks so badly we can hardly breathe, and there are a couple of dead Frenchies. The floor is slippery with blood, clotting in puddles. More is splashed on the walls, along with flesh and brains.

The machine guns are wrecked. No point salvaging them.

Go back out into the fresh air.

Lorenz is just returning, with the flamethrower crew. He looks almost disappointed that we managed without them.

I'm relieved to see him back, though – we're losing enough good blokes.

"Stay with us, anyway," Messner says to the flamethrower boys. "We'll need you before long."

Of course we will – God knows how many of these fucking blockhouses there are in the wood.

Messner and I take stock.

Kessler is dead. Vogelsang should be able to walk back. Weidner has a cut hand but can fight, and the chap with the gashed arm reckons he can too.

"It's the left one," he says.

Messner nods. He looks a bit doubtful, but we've lost ten of ours so far, dead, wounded or missing, plus Pionier Sergeant Schneider. No one saw what happened to him. And we've got almost no distance through this fucking wood.

Off to our right the bugles blow again, followed by sounds of intense fighting.

Kropp and I look at each other.

This is not how it was supposed to be. What was it those fucking artillerymen said? Parade march to Verdun? Like to see anyone try.

The Frenchies set off for our rear, carrying some of those who can't walk. But the French prisoners and our walking wounded are not enough to carry all the stretcher cases. Some will have to wait, for God knows how long.

There's nothing we can do about that.

We have another blockhouse to take, and we're yet another man down, as Schorr's escorting the Frenchies. We can't let them wander about by themselves – there are discarded rifles and ammunition lying about, and God knows what sort of stupid ideas they'd get.

The same sort of stupid ideas that I'd have in their position – re-arm ourselves and fight our way back through to our own lines.

*

And on it went, Max thought. *Blockhouse after blockhouse after machine-gun nest. Trenches dug deep with beams and wattle over the top of them.*

So much for the bombardment killing all the Frenchies. Plenty of them were very much alive and they fought like tigers.

Chapeau, messieurs.

He sat down on a tree stump and lit another cigarette.

*

22nd February 1916, Herbebois

Ahead of us, the wood continues to slope gently uphill. We can see almost no distance. It all looks the fucking same – tangled undergrowth and fallen branches.

Edge forward.

We can't go any further left. The vegetation is dense and curiously solid.

"It's another fence," says Tischert, giving it a push.

"Bollocks," Mersch retorts.

Kropp gives it a push as well.

"Woven willow."

And so it is – with vines and God knows what growing through it.

We know what it means, and what will happen if we carry on beside it.

Maybe we can get through it. "Wire cutters."

"Here, Sergeant Major," says Dachwitz.

After twenty sweaty minutes, I realise it's pointless. I've made a bit of a hole and there's another fence behind the first one.

"Right, boys – we'll have to stay as low as possible."

There is a nasty cold feeling down my back as we crouch low and shuffle forward.

Some fucking Frenchie is waiting for the right moment to kill us, and we don't know where he is.

I do not like this one bit—

Burst of fire.

Throw ourselves down yet again.

Someone screams.

Crawl forward.

Another burst, over our heads.

Stop in the next shell-holes, search the undergrowth with my eyes.

There's a lump in the ground to our right.

And a good number of broken branches and a lot of shell-holes.

"Weidner."

"Sergeant Major?"

"That's the bastard over there. Take half the fellows to the right of it, I'll go left."

No plan survives…

The Frenchies let us start moving.

Weidner's boys get a burst from their right. We get one from our left.

Tischert goes down, so do Bauer and Kirn.

Shit.

Messner comes crawling from hole to hole, with some of his fellows.

"We've got two more blockhouses in front of us," he says.

Hope they're the same two we've seen.

They are – or we think so, anyway.

In front of us is a dirt track going left to right through the wood. The blockhouses are on this side of it.

Between us, we come up with a fresh plan. He'll take his fellows round the back of the one on the right, and we'll do the same to the one on the left.

"You can have the flamethrower boys," he says. "We'll go for the postal service."

"Do you need more 'letters'?"

"Let you know in a couple of minutes."

Grenades for a flamethrower seems like a reasonable trade, though we really could do with more of both.

"Can you spare us five?" Messner asks me.

"I reckon so, sir."

Sit down with Kropp and Weidner.

"So the question is how far back we have to go," Kropp says. "To get round the fence."

"At least the part behind us is cleared."

Creep away from the blockhouses. The Frenchies send us a noisy farewell.

It's au revoir, mes amis, not adieu…

And bugger me, but there's a hole in the fence with a fucking great shell-hole beneath it.

"I'll never be rude about gunners again," mutters Dachwitz as we crawl through.

"Bet you are," says Stadler.

There's barbed wire on the other side, but we can just squeeze under it.

That's made more tears in my tunic and trousers. My arse is going to freeze.

Creep carefully forward, well spread out, keeping low, trying to use the shattered trees as cover.

Which is difficult when you don't know quite where the enemy is…

There's yet another obstacle in front of us. It seems to be just fallen branches.

Nothing in this killing ground is what it appears to be.

Motion to the boys to stop. We all sink into the holes.

All I can see is brushwood, the thin branches and twigs overlapping each other.

But I have a very bad feeling.

Stare and stare—

Fuck me.

Fresh cold runs down my back, settles in my stomach.

There's a Frenchie machine-gun nest.

Only part of it is visible, and thank fuck they haven't seen us. Or have they?

Kropp is about five metres to my right, and I need to talk to him.

This could be interesting.

Crawl on my belly up and over into the next hole.

Nothing happens.

So. Did I imagine them, or haven't they seen me, or are they waiting to kill me?

Crawl up – crackcrackcrack rattle whine—

Tumble into hole beside Kropp.

He raises an eyebrow.

"That's what I need to talk to you about," I say.

He sighs theatrically. "I didn't think you'd brought me lunch!"

"Don't talk about food!"

The nest is even harder to see from this hole. Kropp looks and looks.

"Yes. Got it."

"We'll have to try to get round behind it."

Every way we look there's an obstacle.

Another wattle fence with ivy growing through it.

A wall.

Another dense tangle of brambles. Nature's barbed wire – stems as thick as my thumb, bristling with thorns, curving over and over and looping around and around each other, completely impenetrable.

You'd have to cut a path through, and God knows how long that would take.

We'll have to work our way from shell-hole to shell-hole, until we're close enough to get them with grenades and the flamethrower.

Wonder how Messner's getting on.

"Stealth, this time, I think," I say to Kropp.

He nods. "If we creep round to the left, use the broken trees, that could work."

The artillery really shredded this part of the wood. The fallen timber both helps and hinders us.

But the Frenchies are alert and bullets crack and whistle past us, kick up the earth, chip splinters off the trees—

Ricochet whines past me in a shower of blood.

Hoffmann yells.

His face is split right open, half his lower jaw gone.

Poor bastard.

Throw ourselves into the holes.

We're just close enough for the flamethrower.

The flamethrower boys are nervous, and I don't blame them. They're a prime target.

No one wants to be near them.

There's a hiss and stink of fuel, a 'whump' as it ignites.

The wood fills with vivid orange light and shrieks.

The machine gun position is blazing. At least we're upwind of it.

The Frenchies scream to chill your soul.

Whoever thought up such a weapon?

In no time they're burned to a crisp. As the flames die down, we creep to the nest. The stench of charred flesh is eye-watering.

"Almost enough to put you off bacon," Stadler says with a grin.

"Nah, mate," says Lorenz. "Nothing would put me off bacon."

"Stop talking about food, you bastards!" says Dachwitz. "I'm fucking starving."

"Wonder if the cookers will make it today," Lorenz says.

"They've already been!" says Pieper, gesturing at the blackened corpses.

Lorenz looks at him with genuine disgust. "I'm not that fucking hungry."

"God, no," Dachwitz agrees. "Roast Frenchie? Not fucking likely."

"Overdone, anyway," says Stadler, and we all laugh.

If you didn't, you'd go mad.

We still need to get round the back of the blockhouse.

But where the fuck is it?

Sounds of heavy fighting from both left and right – small arms fire and explosions. Nothing in front, though.

There's a belt of dense brambles on our left.

We're being forced right…

Motion with my hand to keep low.

We don't even get two shell-holes forward. The Frenchies let rip at us.

Three fellows dive to the side, into the brambles.

Where the fuck did that come from?

Broken, blackened branches… brush…

Come on, look harder.

Nothing… nothing…

My eyes are starting to ache…

A thin black rectangle. Another fucking blockhouse.

How many of the bastard things are there?

The flamethrower crew are right beside me.
"Can you get flame into that slot from here?"
"Some of it."
"Go for it."

The jet of flaming oil hits the blockhouse wall, moves up towards the slot.

The Frenchies fire again, and hit the flamethrower boy who's holding the nozzle.

He shouts out and turns and I hit the ground, feel the heat on my back.

Don't let me burn, please—

The flame hits the brambles. They catch light.

Kehrer, Mersch and Schaffer are held fast. The more frantically they try to free themselves, the tighter the thorns grip them.

"HELP!"

Kropp and Stadler leap up and run towards them.

"HELP!"

Terror in their eyes faces voices—

"*HELP!*"

Burst from the Frenchies.

Stadler hits the ground.

Kropp almost reaches the brambles, but the heat is already too intense.

"HEL—" The word ends in a scream.

All we can see is flames and writhing bodies.

The sunlight slants through the blasted canopy, lights the smoke blue.

The stink of burning flesh is choking. The screams chill my blood and sear my soul.

Jesus fucking Christ.

How long can it take?

I look away, and realise the others are doing the same.

It's indecent to watch. That's what I tell myself.

VII

Max shivered in the warm sunshine.

I've never been able to stand the sight of brambles since. They always look malevolent, as if they're reaching out for me.

Those poor bastards. Horrible, horrible way to go.

Think about something else, for fuck's sake.

What's left of the Frenchies' perfect killing ground is laid bare now among the shattered trees: half-collapsed trenches with fallen timbers, bits of wattle fence and stone walls, and those mounds of ruined blockhouses.

*

22nd February 1916, Herbebois

Kropp and Stadler crawl back to me. Burnt flesh is thick in the air, and I don't want to breathe.

For a moment we don't say anything.

I'm desperate for a fag, but can't face lighting one.

Must get the boys moving before their minds dwell on it.

"What d'you reckon, Kropp?"

"We'll have to go back and find a way round."

"But is that the one we were trying to get behind?"

He scratches his stubble. "You know, I don't think it is."

"Neither do I… How many of the fucking things have they got?"

"God alone knows," he says, "and he ain't telling!"

The withdrawal doesn't go badly – they send us a lot of lead but without result.

And by great good fortune we encounter Messner and his boys.

He looks at me, obviously wondering where the rest of us are, just as I'm thinking the same about his lot.

"Another blockhouse, sir – need to get round behind it."

"So how many's that in this group? We found one, but it's got a thick belt of wire in front of it."

"We've found two."

Messner sighs. "Well, this one's closest, isn't it? So I reckon it's round the back and knock it out, then on to the next."

"Sounds good to me, sir."

In truth, it sounds anything but good – but what can we do? We can't leave the bastards intact to kill anyone following us.

We'll have to clear the fucking things one by one – and at the rate we're losing fellows, we'll all be gone before the job's finished.

Creep forward slowly and carefully. This wood is not the place to do anything in haste.

Pass the end of a fence.

There's a lump in the terrain… and a concrete lintel.

"Maybe we can get on top of it and give them some post," Officer Cadet Jahnke says cheerfully, as if it were a game.

We don't have a lot of 'post' left.

Strecker appears out of the ground, smoking his pipe, calm as anything. You'd never think his Company is up to its eyeballs in the crap.

"Sorry we haven't got further, sir," says Messner.

"You're not doing any worse than Scheumann's and Hutten's Platoons – and the Third Battalion's making very slow progress. Lack of support on the right."

Not only calm but a diplomat. We all know he means our neighbouring regiment is lagging behind.

Messner gives him the situation.

"Scheumann's working on another blockhouse," Strecker replies. "So if you deal with this one, we might make some progress."

"Do we know what's beyond them, sir?" Messner asks.

"No – more of the same, no doubt. Well, I'm off to check on Hutten. Carry on."

"Sir."

Strecker vanishes. Messner and I look at each other.

"Better get on with it," he says.

But as we try to creep round the blockhouse we come under fire, from God knows where.

Take cover hastily.

We can just make out the next blockhouse, by the dirt track.

But there is something else…

Try again to move.

Crackcrackcrack hit the ground.

Brehm takes most of the burst and it stops him dead.

Literally.

So where did that come from?

"Stadler."

"Sergeant Major?"

"Any idea where that machine gun is?"

"I think it's off to our right."

Just what I thought, too.

Now what?

Take my life in my hands and leap into the next hole, and the next. Somehow they miss me.

That's another life gone. Wonder how many I've got left…

Kropp looks at me with a raised eyebrow.

"Cunning bastard, Mr Frenchie," he says.

"Indeed."

Obviously, we have to deal with that machine-gun nest before we can storm the blockhouse. But until we've taken the blockhouse, we can't deal with the machine gun.

Bit of a bastard, really.

*

The cigarette burned down to Max's fingers.

He swore and dropped it, then trod it out.

One of the clean-up teams was coming towards him, carrying something in a tarpaulin. Max stood up to see what it was.

More bones, bleached from lying in the open.

He took his hat off and bowed his head.

What in God's name are they going to do with all these bones? No one can tell whose they are, unless there are still tags with them, and even then they'll be jumbled up.

Put them in a mass grave, no doubt. What else can they do?

Such a fucking waste. These were strong young men, who should have had years to live.

Why did we go to war anyway? The Allies blame us, and saddled us with those reparations, but we weren't the first to declare war, and the Russians and the Frenchies mobilised before we did.

We believed we were defending our country, just like everyone else.

He sighed.

None of that changes anything.

*

22nd February 1916, Herbebois

"We need to find that machine-gun nest… Kropp, you search from ahead to left, and I'll look right."

The boys don't need telling not to move.

Look and look until my eyes burn. All I can see is shattered trees, broken, burnt branches lying everywhere, brambles, what might be a wall…

It all looks the fucking same.

"Fucking hell."

I've never heard anyone murmur as expressively as that.

"What have you seen?" I ask Kropp.

"There's another blockhouse, about twenty metres away, that way."

He points and I look along his finger, but I can't see – *shit*. There's a slim black rectangle half-hidden behind a tangle of vegetation.

It and the one in front of us cover each other very nicely. From their point of view, that is.

If we can work our way round behind it…

A few minutes later, Kropp and I have a plan. We'll back off again, then work round to the left.

We all know what happens to the plan.

We manage the 'retreat' unscathed, but when we try the flanking manoeuvre we land properly in the crap.

Schmidt II goes down, the rest of us dive into the holes.

There's another hidden machine gun.

At this rate we'll all be shot.

Again we search and search – and Tiemann spots another aperture. There's a third blockhouse supporting the other two.

I've lost count. How many are there in this group?

And how the fuck are we going to deal with them?

The Frenchies have done a fucking good job, I'll say that for them. I just wish we weren't on the wrong end of it.

Green flares go up, off to our right and left.

No response from our artillery, which is probably just as well.

More flares.

Scream of shell from behind. Our artillery has woken up.

Press ourselves into the bottom of the shell-hole.

Detonation some way ahead.

And another – and another… Closer.

Closer.

World explodes in flame and blast.

Stones rain down, put my arms over my head.

Wish our helmets were steel like the French ones.

No closer, boys, for fuck's sake.

Half an hour later the bombardment stops, and we look up cautiously.

In front of us is a smoking crater, surrounded by burnt branches and chunks of concrete.

A man drags himself towards us, covered in blood and dirt, his face singed black.

"M'aidez, camarades," he croaks. "M'ai – dez…"

I'll give you fucking 'camarades'… you were trying to kill us a few minutes ago.

But that's war, isn't it? And the poor bastard's fucked.

No one dares go to him, though – the other blockhouses are still there, and who wants to get shot helping a Frenchie?

"M'ai – dez… m'ai – dez…"

The agony in his voice is unbearable.

Kropp shouts something to him in French. I catch only, "Your mates will shoot."

"M'ai – dez… m'ai – dez…"

Schmidt II starts screaming, and he's far from alone. The wood rings with cries and shouts for help.

It's enough to drive you mad – especially when you know it could be you next.

It's bad enough that men get killed, but mutilated and screaming is far, far worse. You wouldn't do that to an animal.

God knows when they'll be picked up, the poor sods – if they ever are. Most of them will probably die first, in agony.

And we're going to have to listen to them all night, and it's the last thing any of us needs to hear. Fuel for the imagination, which we'll all have to curb or we'll be fuck all use.

What a fucking shit business this is.

Messner joins us.

"Stuck as well?" Not that he needs to ask.

"Yes, sir."

The sun's almost down, and we are truly stuck. Not even halfway through the wood.

"I'll say this for the Frenchies," he says. "This is a beautifully designed killing ground. They couldn't have done it better."

"Just a real bastard that we're in it!" I reply.

He's right, though, and I can't help admiring what our enemies have created.

"Yes." He grins. "But we are the Brandenburg Corps – so we'll get the fuckers in the end!"

"That's for sure, sir!" says Kropp.

"So what's next, sir?" I ask.

"Strecker's sending a report back to Battalion – hopefully there'll be another bombardment in the morning, sort those fucking blockhouses out."

That's the only thing that will sort them out – a few heavy shells.

If they can hit them. That's going to be fucking difficult when no one knows where most of them are.

"In the meantime, we need to know what's behind this blockhouse line. So I need volunteers for a patrol."

"I'll go, sir," I say.

He looks at me. I can see what he's thinking, but after a moment he says, "Good. Take these." He hands me his opera glasses.

"What's the chances of food, sir?" Dachwitz asks.

Messner pulls a face. "Hopefully they'll get the cookers forward."

"I'm fucking parched," says Stadler, speaking for us all.

"See what you can find once it's dark," Messner says.

Night settles uneasily over the wood. The French barrage is still slamming in behind us, and fighting breaks out sporadically.

Warn the boys to be alert – not that they really need reminding. Everyone's knackered and keyed up at the same time.

Take water bottles from the dead, and iron rations, and Frenchie rations.

A lot of the bottles are holed. Some of the Frenchie ones contain their rough red wine.

"Christ," says Lorenz. "You could take paint off with this!"

"It's alcohol," says Tiemann. "It'll do."

We'd all prefer good German beer, but wine is wine. And it does warm us up, just a bit.

Time to set off. "Right, who's coming with me?"

Tiemann, of course, Lorenz, and Stadler.

Dachwitz volunteers as well.

Think for a moment. *Four of us will have to be enough, given our depleted numbers.*

"Sorry, Dachwitz – I can't risk losing any more."

He pulls a face of mock disappointment. The other three grin at him.

"Don't go thinking you can eat our rations!" says Lorenz. "We'll be coming back!"

"And you can save us some of that wine!" adds Stadler.

"Kropp, you're in charge."

"Sergeant Major."

It's proper night now. If it weren't for the explosions and small-arms fire it would be pitch fucking dark.

Which will help us creep past the Frenchies.

Last night when we crept close to the Frenchies, I nearly got shot.

How can that be less than twenty-four hours ago? Maybe Professor Einstein could explain it.

*

And maybe he could explain where today's going to as well, Max thought.

The sun was well on its way down.

Better get back to Prince – though I left him with plenty of food and water.

I hope I can find my way back – but it's so much easier now. You can see a lot further. If I walk north I'll meet the old French front line at some point, and it's straightforward from there.

And I hope I get back without forgetting what year it is.

That was the least frightening way of thinking of it…

As he left the wood, someone said clearly, 'Stay with us.'

He turned.

"I'll be back tomorrow."

Without realising it, he'd spoken aloud.

Just as well there's no one about – they'd think I was bonkers.

And they'd probably be right.

It was a long slog back up the hill from Soumazannes to the ridge.

To think we came all the way down here under fire. I wouldn't do that now.

Or would I?

I hope I never have to find out. Surely no one would be insane enough to start another war, not after that one. Surely we must have learned…

He reached the top and looked back at the wood. *So many good men lie there, and part of me with them. Why did I live when they died?*

His leg was aching. *That's enough for one day. At least it's downhill from here to Azannes.*

That's what I thought that day, when – keep things in order, Max. That was the second deployment.

Prince was dozing in the shade, his weight on three legs while the fourth was bent, its hoof resting lightly on the ground.

Amazing how they can do that – though we fell asleep standing up when we were knackered enough. Though with only two legs we promptly fell over, and usually woke ourselves up.

"Hello, boy," Max said.

One ear swivelled round, followed by Prince's head.

"Come on – time to go home."

The horse snorted and gave him a gentle push.

It's later than I thought – we'll be lucky to get back before nightfall.

They trotted back past the destroyed villages, cantered through the dark, brooding valley which held the village of Vaux, and trotted up into the evening light.

The city was spread out in front of them, crowned by the twin towers of the Cathedral on its hill, the broad river winding through it.

Verdun.

For all we knew, it might not even have existed. None of our boys caught even a glimpse of it.

As they entered the town, Prince began to skitter again, and had to be coaxed back to the stable.

Not what you expect – not at all.

"You really don't like it there, do you?"

At the turn into the yard, Prince planted his hooves and refused to move, in spite of Max urging him on.

"Come on, boy. There's food and water, and rest."

The horse started to back out.

"Let's not fall out now."

Max had to be very firm indeed to get Prince into the yard.

"Well done, boy."

The stable owner appeared as Max dismounted. Prince laid his ears flat back against his head and skittered again. Then he gave Max a long gaze as if he were saying, 'I'd rather stay with you.'

It does feel wrong, giving you to someone you obviously dislike…

He gave Prince a slap on the shoulder.

"See you tomorrow."

The horse nuzzled his neck and blew softly, and he felt a pair of plaintive eyes following him as he left.

No one else wants me here, he thought as he walked towards the river in search of dinner. *And I can't say I blame them – I'd feel just the same. We invaded their country and smashed it to pieces – but were we any worse than any other invader? What about Genghis Khan and his towers of skulls, or what Napoleon did in Prussia, or the Russians in '14?*

Everyone does exactly the same thing. And we fought here to keep them out of Germany.

We all believed we were being attacked – but where was the truth?

No point pondering that.

Eating by himself felt strange and lonely, even though the restaurant was busy. No Frieda looking at him with her beautiful eyes, no lively chatter from Ernst and Peter.

How I miss them. Maybe they miss me too, in spite of everything. At least I'm not waking them up at night. It must be nice and quiet.

It's too bloody quiet here, without them and with no comrades to share a joke with…

They're up there on the battlefield.

His room was too bloody quiet as well, and the Frenchie officer was watching him and waiting.

Waiting for what?

'For you to go to sleep.'

VIII

Fuck you, Max thought. *I'm not scared of you.*

But he lay awake for quite a while, wondering what the Frenchie planned to do while he was asleep.

His eyes closed – and he was back in the wood, the air filled with bugle calls and the cries of the wounded.

The brambles caught alight as the flame hit them, and the men screamed as they burned—

Max jolted awake, running with sweat.

The French officer's presence was stronger than ever. Max could almost see the bastard sitting in the corner, staring at him with his empty sockets.

And on it went – every time he fell asleep he was in the wood, and when he woke he was in the room he didn't want to think was haunted.

Some time in the early hours he got up and opened the curtains a little, laughing at himself.

I'm just like Peter, wanting a fucking nightlight. At my age.

He didn't get back to sleep, but lay waiting for the dawn. It took a long time to come.

That's a night I'm glad to see the back of, he thought as he left the hotel. *Hope they won't all be like that or I'll be wrecked.*

He let Prince gallop up the hill again and felt something like happiness, as if the frozen part of him were starting to thaw.

I wish it would. Frieda and the boys deserve more than I can give them.

I wish I could remember how I was before the war… And before I was in this fucking slaughterhouse.

He walked again from Azannes to the wood.

A kilometre is such a short distance in peacetime, and such a fucking long way when they're throwing crap at you.

As he entered the wood, he had the strong feeling again that Axel was close by.

You can't be in that grave – not all of you, anyway. Some of you must still be here.

The clean-up teams were carrying yet more bones towards the pile. He wanted to ask what would happen to them, but didn't want the reaction his accent would produce.

I'll find out another way.

"Bonjour, monsieur!" one of them called out. "Vous êtes encore ici."

You're here again.

"Oui."

The man didn't seem surprised.

They must get a lot of veterans, from both sides – trying, like me, to pick up the pieces they left behind.

Strange, isn't it? Eight years ago, we'd have been trying to kill each other, because the idiot politicians chose to have a war, and now we exchange greetings instead of bullets.

Here I am, where I finished yesterday, close to where we set off on patrol that second night in the wood.

*

22nd February 1916, Herbebois

We'll have to be as quiet as mice – and somehow keep track of where we are and how to get back in the darkness.

My compass won't be much use with all the lumps of iron lying around.

Better not get lost. It would be too fucking stupid to end up prisoners...

The night's far from quiet: there are enough explosions and bursts of fire to hide the stealthy movements of a few men.

Creep unseen past the two blockhouses.

There are two more lumps in the ground behind them – and no doubt more hidden in the darkness. All supporting each other.

No wonder we're fucking stuck.

And then there's a belt of wire – with a break in it. Motion to the others to follow me through the gap.

Behind it there's a trench. It's rather battered but mostly intact, with sides of woven willow and sandbags, and logs laid across the top.

Stop.

The sentries will be alert. The least noise, and someone will call out 'Qui vive?' and none of us will be able to answer.

And then we're quite likely to get shot.

Part of the trench is filled in by the shelling, a tumbled confusion of earth and wattle and sandbags and bodies.

Softly, softly... Creep down and up the other side, pass by like ghosts.

Not twenty-five metres later there's another belt of wire.

My nerves are all on the outside. My breathing sounds like a train, and my heartbeat must be audible to everyone within fifty metres.

The wire is unbroken.

Fuck.

If I start cutting it'll go 'ping'.

Left or right?

Motion to the boys to follow me to the left.

The wire goes on.

Thirty paces. Forty.

Still no breaks.

Motion 'stop'.

"Back the other way," I murmur voicelessly.

Forty paces. *This is where we came in...*

Twenty.

Rustle.

Freeze.

Something scurries past my feet.

The Frenchies step up their shelling. Heavy shells moan overhead to burst in the valley behind, lighter ones shriek and explode volcanically in the wood. *Fucking bloody 7.5s – I hate those fucking things.*

Sink into a shell-hole.

Wish our artillery would keep the buggers' heads down a bit better...

Crouch low and creep on.

Thirty-five—

Lorenz tugs at my sleeve.

Stop.

"There," he murmurs, pointing.

There's a hole under the wire.

Wriggle through. It snags my tunic and I feel it rip.

The others follow. What's next?

It starts snowing, big fat flakes that stop me seeing more than a few metres.

If we can't see them...

Here's another fucking trench. Half-full of dead Frenchies.

Best not tread on them – I'm not squeamish, but I've heard a corpse grunt under a foot.

Lower myself softly in beside them, climb up the other side, the wattle creaking under my weight. The others are close behind.

Jesus, we're making too much noise. Where are their sentries?

"Qui vive?!"

Freeze.

"*Qui vive? Répondez ou je tire!*"

And shoot he does – well wide of us.

But he's spooked, and his mates will be too. We have to get away from here.

Scream of shell.

Move forward as it explodes.

And again.

Babble of French voices just ten metres behind us.

They open fire—

Towards our lines. Away from us.

Thank fuck for that.

The snow stops and the night is clear again.

In front of us, the ground drops away steeply. This must be the ravine that cuts through the wood.

So how deep is it and what's on the other side?

The second question is answered very quickly.

CRACK.

Hit the ground.

No 'thump' – but there's too much shelling.

That was bloody loud.

Someone on the opposite slope is doing my old job. And he's seen us, or he wouldn't have fired.

"Tiemann."

"Sergeant Major?"

"See the flash?"

"No."

"Lorenz?"

"No."

"Halfway up the slope," mutters Stadler. "Straight ahead."

Wonderful.

Now we have some fucking Frenchie sniper watching us, and I know how much brighter everything will look through his sight.

Wish I had my old rifle and my Zeiss four-power...

This is a bit of a bind. We're well behind the French lines, and we'll need to go home soon. But the moment we try to leave, our friend will shoot.

"We'll stay here for ten minutes," I murmur, "and observe."

Get out Messner's opera glasses, shading them with my other hand. One glint of reflection from the objective lenses, and I'm dead.

I do not like what I see.

The ravine is narrow, and the opposite side slopes up steeply right in front of us. In the light from the shell bursts and the flares, I can see broken trees, trenches, wire, and suspicious lumps in the ground.

There are also Frenchies moving stealthily about.

Their positions are very thoroughly occupied.

I've seen enough.

Put the opera glasses away, glance at my watch.

Footsteps, rustling through the undergrowth.

Crash of falling body.

"Merde!"

Tiemann's knife is in his hand.

The Frenchie gets up, curses a bit more, moves away from us.

Good. I don't want trouble.

It starts snowing again, the dancing flakes lit to a swirling curtain by the explosions.

I can't see across the ravine.

"Let's go home."

Even Mr Frenchie Sniper won't see us creep away...

And with a bit of luck nor will that sentry.

The snow keeps falling. It hides us, but also makes it difficult to find our way.

We make it across the first trench and through the wire.

Reach the second trench.

There's a fucking Frenchie, hugging himself and stamping his feet in a vain effort to get warm.

He turns towards us – and stares.

Shit.

Tiemann is a handy fellow with a knife, but if that Frenchie makes a sound we're fucked.

The Frenchie smiles and lets out a torrent of words.

The only one I catch is, "Froid."

Cold.

"Oui, vraiment," I reply. Yes, really.

Hope my accent was good enough. He might think I'm from the borderlands.

Can't think why he thinks we're Frenchies too, but then it's mostly fucking dark.

We all climb down into the trench and start up the other side.

He lets out another cheerful torrent, and as we leave I say, "Oui," hoping like fuck that it's the correct response.

Hold my breath as we creep away from him.

He doesn't fire, and the falling snow soon hides us.

"What the fuck was that about?" whispers Lorenz.

Motion to him to be quiet.

Now which the fuck way do we go?

The wood is acquiring a carpet of white, glowing in the shell-bursts. Everything looks the same – what we can see of it.

The compass needle swings... North-ish will do.

There's a blockhouse in front of us.

We could walk right up to the door.

Yes – and make a hell of a row trying to take it, and probably end up dead.

Our job is to get the information back to Messner.

Beside the blockhouse is a wattle fence. Creep along beside it.

I will be so glad to get back.

If the snow will only keep falling…
I'm sweating in spite of the cold.
We'll bloody freeze when we stop – it'll be fucking horrible.
There's a fine assumption, Max.
And then, to my great joy—
"Who goes there?"
"Schelling." Give my rank, company and regiment number.
"Password?"
"Crown Prince."
"That was yesterday's."
It's after midnight, then. What's today's? Ah, yes. "Friedrich Karl."
"Pass, friends."
Bloody hell. We made it back without trouble. And to the right place.
"Well done, boys. Very well done."
Hand round my hip flask and share out some fags.
We go together to report to Messner.
He's plainly relieved to see us.
"There are at least four blockhouses by the road, sir, and a double line of trenches behind them – quite a bit of damage but still well manned. Then there's the ravine – it's narrow and looks steep, both down and up. On the far side, there are trenches and what appear to be blockhouses, all full of Frenchies."
Messner does not look thrilled. "So they've got positions all the way up the hill."
"It looks that way, sir."
"Shit. Is there any dead ground?"
"I can't say for sure, sir – we got stopped by one of their snipers. There might be, in the bottom."
He doesn't need to say that as soon as we reach the edge of the ravine, we'll come under a hideous weight of fire from the positions stacked up the hill.

If the Frenchies shoot straight they'll do for us all in a few minutes.

Those of us that have made it past the blockhouses and the trenches, that is.

I'm starting to wonder whether I'll ever leave this wood, or whether I'll lie here forever like those it's already claimed.

Put that thought aside, go to find the rest of my fellows.

"Ah, you're back," says Kropp.

"Yes – you'll have to wait for promotion!"

"Bugger it! So what did you find?"

"Give us all some of those Frenchie rations and wine, and I'll tell you."

He listens in silence, but his eyebrow signals its misgivings. After a pause, his voice joins it. "You know, I don't think I'm pleased to see you."

"Don't blame you."

Suddenly realise how cold and tired I am. The icy air comes through the tears in my uniform, and my sweat is close to freezing.

In spite of that, I fall asleep sitting in a shell-hole.

And dream about Frenchies, and trenches and blockhouses – someone gets hit and starts crying out and calling for help—

Wake with a jolt.

The cries are real, and so is the shelling.

Anyone who can't walk back out has to wait to be picked up – and there are so many that it'll be a very long wait. And a lot of them won't make it.

Poor sods. It's a pitiful chorus and it makes your hair stand on end.

And tomorrow we happy survivors have to do it all again.

The first violet light comes through what remains of the trees. I do not greet it with gladness, but with a cold, sick feeling.

This will be another day like yesterday, getting hammered from blockhouses and machine-gun nests.

God knows how many of us will be here at the end of it. God knows what state I'll be in.

Not like one of those poor bastards, I hope…

Don't think, Max. For fuck's sake, don't think.

Messner appears in my shell-hole.

"How many of yours are left?"

I tell him and he pulls a face.

"That makes thirty-five for the Platoon."

My turn to pull a face – we're twenty down already. I wonder what the company strength is.

"We're pulling back to the French second line," he says. "The artillery's going to shell the wood again."

"Let's hope they don't drop shorts."

"Quite."

Wonder how the orders got through the barrage – someone must have run like fuck and been bloody lucky both ways.

"And the General's ordered that the wood is to be cleared of the enemy today, regardless of casualties."

The faces around me say it all: 'What the fuck does he think we're doing anyway?'

But he knows us – the order's probably for effect. Hard to remember that the General – God Almighty to us – also has superiors.

"So we've got more grenades and ammunition—"

"Thank fuck for that!"

Messner grins. "…and coffee!"

"Bloody hell!"

Hot coffee. Bloody wonderful.

He hands me a water bottle. I open it, put it to my mouth and tip it…

Nothing.

No nice, hot coffee. Not a drop.

It's too heavy to be empty.

Messner is looking at his bottle in bemusement.
"Any luck, sir?"
"No. You?"
"No."
We shake the bottles. They remain silent.
"Fuck me," Dachwitz exclaims. "The fucking coffee's frozen!"
"Oh, bloody hell," says Kropp. "What the fuck use is that?"
No wonder we're all so fucking cold.
Messner sighs, and puts his bottle down. "And we can have one more day's iron rations," he says.
Cold food again. Better than nothing.
Light a fag in the vain hope that it'll warm me up. Put my coat on, but it's as full of holes as the rest of my uniform.
"You know what I really don't understand," says Tiemann, "and that's why that Frenchie chatted to us and let us go."
"Must have thought we were Frenchies too," Lorenz says.
"You still got that Frenchie helmet?" Kropp asks Tannwitz.
"Yeah."
"Put it on for a mo."
"But Sarge—"
"All right, give it here."
Kropp sits beside Lorenz and puts the helmet on.
"Fucking hell," says Tiemann.
"Give it to me," I say. "Kropp, you need to see this."
Put the Frenchie helmet on.
"Fuck me," says Kropp. "You look like one of us."
In the dim light, it's almost impossible to tell the difference between a French steel helmet and a Prussian helmet without the spike.
Bet no one thought of that when they told us to unscrew the spikes – all anyone was worried about was us getting caught up in the undergrowth.

Kropp goes over to Messner.

"Sir, you need to see this."

"Bloody hell," he says. "I'll tell Strecker."

Take the helmet off and hand it back to Tannwitz.

There is no need to spell out that we have to be certain before we fire.

Wonder how many have already got it wrong.

Just as I'm pondering that, our artillery starts up.

Shells of every calibre whine and moan and roar over our heads, and explode with stunning force ahead of us.

The ground shakes as the wood lights up incandescent.

Don't drop shorts, boys, for fuck's sake…

How can anything survive this?

That's what we thought the first day. Remember how thick the concrete is on those fucking blockhouses? It'll take a direct hit from a heavy to knock those fuckers out, and no one knows where they are.

The French artillery responds.

Can't someone kill those bastards?

Press myself harder into the frozen ground, try again to dig in but without success.

Stadler's praying again.

Time stands still.

We're going in at 12:30, almost exactly like yesterday.

Let's hope it's not like yesterday.

IX

The bombardment lifts.

'Potato soup potato soup—'

I'll hear that in my dreams for the rest of my life.

Rest of my life? That's a good joke.

Jump up, rush forward—

CRACKCRACKCRACKCRACKCRACK

Dive into the nearest hole.

There's nothing wrong with that blockhouse.

"Kropp."

"Sergeant Major?"

"Let's get past this blockhouse. That'll put us behind the others."

We manage two shell-holes forward and Zeitler gets hit in the process.

And that's it.

Every time we try to move, or even raise our heads, the Frenchies shoot.

None of the blockhouses has been touched by the bombardment. And then there are the machine-gun nests.

Some of them have been hit – we can hear that – but not all.

They're well hidden in the undergrowth and we can't see them.

They can see us.

I'll give His Excellency 'without regard to casualties' – if we try to storm those blockhouses we'll all get killed, and they'll still be full of Frenchies. Bugger-all use that will be.

So now what the fuck do we do?

"Over there," Dachwitz murmurs, and points.

Through the confusion of broken branches, I can just see a French steel helmet, and a bearded face beneath it.

He's only about thirty metres away.

It's a tricky shot with all those branches in the way. If the bullet even grazes one, it'll be deflected.

But I have a thought.

If the others are ready to go when I shoot, they might get close enough to throw them a grenade or two…

"Weidner."

"Sergeant Major?"

Explain.

He nods.

They're ready.

The Frenchie hasn't moved.

I must get this right…

He drops.

Weidner and the other four leap up, run forward, drop into another hole, and another, and their grenades fly into the Frenchies.

That's the end of that nest – but when we try to take possession of it, the guns in the blockhouses force us into cover.

Good to know I can still shoot, though.

There is respect in Dachwitz's eyes.

Yes – your bastard Sergeant Major's not just braid and discipline. He can actually use a rifle.

"I was a sniper in my old regiment."

His expression changes as reserve is added to the respect.

I'd forgotten about being looked at that way. Never did like it.

"Oh, right," he says, reserve in his voice as well.

His problem – and the very least of our troubles.

We're stuck again.

How in God's name are we going to clear this fucking wood? Every time we try to move, we get shot at and lose more blokes. What if it's like this all the way to Verdun?

Laugh to myself. *If it is then I won't need to worry about it. Axel's wallet will be quite safe.*

I need to talk to Messner—

Suddenly there's movement on our left.

Weidner and I look at each other.

Are the fuckers counterattacking?

Strecker appears out of the ground.

"The Sixth has got behind the line of blockhouses," he says. "So we can join in rolling them up."

Thank fuck for that.

But as always, it's easy to say.

The blockhouse left forward has stopped firing – and I can just make out grey figures beyond it. Go for the next one, then.

A few flakes fall from the sky…

"Come on, boys!"

Leap up, run forward—

CRACKCRACKCRACKWHINE

Dive into the nearest hole.

I'm alone. *For fuck's sake—*

"Where are you all, then?! COME ON!!"

Four men dart across the open ground, join me.

The others are bolder now, and as their heads appear I jump up—

Another burst, something tugs at my sleeve—

Into the next hole.

The others have all followed.

At last we're making progress. At long fucking last.

There's another lump in the ground to our right.

Wriggle onto the roof and post a 'letter' through the slots.

The detonation shakes the concrete.

Weidner bangs on the door with the butt of his rifle.
"OPEN UP!"
Silence.
Does that mean they're all dead, or that they're holding out?
"One more."
A few seconds later, the door opens.
Out stumbles a small group of Frenchies, covered in blood and well singed.
Disarm them and send them to the rear. Lose another man as the escort.
"Pieper, Tiemann, check it's empty."
"Fucking hell!" says Pieper, his voice echoing.
What he's seen he never says, but his face is actually pale when he comes out. Tiemann looks rather subdued, which is most unlike him.
Frankly, I don't want to know what sort of mess they found.
Comrades are passing us.
"Come on, boys! Or they'll get all the glory!"
Ahead, I can see Messner and his boys on top of another blockhouse. Everything beyond that is hidden by the falling snow.

*

Max sighed.
We didn't find out until much later how the Sixth got behind the blockhouses. Their Leutnant Rassow charged a machine-gun nest – armed with his pistol and walking stick, the fucking lunatic.

Got shot dead, of course, but the few fellows who'd gone with him overran the thing and put it out of action – and that opened the way.

So the Seventh owed Rassow our lives – temporarily, in most cases.

Someone told me the Tommies give posthumous decorations. Seems a waste of time to me as the fellow hardly knows about it

– and how can you give a gong to someone who doesn't exist any more?

They'd probably have given Rassow their Victoria Cross for that. If he'd been a Tommy, of course.

You're rambling, Max.

He was a bloody good bloke, though, Rassow, and I'm eternally in his debt. And it was a bloody good way to go, a fine soldier's death.

Amazing how I can still think that – and how often I wish I'd found such a death myself, instead of having to try to find my way back to 'normal' life…

Getting behind the blockhouse line wasn't the end of it. Not by a long way.

Max got up and walked south through the wood, past the blockhouses that had held them up for so long.

There was another black hole of an entrance, under a thick layer of broken concrete. The top of the blockhouse was shattered into pale chunks, and more were scattered all around.

Those would have given you quite a whack. Our gunners must have actually hit this one. Fucking great bang that must have been.

Fun for the poor bastards inside…

He didn't want to imagine that, or the resulting mess, or the broken skeletons that must still be down there, clad in stained and tattered horizon blue.

Strong young fellows like ours, with families back home. What shit war is.

A short distance away, men were cutting the remains of shattered trees down into stumps, the axes hitting with solid thunks. Someone shouted to them urgently, waving his arms, and they stopped and joined him, peering at the ground. Then they started poking it cautiously.

Max approached and watched with curiosity – and realised with a cold shock that they were digging carefully around an unexploded shell, 10.5 cm from the look of it.

Jesus – better look where I'm putting my feet.
For more reasons than one. Better not fall into that trench.

In front of him, a trench snaked through the wood, quite deep in spite of all the later shelling. It was still lined with wattle panels, some fallen in, and topped with sandbags, green with moss. In front of it, stretches of rusting wire were looped through screw pickets.

I didn't think this would still be here. I'm almost at the top of the rise, so it must be the first of that double line.

Taking those was real fun as well.

*

23rd February 1916, Herbebois

Hit the ground as we come under fire again – from straight in front.

What did we find last night on patrol?

Come on, Max – it's only a few hours ago.

A double line of trenches, just before the crest of the hill.

And there's the first trench, with a belt of wire in front of it.

There's no sign of the gap we found last night – but we're some way left of it.

Spread out.

Creep forward.

CRACKCRACKCRACK. Over our heads.

Hole to hole…

"Over here, sir!" calls Weber, beckoning urgently to Messner.

There's a hole under the wire.

The trick will be to get everyone through it without getting shot.

Or blown up. Because of course the Frenchies are not pleased to see us, and greet us with their egg grenades.

Weber's reward for his sharp eyes is a belly full of fragments.

Leave him lying there groaning and scrabble under the wire.

There's someone off to our right—
Grey uniforms.
"Sir."
Point them out to Messner.
"Lorenz," he says.
"Sir?"
"Go and find out who they are."
"Yes, sir."
Hold our breath as he makes his way from hole to hole. Knows what he's doing, does Lorenz.

He creeps back. The Frenchies fire over his head a couple of times, but fortunately even the ricochets miss.

"It's Leutnant Scheumann's Platoon, sir."
"Thank you, Lorenz."
Messner turns to me.
"I'm going for a chat with Scheumann. You're in command until I get back."
"Sir."
We both know what he really means.

Ten long minutes later he returns, leaping from hole to hole, pursued by French greetings.

"Right," he says. "We have a plan."
It's a very simple one and it doesn't take long to pass on.

Both Platoons are inside the wire and close enough to storm the trench. The only question is how many of us will get there…

"Five minutes," says Messner.
An eternity later, 'potato soup' rings from the bugles, and we leap up and run forward.

The Frenchies don't like it, not one bit, and their indignation is loud round our ears.

Jump down into their trench, knife in hand.
Stick the nearest Frenchie.
Blast in the next bay.

Fragments over the traverse. Metal, bone, flesh.

Flatten myself against the wattle wall.

Round the traverse—

French officer trying to get up pistol in his hand aims at me Stadler clubs him.

Who's round the next traverse? They won't be friendly…

Try to lob a grenade in, but it bounces off the logs laid over the top of the trench.

Shit—!

And flies off into the wire. *Thank fuck.*

Deep breath. Run into the next bay.

Frenchies.

Stab another. Blood spurts over me.

Club stab shots grenades.

Bottom of trench filling with bodies, alive and dead, blue and grey.

Blood. Brains.

Remaining Frenchies have their hands up—

Stop and draw breath.

My hand is red and sticky, and my sleeve is sodden. So's the front of my ragged tunic.

There's something sticky on my face too, soaking into my stubble.

Frenchies jabber something.

Their Sergeant is lying against the parapet, soaked in blood, trying to shove his guts back into his body. The glistening loops slither through his hands, stinking brown liquid drips from his fingers.

He looks up at us in terror and despair. The pain hasn't hit him yet.

If he were a horse, you'd shoot him now, before it does.

"Poor fucker," mutters Kropp.

The Frenchies don't seem that bothered about him.

"Take him back with you," Kropp tells them.

They roll him up in his coat, and pick him up with indifference bordering on roughness.

Wonder what the story is there...

As they carry him away, Dachwitz says, "What's the point? He won't last five minutes."

"What the fuck else can we do?" asks Weidner.

What indeed?

Our wounded will have to wait – we have another trench to take.

And then we'll get to the edge of the ravine and the bastards will shoot us to pieces.

We'll just have to get down to the bottom as fast as we can.

You really are getting ahead of yourself, Max...

The next trench is crammed full of steel helmets, and they're waiting for us.

But our blood is up.

*

I hope my sons never have to go to war, never have to find out what it really is, Max thought. *Everyone writes about 'glory' without mentioning its hideous cost.*

He lowered himself into the trench, taking care not to snag himself on the broken edges of the wattle.

It's so peaceful here now. You'd hardly think this was full of dead and wounded, and soaked in blood and God knows what.

He climbed up the other side, his boots slipping in the loose earth.

And for one horrible moment thought he was about to be shot.

He stopped, gasping for breath, his heart pounding.

The peacetime wood had vanished, and he was standing in the open between the two trench lines.

23rd February 1916, Herbebois

"How many grenades have we got?" asks Messner.

Quick count.

"Ten between the lot of us, sir."

"Bugger."

He squeezes along to Scheumann, comes back.

Just as he reaches me, the Frenchies chuck their eggs at us.

Most land behind us, but two arrive with Scheumann's lot and one off to my left.

Explosions, screams.

No point staying here.

"We'll give them five of ours five minutes from now and then go for it," Messner says.

Let's hope our boys' aim is better…

'Potato soup potato soup—'

Up and at 'em.

Jump down into their trench.

This lot don't have as much fight in them. Can't say I'm sorry about that.

Send them to the rear.

This trench too is full of corpses, and men torn open and groaning.

Blood all over me, all over all of us.

What a fucking shit business this is.

Schlenk and Tannwitz are still busy with our casualties in the first trench.

Pause to sort ourselves out.

"Better go through the Frenchies' equipment," I say, "see what's useful."

"Hey!" says Lorenz. "More Frenchie rations!"

"Hot?!" asks Stadler.

"Don't be so fucking stupid."

There's more of their rough red wine in their bottles.

"Hey, this'll—"

French bugles, sounding the assault.

"Sound the alarm!" shouts Messner, and our bugles ring out as well.

Line the trench, waiting.

"Here they come!"

Steel helmets, blue uniforms, bayonets—

"FIRE!"

Send them a wall of lead. Jahnke jumps up out of the trench and throws a grenade, then fires at them, standing.

Many go down.

The rest falter.

Their Lieutenant turns, shouts, and beckons them forward.

Can't have that.

Shoot him. He staggers and falls.

Moments later their Sergeant goes down as well.

The rest turn and run, and we send them on their way. Several more fall before the survivors disappear from sight.

"Must of known we was drinking their wine!" says Stadler.

"No sense of humour," says Dachwitz.

"They'll try again." Messner knows he's stating the obvious, but it has to be said.

"Better drink their wine and eat their food quick, then!" says Lorenz.

"Nah, mate – they'll never get their hands on it," Tiemann retorts.

Jahnke leaps back down.

"Mad bastard," I say. "They don't give epaulettes to a corpse."

He grins at me, with all the cheeky confidence of his eighteen years.

I must have been like that once…

The ground in front of us is covered in French dead and wounded. They'll have to stay there. No one wants to risk leaving the trench when their mates might turn up at any moment.

One raises himself cautiously, waving a white handkerchief.

"Leave your weapons and come in with your hands up!" Kropp shouts.

At least I think that's what he said.

Twenty Frenchies get up, hands in the air.

"Can we bring our wounded?" asks one.

"Yes," shouts Messner.

They reach the trench and we send them rearwards. They can patch their fellows up somewhere quiet.

Hope they behave themselves – we can't spare anyone as escort.

Share out the French iron rations, put them in our packs.

Drink the wine.

Messner turns to the men beside him.

"Keller, Grumach – go and pick up the French weapons. But stay alert."

Quite a haul, on top of what's in the trench.

French rifles, ammunition, bayonets. Two machine guns, undamaged.

Knives – very handy. Knuckledusters, likewise.

No grenades, though. Would have been very useful, those. God knows when we'll get more of our own.

They attack again an hour later, but without much enthusiasm.

The fight seems to be going out of them. How sad.

More prisoners, more booty.

Time to take stock.

"Number," orders Messner.

Twenty-eight.

This time yesterday, there were over forty of us.

And this time tomorrow? We're not halfway through this fucking wood yet.

In front of us is the ravine and all those positions stacked up the other side... All those Frenchies, well dug in and waiting to kill us.

"Fuck me," says Rausch suddenly.

"What's wrong?" asks Wredow.

"I'm bleeding. Look."

His right trouser leg is soaked with blood.

"I thought it was French," he adds.

But there's a long cut in the fabric – and when Wredow rips it right open, there's a matching one in his thigh.

"Better make that twenty-seven, sir," I say.

Messner swears.

X

Max was standing between the two trench lines.

Shit – I'm out here in the open!

He threw himself into the nearest hole, his heart thumping.

Thank fuck for that.

Wonder where the boys are.

The next trench will be full of Frenchies, all waiting for us – but it has to be done.

Don't think. Just go.

He steeled himself, jumped up out of the hole and into the wreckage of the second trench.

The bay was empty.

He crept cautiously round the traverse into the next bay, and froze in terror as the collapsed wattle parapet broke under his feet with a loud crack.

Jesus fucking Christ!

Nothing happened. There were no Frenchies, either alive or dead.

None of his boys were there either.

"Where are you all then?"

No answer.

Just the rustle of small creatures in the silence, and the cry of a buzzard overhead.

Strange...

What in God's name is going on?

He sat down and tried to light a cigarette. His hands shook

so badly he almost dropped it, and then the flame trembled so much he couldn't get it lit.

Finally he succeeded.

Jesus, the state I'm in!

He leaned against the side of the trench and took a deep drag, sweat pouring down his back.

'It's all right, Max,' said Axel. 'It's all over. You're safe.'

"What?"

'Just listen.'

Max listened.

Silence.

No sounds of fighting, just the clean-up teams calling to each other.

Slowly his vision cleared, and his heart rate returned to normal.

Jesus, that was a bad one. Maybe I shouldn't have come. Maybe I should get the next train home.

'You've come to see us, haven't you?' said a voice. 'Don't go yet.'

"All right."

Hope no one heard – or they'll think I'm crazy and take me away.

What do you mean, they'll think you're crazy? What sort of sane man are you?

Best not thought about.

He climbed out of the trench and continued to the edge of the ravine. In front of him, the ground dropped away sharply.

I wonder where that Frenchie sniper was, that night. And I wonder what happened to him.

Probably went the way of most snipers. That job's fucking dangerous and the bastards get you in the end.

Jesus, it is steep, though. Not surprising I slid down it.

*

23rd February 1916, Herbebois

The edge of the ravine is close ahead.

Stop everyone.

Crawl from hole to hole with the same order: "Don't hang about. Fast as you can to the edge and down to the bottom."

And hope we don't all get shot.

Run like fuck. Reach the edge. Start down.

It's fucking steep.

Any moment the fuckers opposite will shoot me—

Stumble slip slide on my backside down to the bottom.

My trousers and underpants rip, and my bare arse scrapes over stones, frozen earth and twigs.

"Thought you'd had it, Schelling," says Messner.

"Thought I was going to lose my virginity!"

He laughs.

I take another step – my boot crashes through snow-covered ice and I go arse over tit into the hidden stream.

"Shit!" Can't help laughing, though.

Messner laughs and pulls me up.

Dachwitz chuckles to himself, clearly seeing justice in a dripping Sergeant Major.

Unbelievably, we have all made it down.

And even more unbelievably, we're in dead ground.

The slope rises in front of us at some stupid angle.

At some point the gradient will slacken, and our heads will pop up in front of the Frenchies. And then they'll blow our brains out.

So we'd better use them while we've still got them.

Time to pause and plan…

Fuck me but I'm cold.

My uniform is torn to rags now and soaking wet, and starting to freeze solid. It cracks when I move.

The others aren't much better.

God knows what the temperature is. The snow's stopped, but the sky is still clouded over.

"Better not stay here much longer," Messner says. "We've all got our breath back now."

And moving will warm us up – especially when the Frenchies see us.

After which some of us will be very cold indeed.

Except…

"They didn't fire," I say.

Messner looks at me. "No, they didn't."

He's just as puzzled as I am.

"Forward with caution, then," he says.

Start edging our way up the slope, well spread out.

After about fifty metres, the angle lessens a little. High up, the slope is cratered by the triple bombardment, but before that there's a clear band of about twenty metres that the shells didn't reach.

Not really the artillery's fault, that – the ravine is very steep-sided and narrow. Even high-trajectory fire wouldn't reach all of it.

We're going to have to cross the untouched patch flat out – as flat out as we can manage up a hill like that. And God alone knows what's hidden in it.

How many of us will get to the cover of the shell-holes?
And who will make it to the top of the hill?
No point thinking, Max.

On Messner's signal we leap up and run forward—

No reception.

No bullets cracking and whistling round our ears.

No grenades.

Reach the shell-holes, gasping for breath.

This does not make sense. No enemy in his right mind would miss an opportunity like that.

Messner beckons me to his shell-hole. No one tries to shoot me.

"What d'you reckon, Schelling?"

"Send a patrol forward, sir – find out what the hell is going on."

"My thoughts exactly. Not you this time… Jahnke! Over here!"

Five minutes later, Jahnke and three men start creeping up the hill.

As they leave, Strecker appears out of the ground. His use of cover is superb.

He'd have made a good sniper – assuming he can shoot well enough, of course.

He's covered in mud, and his trousers are almost as ragged as mine. He looks like a scarecrow.

"You get fired on?" he asks Messner.

"No, sir."

"Nor me. Same with Scheumann."

"I've just sent a patrol up the hill, sir."

"Good."

None of us dares voice the possibility that the Frenchies might have withdrawn.

I don't want to start thinking like that.

Strecker passes his hip flask to Messner, and then to me.

Schnapps settles with a warm glow in my stomach, starts to run through my veins.

Jesus, I am so fucking cold and hungry and tired – and on edge at the same time.

I will be so glad to get this job done. I could sleep for a week.

See the same in the boys' eyes. They've had enough, and who can blame them?

Two hours later, the patrol returns.

"Well, Jahnke?" asks Messner.

He gets a grin in return. "They've all gone home, sir. We went right to the edge of the wood and had a good poke about, and didn't see hide nor hair of the buggers."

Thank fuck for that – unless it's a trap.

"Well done, Jahnke. I'll pass that on," Messner says.

He doesn't need to remind us to be vigilant.

Creep carefully up the hill, past trenches and blockhouses.

Nothing.

No one apart from the dead.

It's impossible to believe.

Towards the top of the hill, there's a deep trench with a thick belt of wire in front of it and blockhouses set into it, their doors wide open.

Most are completely untouched by the bombardment, and we approach them very carefully – but they really are empty.

Beyond that, the crest is crowned with more blockhouses and trenches behind them.

Jesus, but these are commanding positions – anyone attacking has to come up the hill, and a handful of men with machine guns would slaughter them all.

It's a fucking fortress, but empty and abandoned.

"Why?" asks Dachwitz.

"Off their fucking heads," says Stadler.

"They'd have had us all if we'd had to fight our way up here," says Lorenz.

I do not want to imagine what that would have been like.

The sun is low as we reach the southern edge of the wood. It has taken two full days to clear, and cost scores of lives.

And then there are all the poor mutilated bastards who will never be right again.

This was only the beginning. If the Frenchies carry on fighting like that, we'll be wiped out.

As long as those behind us get to Verdun, we'll have succeeded.

"Why in God's name did they leave positions like those?" Messner asks me.

"Fucked if I know, sir – maybe we should just be grateful!"

The trenches are badly damaged by shellfire, and there are dead Frenchies everywhere. Multiply that by three for their wounded…

"Maybe they'd lost too many and thought they wouldn't be able to hold us off," I say.

"Maybe. Or maybe they're regrouping to counterattack properly."

"Quite."

*

Almost without realising it, Max had climbed up the further side of the ravine.

The ruins of the blockhouses, and the trenches at the top of the hill, showed up clearly in the ruined wood. *So misleading, it is now – you can see everything so easily.*

He shivered as he looked at them.

If we'd had to fight our way up here, I doubt any of us would have made it. We'd all have been dead or mutilated or pinned down in shell-holes.

Two whole days, and it was our objective for the first day.

Someone should have realised then that the whole thing was misfiring. But apparently it was different in all the other sectors – big, easy gains on the first couple of days.

We got the hardest task of all – but then we were the Brandenburg Corps, and if it was so difficult for us then no one else would have managed it at all.

He smiled at himself. *Still bloody well Corps-pissed after all this time, even though there is no Brandenburg Corps any more.*

He sat on the remains of one of the blockhouses, looking down the hill, and lit a fag.

Just because the Frenchies had left didn't make this place safe. They stepped up the shelling once they realised their own boys had abandoned it.

This wood is so full of ghosts. So many good men we left here… And they're still here. It was difficult enough getting the wounded back. No one was going to risk his neck for a corpse. And even if the clean-up teams collect all the bones they can, there are plenty of fragments too small to pick up, and all the flesh is part of the earth now.

Dust to dust…

*

23rd February 1916, Herbebois

In front of us, the ground slopes down sharply again.

"Let's get down into the bottom," says Messner, "get a bit more protection from the shelling."

And indeed the Frenchies are dropping their 'presents' ever closer.

The bottom of the ravine is dark and muddy. The light's fading and the place feels hostile. You could almost think it was haunted.

Laugh at myself.

There are thousands of Frenchies here, itching to kill you, and you have to start imagining ghosts. Fucking idiot. What could ghosts do to you, anyway?

There should be ghosts, though. There are dead Frenchmen lying everywhere.

Their abandoned equipment gives us another good haul of booty – and more Frenchie iron rations and rough red wine. That'll keep us going.

Post sentries and settle down for a quick kip.

The cold wakes me after a few minutes.

Messner sits beside me.

"We're to go back up the hill into the wood," he says. "The Fifth and Eighth are coming to relieve us."

Thank fuck for that.

*

Relief was the right word, Max thought as he gazed down the hill. *We were all completely fucked. All anyone wanted was to get some hot food and go to sleep. It was the sort of exhaustion where you don't even take your boots off – you just lie down and pass out, or even the other way round. I've seen men fall asleep on their feet and just keel over, and not even feel it when they hit the ground.*

*

23rd February 1916, ravine south of Herbebois

It takes forever for the relief to reach us.

I'm half-asleep when a hand shakes my shoulder.

Leap up.

"Sorry, mate. Klein, Fifth Company."

In front of me is a Sergeant Major, in a proper uniform that's somewhat muddy but intact. His face is fresh and unlined, unlike those around me.

We are all filthy and unshaven, and we look about fifty.

Their Platoon Commander is talking to Messner.

I almost laugh at the contrast. Messner is dressed in bloody, grubby tatters like the rest of us, and you'd hardly recognise him as an officer.

Klein looks me up and down.

"I heard you'd had a bit of a time of it," he says.

"That's for sure."

That's another thing that strikes me – how many of them there are. A full company. And they're fresh and full of energy, just itching to get stuck in.

We looked like that two days ago. Now half the boys have gone, and what's left of us can barely stand from sheer exhaustion.

Get the fucking handover done with so we can get some bloody rest.

Klein's fellows don't want to look at us.

No – this will be you in a couple of days' time, and you don't want to think about that. I wouldn't either.

"Got the Frenchies moving at last, though," Klein says.

I barely have the energy to answer him. "Yes."

Finally the talking's done.

"Come on, boys," says Messner.

A handful of men climb wearily to their feet, put on their packs, pick up their weapons and the booty, and start trudging back up the fucking hill.

I swear this is the steepest one of all…

It goes on and fucking on, and our boots slip in the loose earth.

Dachwitz stumbles and knocks Kropp flat.

"Sorry, Sarge."

"Clumsy bastard," Kropp says kindly as Dachwitz helps him up.

Lorenz is almost out on his feet.

Put my arm round his waist to help him up the steepest part, but my feet can't get much grip.

Pause for breath, wait for the stragglers.

"Come on, boys. Just back up the hill and then we can rest."

The Frenchies send us a few shells to speed us on our way, but miss by quite a margin.

Just as well.

Finally we reach the top. Ahead of us, the ground slopes gently down.

We all stop, well out of breath.

I haven't felt this fucked since last summer.

"Where are we going, sir?" asks Kropp.

Messner grins. "Nowhere much. Back beyond that line of trenches."

"Any chance of the cookers making it up, sir?" I ask.

"Let's hope so."

But they don't, and it's cold iron rations again, plus what we scavenged from the Frenchies. That, of course, is also cold.

Sit down. Wince as my bare, scratched arse meets the frozen ground.

"My feet are like lumps of ice," grumbles Stadler.

"Mine too," says Lorenz.

Better check their feet, now we're out of it for a while.

"Foot inspection, boys." Kropp and I are like twins, saying the same thing together.

Wredow has white patches on his feet, and so does Dachwitz.

"Off to the medics, boys, before that turns to frostbite."

My hip flask is empty. Drink some of the rough French wine, eat a tin of their stew and beans. Quite tasty. Bit heavy on the onions and garlic, though, and no doubt the beans will make me fart.

Laugh to myself. *The Frenchies have made me fart, all right, but luckily that's all.*

Light a fag.

The Frenchies leave us in peace – their infantry, that is. The shelling continues.

Another pitch-dark night in the wood, lit only by the incessant explosions, and fighting some way to the west.

Wrap myself in my coat and a tent quarter, and try to sleep.

I'm so fucked I feel like I've been hit on the head, but at the same time my nerves are strung out and I can't relax.

Fall asleep in spite of the hideous cold.

Wake with a jolt.

Shells.

Sit up, reach for my rifle—

No need to fret, Max. You're behind the front line now. If there's trouble, the Fifth and Eighth will deal with it first.

Maybe, but God, I hate fucking shells. Death at random from the sky.

Wonder if the Sixth is as smashed up as we are. And what about the Third Battalion?

Hope it's not going to go on like this...

Won't last much longer if it does. God alone knows how I've made it this far.

Screams. They're slowly clearing the wood of wounded, but so many still lie out in the bitter cold – especially those who…

Kropp sits next to me.

"If I get any colder my blood will freeze," he says.

Peer at my watch.

"Time I checked on the boys," I say, and pass him the tent quarter.

"Cheers."

The sentries are alert. *Good blokes.*

Most of the others are out cold. Exchange a few words with those who are awake.

No one complains. They've just had two days in Hell, they know there's more to come, they're fucking frozen with nothing warm to eat or drink, but there's not one word of complaint.

Good blokes. Bloody good blokes.

With men like these, you could walk on water.

Give us a couple of days out of the line, reinforce us, and we'll smash the crap out of the Frenchies and take their fortress city. The battering ram of the Brandenburg Corps will do its job.

XI

24th February 1916, Herbebois

In the morning, we move back into the ravine in the wood. It offers some protection against the French artillery, which is becoming ever more active.

*

Max sighed.

We lost more than half our strength here, in just two days. The Company was never the same again. The men we'd lost were battle-hardened and had trained specifically for Verdun, and they weren't easy to replace.

Worst of all was the loss of experienced NCOs, the men no army can do without...

He got up.

I've seen everything there is to see here. I could walk over into the next ravine and along to Ornes, but it would make more sense to go back to Azannes and then ride there.

As he turned to leave, someone said, 'Stay with us. You don't have to go.'

"I have to go back."

'Not yet.'

There will never be a right time to leave here.

"I'll come back."

Oh, Max – what have you said? That was a promise and you have to keep it.

This wood is full of the dead...

Once again, as he walked along the old French front line, he felt Axel beside him.

He stopped.

You can see the Knochgraben from here – or rather where it ran along the hill, parallel to our line of advance. How were we expected to take this, when that was still in French hands and nicely positioned to give us flanking fire?

He started down the hill with a profound sense of loss. It intensified as he climbed up the other side to the former German front line.

All the good men who died here, and for absolutely nothing. A lost battle, in a lost war that should never have started.

If only we'd been victorious, their deaths wouldn't have been in vain.

I wish someone could tell me what it was all for.

King and Fatherland, of course – but how did either of those benefit? The King has gone, and the poor Fatherland...

I never, in all my youth, imagined thinking 'poor Prussia' as I do now.

It's barely Prussia any more – no king, no army worthy of the name, no money, so many cripples and widows and orphans, an apology of a government.

What sort of life will my sons have?

That was far too depressing.

Max reached the edge of Azannes. Prince was lying in the shade, and as Max watched, he rolled and gave his back a good scratch, then got up and shook himself, dust flying in the sunlight.

"That better, is it?" Max asked.

A black ear swivelled towards him, followed by Prince's head.

Two large, liquid brown eyes regarded Max gravely and steadily. After a moment, both ears pointed forward.

"Do I pass the inspection, then?" he asked, and got a quiet snort and a soft muzzle pushed gently into his neck.

"I'll take it that was 'yes'. Your whiskers tickle, by the way."

Have to get you some carrots from the market, he thought as he saddled the horse up.

Five minutes later, they were trotting along the road towards Gremilly.

This was our left flank at the beginning, and everyone was worried that we'd be attacked. Luckily the Frenchies only made a token effort.

Not that it made any difference in the end...

I suppose I should be glad I'm alive – but I've forgotten how. I can't remember what I was like before the war. Very young, that's all I know. I was nineteen when I volunteered, not even fully grown. What a way to come of age.

I really should get myself a horse when I get home, though – there's something about looking between a pair of pointed ears, and that mix of strength and spirit and gentleness. Much better creatures than man – and they don't judge you or expect anything more than kindness and decent horsemanship.

It's a while since I've had company that didn't want explanations, or didn't obviously wonder just how many marbles I still possess.

*

24th February 1916, Herbebois

Towards evening, we get orders to move forward to the edge of the Caurières Wood – the blasted remnants of it, anyway. It's full of wrecked trenches running between the splintered trees, and there are dead Frenchies everywhere.

Fortunately it's too cold for them to stink – and dead Frenchies are better company than live ones.

Strecker has quite a smile on his face.

"You'll all be pleased to hear that our First Battalion has made excellent progress, got the enemy properly on the run, taken quite a few prisoners and machine guns."

He's right. It lifts our spirits no end.

And apparently the village of Ornes has been taken by another regiment.

Our sacrifices in the wood will have been worthwhile…

It's *almost* enough to make you not mind eating cold food, while sitting in a freezing hole wearing rags. I've cut a sandbag in half and stuffed it down the back of my trousers. It's rough but it keeps my arse off the icy ground.

"I'm sure tramps have it better than this," says Stadler.

"And no one tries to kill them," adds Lorenz.

I don't feel inclined to argue.

"At least the cold keeps the lice down a bit," says Kropp.

I'm still itching, though.

Have to burn off my short and curlies again once we're out of the line. Maybe do my armpits as well, and my chest…

We stay in the Caurières Wood, and the next day we get hot food.

HOT FOOD. And COFFEE. I swear nothing has ever tasted so good.

The cold penetrates just a fraction less.

"If I could get a fresh uniform I'd be in Heaven," Kropp says.

"Maybe we should just be thankful that we're in one piece," I reply.

"There is that."

The Company is wrecked. So many good men lie dead: Degenhardt, Bloch, Fürst, Kessler, Kehrer, Mersch… and then there are all the wounded, and the missing.

God knows how many men must have died waiting to be carried out.

*

It didn't take long to get from Gremilly to the sign that said 'Ornes. Destroyed village'.

That's the most heart-breaking thing of all, Max thought as they took the turning. *How fucking small the battlefield is, how quickly you can cover the distances.*

So many men dead in such a small space…

The stream burbled on his right. Ahead of him, the dirt road led between mounds of rubble.

Fucking hell. These were houses when I was here last – battered by shelling, but mostly still standing. Now you'd hardly even guess there'd been a village.

The Frenchies must have done this when they were making their big attacks in the autumn and winter. Can't blame them for wanting rid of us.

'DANGER' read a large sign. 'UNEXPLODED MUNITIONS'.

I have been warned.

Better leave Prince outside the village – don't want the poor fellow unearthing something and getting blown to bits.

This must have been the main street, he thought as he walked slowly past the ruins. *Built over centuries, and so quickly destroyed.*

This is where they sent us after the wood, to keep the traffic flowing.

*

25th February 1916, Ornes

"We're to do *what*?" Kropp sounds as disgusted as I feel.

Says everything, really – a company from an elite regiment directing the fucking traffic.

The village is a real mess. It looks as if it was quite prosperous, but most of the houses are damaged. Many are minus their roofs or have large holes in the walls, and there are big piles of debris everywhere – bricks, roof tiles, timber, chairs…

The church is mostly intact and is being used as a dressing station. There's a long queue of wounded waiting outside, and an endless stream of ambulances.

The suffering is all too evident, and none of us want to linger there.

Hutten, Kropp and I are billeted further up the hill, sharing the upstairs rooms with three NCOs from Scheumann's Platoon. The house isn't too bad – part of the roof is off and the windows have all gone, but it'll keep the worst of the weather out.

We break up some of the furniture and make a fire, and it gets quite cosy.

Creep through the woods – scream of shell – hit the ground – thunderous bang—

Dark room, stars above me, sounds of intense shelling and fighting some way off.

Lie wide awake, running with sweat in spite of the cold.

Don't want to go back to sleep, though the bed's quite comfortable – or would be if Kropp hadn't sprawled into my side of it.

Wonder who lived here. It's quite a big house, so they were doing well until the war came and they had to leave. Now their home's half wrecked, and full of enemy soldiers who've smashed the furniture.

We're fighting to stop this happening in Brandenburg, like it did in East Prussia in '14.

Give Kropp a shove. He grunts and rolls away from me.

Curl up with my back against his, feel the warmth radiating from him even through our clothes.

Good bloke to sleep with, Kropp – like having your own personal stove.

Funny how we use language. 'I like sleeping with Sergeant Kropp' is a sentence that would raise eyebrows, but 'sleeping' means exactly that.

Whereas if I were 'sleeping' with the lovely Frieda, it's the last thing I'd be doing – no more than I had to, anyway...

Actually feel faintly human in the morning, especially after a decent breakfast and a mug of coffee.

Messner sets the boys to shovelling the rubble out of the road. That should stop them thinking.

The officers and NCOs direct the traffic, and it's quite a job.

The road through the village is churned to crunching axle-deep mud.

Supplies and reinforcements for the front line all have to move up as fast as possible.

The artillery is trying to move forward, the horses straining in the harnesses as the guns break through the frozen crust and sink into the sludge, the crews pushing the limbers from behind.

Ambulances and walking wounded come down the hill to the church, and go from the church towards the main road and the light railway.

Relieved troops trudge wearily back out of the line, the effort of pulling their feet out of the mud almost too much.

The whole bloody lot clots every five minutes. By halfway through the day I'm hoarse from shouting, and truly thankful to have a break and a fag.

Sit carefully on the remains of a front wall and stretch. The scratches on my backside are still raw, and I just stop myself wincing.

Thank God they've managed to replace our rags.

My new trousers are rather big round the waist, but at least my arse isn't hanging out. The tunic's a bit snug on the chest and shoulders, but it's clean. Stadler has sewn the braid on for me, so I look like a Sergeant Major again rather than a vagrant.

Still have lice, though.

Strecker surveys the traffic, shakes his head slightly, and comes towards me.

His face is very grave.

Shit. I never like that look.

"Schelling, Hauptmann Gneist wants to see you."

For a moment I wonder what I've done, which is really stupid.

I haven't done anything – and even if I had, what can they do to me?

Find the Battalion Command Post.

"Ah, Schelling," says Gneist. "Have a seat."

"Thank you, sir."

His face is grave as well.

What in God's name has happened?

He hesitates, then says quietly, "I'm very sorry to have to tell you, but Leutnant Paetow is dead."

Oh shit. Shit. Like being thumped in the stomach, again. Another cousin, another childhood friend.

"I see… May I ask what happened, sir?"

"Yes, of course. It was the early hours of the 22nd – I'd sent him to find out what was going on, how far you'd all got. He never came back. Apparently Leutnant Ziegler of the Eleventh saw him at the northern edge of the wood, they came under machine-gun fire, Ziegler got hit in the legs, and he said Paetow went down and never moved again."

"Was he able to get to him?"

Gneist looks very uncomfortable. "No. I'm afraid not."

So how did Ziegler know Axel was dead?

Or did he lie there dying all night?

Christ, I hope not.

"Have they recovered his body, sir?"

"No… I'm very sorry, but it wasn't brought back before the French stepped up their bombardment, and – well, they looked, but they weren't able to find it."

And that's it. All I'll ever know. That Axel got shot, and no one knows how long it took him to die or where he is.

"Thank you for telling me, sir."

"Not at all… He was a damned fine officer. It's a great loss to me as well."

"Is there anything else, sir?"

"No, Schelling."

"Thank you, sir."

I hope you got the whole fucking burst. I hope you were dead before you hit the ground – or so far gone that you never felt anything.

But I've seen too many men die…

Oh, Jesus. Axel.

"Bad news?" asks Strecker.

"Yes, sir – my cousin, Leutnant Paetow. Dead."

"Very sorry to hear it."

Strecker means it. I can see that.

*

Max sat down on a mound of rubble and lit a cigarette.

That was another letter I had to write, and the hardest of all. I was so used to writing to men's families. I could almost write the bloody letters in my sleep.

'Dear Herr X, it is my sad duty to inform you that your son…'

And then it was always 'died a hero's death' and 'instantly', plus a few lines about what a good comrade he was and how much he'd be missed. All true except 'instantly'.

Hardly anyone dies instantly – but what else did they want to read? That the poor bastard got mutilated and died slowly in agony, which is what usually happens?

The last thing you want the man's mother to know is what really happened to her son.

And so I wrote the usual thing to my Aunt Ingrid, knowing it would break her heart.

I had to fib a bit about his 'burial' – just said he'd been interred where he fell, knowing that she wouldn't be able to come here until after the war, whenever that might be.

She was never the same, said Uncle Simon, and she died a few months later without knowing that Axel – or rather some bones with his tag – had been found and buried properly.

*

26th February 1916, Ornes

"Give me a hand with the letters, Schelling?"

"Of course, sir."

Messner tears the list of the fallen in half, and hands me one part.

We both know it's incomplete. So many men are still unaccounted for, and likely to stay that way.

'Dear Herr Kirn… Dear Herr Mersch…'

Christ, this is a dismal job.

Messner hands me his hip flask.

"Thank you, sir."

"Don't mention it. Makes the job a bit less… well, you know."

Don't I just. Especially when writing the name brings the man's face to mind. Especially when I can hear him screaming.

I hope to Christ Axel died quickly.

I wish I could stop thinking about Axel. He's there every morning when I wake up.

Ironic, really – I got sent in while he was on the Battalion staff, and I'm here with a whole skin and he's dead.

'Don't forget me, Max…'
How could I?
'Dear Herr Fürst,' I begin.
Loud cheering.

Very loud cheering. Everyone in the village seems to be shouting.

Messner and I look at each other.

"Go and find out what's happening," he says to Walther.

Before Walther reaches the door, Jahnke bursts in, jumping with excitement like a large puppy. All he needs is a tail to wag.

"The 24th have taken Fort Douaumont!"

We all stare at him.

"Where'd you get that?" asks Messner, laughing.

"It's official, sir – from Battalion."

Fuck me.

The biggest fort of all, on the highest ground, commanding the entire battlefield – and it's in German hands.

Surely now we can't lose.

"So what happened?" Messner asks.

"Apparently some of their chaps just walked in. There was practically no garrison."

"*Just – walked – in?*" Messner repeats, with all the disbelief I feel.

"That's what they say. There was a hole in the fence from the shelling, and some of them made it into the ditch and through the door."

Messner and I look at each other.

"Pity they pulled us out," he says.

"Isn't it."

And it is a bit ripe that those buggers have such a victory, while we're glorified traffic policemen.

"Wonder who'll get the Pour le Mérite," Scheumann says later.

I'd forgotten all about that – capturing a fortress gets the lucky officer Prussia's highest decoration. Almost automatically.

Not that it concerns me, or is ever likely to. I'm down for a commission at some point, but on the form to date I won't live to get it. And who wants the Express Ticket to Eternity anyway?

"Well, it won't be us," Messner says with regret.

"There'll be gongs a long way down," says Hutten glumly.

He's thoroughly pissed off – Jahnke has temporary command of the late Chrobak's Platoon and will get his epaulettes if he makes the grade, while Hutten might make acting officer one day. A gong would cheer him up no end.

"No point thinking about it," I say.

"No – we'll get our own opportunities," says Scheumann.

It'll be a while before we're ready to fight again, though.

The reinforcements are just as Kropp feared – youths from the homeland, who've done their training but have no experience of battle.

So now almost half the Company consists of men who've never fought – not quite the same thing as a hundred and sixty experienced, battle-hardened men.

We need to get them trained up – and fast – but to do that we need to be out of the line. And God knows when that will happen.

The Frenchies may be falling back, but their artillery is much busier. So many shells land in Ornes that we move into the cellar.

The next evening, Strecker summons all Platoon and Group Commanders to the Company office.

"The Battalion's to go up to Fort Douaumont tonight," he says, "to relieve the garrison."

That'll be interesting – to see inside the Frenchies' big underground fort.

And getting there could be very interesting indeed.

The Frenchies are not pleased at losing their Fort, and would rather like it back. And so they're shelling the crap out of it and everything around it, as we can hear all too clearly.

"So we'll be going up the Hassoule Ravine," he continues, "and then on to the north-east corner of the ditch, where there's a 42 cm shell crater. We use that to enter the ditch and then the Fort itself."

As easy as that…

XII

We weren't sorry to leave here, Max thought as he walked out of the ruined village. *And it doesn't have good memories for me.*

I'll never forget Gneist's face as he told me about Axel. Can't have been easy for him, especially when he didn't know the full story…

The shadows were getting long.

"Time to go home," he said to Prince. "You always wait so patiently."

Maybe I'll get you an apple as well.

He handed Prince back with mutual reluctance, and went straight to the hotel.

The room was in darkness as the chambermaid had closed the shutters, and the atmosphere was most unwelcoming.

Max opened them wide, and the bright early-evening colours flooded in.

Home. My family's villa, the sun going down across the lake, and the water reflecting the light… Frieda and the boys, in our snug little house in Potsdam. I miss them so much.

I wish I could call her – it would be so lovely to hear her voice… but back then we couldn't call home, and sometimes it took days for letters to reach us.

Though I wasn't waiting for letters from Frieda when I was here. That came later, and I am so glad it did.

Ah, Frieda, Frieda, my darling – I do love you. To the best of my ability, with what remains of my heart. I wish I didn't feel so frozen inside.

He sighed. *Best get out of this room for a while. Not good to be on my own too much.*

The streets were still busy, and he found a grocer's and bought the treats for Prince. A few minutes later, he saw a newspaper headline.

'Construction of the Douaumont Ossuary continues.'

He bought the paper, and read the article over dinner.

It included a short interview with the Bishop of Verdun, who spoke of his determination that the bones found on the battlefield should have a Christian burial, and of the progress of his fundraising.

That's a good idea. I don't believe in God, but the dead should still be respected and honoured.

There was a drawing of the design for the building, and photographs of the construction work and of the Provisional Ossuary, where the remains were currently housed.

So that's where they put those piles of bones.

That's going to be quite a monument. Some of my boys will be in it. Maybe part of Axel will be too.

I'll visit the Provisional Ossuary, once I've been to all the places where the Seventh was.

By the time he got back to the hotel, the last of the daylight had faded.

'Didn't think I'd go away, did you?' said the voice.

"Oh, fuck off."

But he left a gap in the curtains again, and was glad of the dawn after a night of bad dreams.

Prince seemed pleased to see him, and nuzzled his pocket.

"You only love me for my carrots," Max said.

He pulled out a carrot and broke it in half. Prince demolished it.

"Didn't touch the sides, did it? Want another?"

That was a very silly question.

Wonder when anyone last gave you carrots.

"That's it for now, boy."

The sky was cloudy, and as they cantered up the hill a fine rain began to fall.

I don't mind getting wet, but I don't want Prince standing around in the rain. If I change my plan, go to the Provisional Ossuary and then to the cemetery, maybe there'll be some shelter for him.

They took the dirt road up towards Douaumont, through a devastated landscape of overlapping shell-holes part full of water. Grass and scrub were slowly covering the bare earth, and there were splashes of colour where wild flowers bloomed.

Jesus fucking Christ – I've never seen so many craters. It's even worse than when we were here.

But then we left the battlefield in late May, and the fighting went on until December with the same ferocity.

God alone knows how many men lie here.

Max took his hat off.

This must be the largest graveyard in Europe, if not the world.

And what on earth are they going to do with this ruined land, even after all the munitions and all the bodies have been removed?

All the bodies will never be removed. Thousands and thousands of men rotted into the ground.

Have you forgotten how the place stank? How we all stank when we came out of the line?

The cold rain ran down Max's neck.

It's only right that I should feel uncomfortable.

There's Fort Douaumont, right on the top of the ridge.

That's for another day…

Bloody hell, look at that!

Part of a huge stone structure was rising out of the ground, a hollow vault with a massive tower, surrounded by scaffolding.

That's the new Ossuary. God, it's going to be enormous, far bigger than I realised from the drawing. But then it needs to be

– enough men disappeared here to populate a decent-sized town. There must be millions of bones…

Another sign: 'Fleury. Destroyed village'.

Just a wasteland of craters.

More clean-up teams were working, and there were piles of shells and of bones beside the road.

Those won't be our boys, though – it was the poor old Bavarians who got slaughtered here. And of course they blame us, seem to forget that they were here because we'd been slaughtered first.

The buggers are still causing trouble, with those right-wing lunatics trying to seize power. And what's even worse, Prussians are joining in. Again.

When you think what value we used to place on tolerance and the rule of law – but we had a government in those days.

At least we didn't turn into a Bolshevik republic like Russia – though if you ask me the extreme right and the extreme left are exactly the same oppression, just in different clothes and with different slogans.

He sighed. *Fucking politicians – all the bloody same…*

Here's the Provisional Ossuary. Time to pay my respects.

Max tied Prince up in the lee of the wooden building, hoping he'd get less wet there, and walked round to the front.

As he approached the door, he saw a black-clad woman climbing out of a cab.

"May I help you?" he said, offering his arm. "It is rather muddy."

She stiffened at his accent. "No, thank you."

He bowed and retreated, allowing her to enter the building alone.

I'll wait until she comes out – but she was quite some time, and his jacket was almost soaked through.

It's only water, Max – and she's probably trying to find her husband.

Eventually she emerged, and got back into the cab without glancing at him.

He went into the Ossuary and stopped dead. It was full of the standards of French regiments.

We had colours once. Now the Regiment's been disbanded and they'll never fly again. The difference between victors and defeated…

At the far end was an altar.

Lucky people who can still believe. You can forget that crap about there being no atheists on the battlefield – I was in more tight corners than I can count, and it never even occurred to me to pray.

Not after Diksmuide. What faith I'd had died there along with my comrades. No loving God would permit such slaughter and mutilation.

Where are the bones? They must be in these huge boxes, marked with signs for the sectors of the battlefield.

I wonder how many belong to my boys.

He paused at each of the places where the Regiment had been deployed, then paid for a candle and lit it, the flame bright. He stood in silent remembrance for a few minutes, then brought his heels together smartly and bowed to the dead.

As he turned to leave, there was a loud, sharp knock, right next to him.

He started and looked round.

There was no one else in the building. Nothing had moved.

There was just a very strong sense of someone standing beside him.

Axel.

'Would you find the rest of me, Max, in the wood?'

That's an impossible task. I don't even know where to look.

'It would mean a lot to me.'

You'd still be in two places – and what remains of you in the wood is with our comrades.

Silence.

I could spend the rest of my life here looking for your bones – and how would I know when I'd found them?

Further silence.

I'll come back, Axel, as often as I can, but I have a family and I have to look after them.

'Yes, of course you do…'

Axel accompanied him back outside, and then was gone.

The rain had almost stopped. Prince gave him a rather accusing look, though he was only a bit damp.

"Prima donna," Max said. "It's only water."

The horse snorted and shook himself, showering Max with fine spray.

"All right, all right – I deserve it!"

Leave the cemetery for another day – then I can do all the rear areas at once.

So – time to head towards Bezonvaux and retrace our steps up to the Fort through the Hassoule Ravine. I really should go up from Ornes, but my leg won't like it. Bezonvaux to the ravine is much shorter.

I suppose we could take a straight line there – don't be stupid, Max. Stick to the roads. It would be a right bastard to get blown up now.

Sticking to the roads meant going again past the village of Vaux.

Max shivered as they neared the bottom of the valley. *If I keep up the chronological order, then I can put this place off for a couple of days.*

The ghosts called out to him as he rode past, and Prince skittered again and cantered sideways.

"Easy, boy…"

It's not just me, is it? You can hear – or sense – something as well.

Max tried to close his ears, and carried on to Bezonvaux.

There's a bit more of this place than there is of Ornes, but not much. And this too still looked like a village when we were here.

It deserves a longer visit as well, but not today. That was the second deployment.

He unsaddled Prince.

"Well, boy – you've got food and water, and it's stopped raining, and I don't suppose you'll miss me. Though I have got an apple for you if you're good."

He oriented himself, and set off towards the entrance to the Hassoule Ravine.

*

27th February 1916, Ornes

Up to the Fort – that'll be quite something…

Go back to our billet, and tell Kropp and the other NCOs that we'll be heading up to Fort Douaumont to relieve the garrison.

"At least we can do something useful," says Kropp. "I'm sick of being a traffic policeman."

"And it won't be snowing in the Fort," adds Hutten.

"And with a bit of luck there's a kitchen," says Unteroffizier Richter.

"All you think about's your fucking stomach!" Sergeant Otten says.

"Enjoyed cold iron rations, then, did you, Sarge?" Richter retorts.

Otten pulls a face.

"We have to get into the fucking Fort first," says Feldwebel Kiepke. "And the Frenchies won't like that idea much."

He is, of course, correct.

We leave Ornes once it's dark, in Company order.

The Seventh looks almost as it did a week ago – but that's only appearance. The new boys will hear shells screaming and whining overhead, but with no idea which way they're going or where they'll land.

They'll be slow to hit the ground when we get shot at, and even slower to shoot back – and probably too scared to hit anything.

To top all that, we're heading for a real witches' cauldron.

The night would be pitch-dark but the shelling is continuous, the sky alight with brilliant flashes and rolling thunder.

The new boys skitter like nervous horses, and try to pretend they're not scared.

You should be scared. You have no idea what shell fragments do to men's bodies.

The next village, Bezonvaux, and the strongpoint above it are in German hands – which is just as well. Flanking fire on top of the barrage would be just a bit much.

And the barrage seems to increase in intensity every day. The Frenchies are getting their arses into gear properly.

Hit the ground a few times, but that's all. Everyone gets through unscathed, and the new boys are already reacting faster to "Get down!"

Jahnke's doing a good job of encouraging them. Maybe there's more to that boy than I thought.

The valley sides close in as we enter the Hassoule Ravine, and the racket is unbelievable. It's like being inside a massive thunderstorm. French shells of every calibre scream into the valley, and the explosions merge as they reverberate. Somewhere our artillery is also firing.

It's hard to see where we're going – the ravine is full of lightning, and the split seconds between the flashes are dazzled blackness.

Scream of shell.

"GET DOWN!!"

Can't even hear myself.

Hit the ground.

BLINDING LIGHT MASSIVE FLAT DETONATION

Fragments of steel lumps of earth bounce off my back. Soft lumps follow.

Screams, barely audible.

Smoking crater.

Wrecked bodies.

All but two of my boys get to their feet, stunned and unsteady.

Try to shout reassurance but it's futile. Even when I bellow right into Nehring's ear, he can't hear me.

Leave Tannwitz and Schwenk to patch up who they can, and trudge on.

Burchartz looks at me, appalled.

No, we don't stop for them. You were told that.

Up and up. It's not steep but we're carrying so much stuff, and the mud holds our boots when they break through the icy crust. It's fucking knackering.

The noise has, incredibly, got even louder – it's a physical wall of sound that vibrates in my chest and presses in waves against my head. My brain's reeling.

Multiple thunderous flashes off to the right.

Shells roaring overhead towards the enemy.

Across the ravine are howitzers. Twelve guns, firing as fast as they can to defend themselves, while the Frenchies fire as fast as they can to try to obliterate them.

No wonder it's so fucking loud.

*

Max paused and looked around. *This is the ravine proper, and it's narrower than I realised in the dark.*

What's that over the other side? A scattering of lumps of concrete, and another... Maybe those were the howitzer positions.

There are craters everywhere here, too. But then it did turn into a real death trap. 'The Ravine of Death', it was called, and men avoided it if they could.

He had to laugh. *The whole Verdun battlefield was a death trap – it's just that some parts were deadlier than others.*

He continued up the hill, the sky widening.

*

27th February 1916, Hassoule Ravine

As we reach the top, the ground opens out and the noise diminishes, but now we're exposed to the full force of the French bombardment.

We'll be lucky to get to the Fort at all.

And yet – we have quite a few scares, but reach the high iron fence that surrounds the ditch.

There's a massive shell-hole, metres wide and deep, and in it all structure has vanished – the railings and the steep outer wall of the ditch have been blown to fragments.

Nehring and Burchartz stare at it.

"*Forty-two*," Kropp shouts at them.

Forty-two what? I can see them thinking – and then they understand.

And I can see them wishing they hadn't.

They'd like it even less if they saw a 42 cm shell, standing well over a metre tall – and no one wants to be anywhere near one when it explodes. Not that you'd know anything about it.

"The Frenchies only have 40s," Kropp shouts cheerfully.

They fail to look relieved.

Let's hope we don't get any of those – what the Frenchies are sending over is quite bad enough.

In the flashes I can see down into the ditch.

Away from the huge crater, the outer wall is six metres high and lined with stone blocks, many dislodged. On the inner side, the ground slopes up to the top of the Fort.

I do not want to stay here.

Let's get into the fucking Fort before we get blown to bits.

But it seems there's a problem. We are not going anywhere.

Spread out, and take what cover we can in the shell-holes.

*

Jesus, thought Max as he picked his way along the path. *The Fort's had the crap shelled out of it all right. Yes, we knew it was happening, but the damage is unbelievable.*

The craters had multiplied to an unimaginable extent. The land looked like a stormy sea that had been instantly frozen.

Each one of these holes was caused by an exploding shell, fired with the intention of killing and maiming as many men as possible.

Each one marks a shocking toll of pain and death.

Most were at least half-full of stagnant greenish water, and he shuddered as he looked at it.

When the vegetation reclaims this place, it'll grow good and lush – all that fertiliser…

All those lives, their boys and ours.

You'd think the 42 cm crater would still show up – ah, here it is. A bit battered but still visible.

The outer wall of the ditch has lost its stone lining completely, though – it's just a bank of earth, and the ditch itself has got shallower.

And it's so quiet, not like then with the shells raining down.

The dead are all around, though.

*

27th February 1916, near Fort Douaumont

"Stay here, boys."

Take my life in my hands and go in search of Messner, or Strecker.

Find the latter.

He gives me a wry look. "No room at the inn," he shouts into my ear.

"How about the stable, sir?"

He laughs. "We're waiting to hear! The Fort's crammed full. Hauptmann Gneist's gone in to talk to the Commandant."

"We'll make ourselves comfortable, then, sir."

Make it back in one piece, brief everyone.

Kropp's eyebrow goes up and down. "Why the fuck have they brought us up here, then?"

"God alone knows."

Spend time with all the new boys in turn, try to teach them what to listen for as the shells arrive.

Hope they're taking it in.

Braun looks terrified. The poor bugger's actually shaking.

Try to remember the first time I was shelled, and fail.

I do know what it is to be scared – though I'm used to that as well. He will have to learn for himself how to deal with it.

The night is wearing on.

I do not want to be on this high point in the daylight, outside in the shelling. Wasn't there something about machine guns in the church tower in Douaumont village? That'll be fun.

Messner dives into my shell-hole. "We're going back down."

"When, sir?"

"Right away."

Pass it on. Kropp's eyebrow is very expressive. The new fellows look completely baffled, and I don't blame them.

Let's at least get into the fucking ravine before it gets light.

Nearly all of us make it.

Tramp back down through the infernal racket of French and German shellfire.

Hit the mud several times.

Another of the new fellows is writhing on the ground – I barely had time to learn the poor bastard's name, and now he's smashed up to buggery.

If he makes it, he'll be home for good... after being here five minutes and doing fuck all.

By the time we get to the bottom of the ravine, it's well past dawn.

"We're staying here, boys," says Strecker.

No more directing the traffic, then. They must have something livelier in mind for us.

XIII

28th February 1916, Hassoule Ravine

"I could have done without that," Kropp says as we queue for breakfast at the field cooker.

"Indeed. Useful training for the new boys, though." *Those that survived, anyway.*

"There is that."

I'm covered in mud again, and there are red patches as well.

"So much for a fresh uniform," says Pieper.

"At least this one's not rags," says Kropp.

"Mine's got lice, though," Pieper replies.

We all have. As bloody usual.

"Pity they don't eat the bloodstains," I say.

I don't mind being covered in mud, but I've never got used to blood. It's always disgusted me, and globs of flesh are even worse…

We stay in the bottom of the ravine for the rest of the day. The French artillery gets livelier as the hours pass, and our howitzers further up have stopped firing.

Towards nightfall, a few singed and tattered gunners make their weary way past us. No one asks where their guns are, or their comrades. We can guess.

The night is cold, but the Frenchies keep sending us shells to warm us up. Finally it gets light.

I'm getting sick of waiting around.

"Hey," says Stadler, "you know what today is?"

"What?" asks Lorenz.

"29th February."

Lorenz laughs. "Well, make the most of it – you won't see another!"

"No," says Stadler. "It's my birthday."

"How old are you, then?"

"Six!"

We all laugh.

"Well, mate, you bloody act it!" says Tiemann.

"Beer's on you tonight, then!" says Lorenz.

"Beer?" Stadler says. "Where the fuck am I going to get that, then?"

"Dunno, mate," Lorenz replies, "but you've got all day to work on it!"

An hour or so later, no one is thinking about beer. The French really don't like us being in the ravine, and step up the shelling.

"See?" shouts Tiemann. "Even the Frenchies know it's your birthday!"

"I don't like their presents much!" Stadler retorts.

No one does.

In no time heavies are slamming down, mixed with 7.5s and shrapnel, and our cover is hopelessly inadequate.

We're well spread out and dug in on the reverse slope, but the bastards are still getting us, the splinters flying across the ravine. It's like being in the middle of a volcano.

Wrap my arms around my head as one screams in close.

Oh, for a steel helmet.

In between the detonations I check on my fellows.

Poor Braun is chalk-white and shaking. There's not much I can say to him – this is how it is and he has to learn to deal with it.

Kropp looks at me, and his right eyebrow waggles again.

That eyebrow should be on the stage. Laugh in spite of the situation.

He puts his mouth to my ear. "What's so fucking funny?"

Put mine to his. "Tell you later."

It really isn't funny, though, any of it. The thunderous explosions leave my brain hanging limp between my ears.

I'll be lucky to get out of this.

"MEDICS!"

For about the fortieth time...

Messner dives into my shell-hole, just makes it before another heavy slams in.

"We're moving to the Brûle Ravine," he shouts into my ear.

"Which one's that?"

"The—"

Another heavy arrives.

"... next one back."

Thank fuck for that.

Most of us are moving back, that is. Not everyone is able to leave – and of those that can, not all will make it out.

I am so sick of the sight of lifeless grey shapes, and even sicker of seeing men mutilated and in agony.

I have had enough of razor-sharp red-hot fragments of steel whirling singing through the air, and of the appalling injuries they inflict.

Metzler's arm gets sliced off.

Blood spurts from the stump in scarlet jets and he stares at it, his eyes wide, screaming like a lunatic.

Weidner rips his scarf off and pulls it tight around Metzler's upper arm.

The blood stops spurting, but Metzler is still screaming in panic.

Weidner slaps him, hard, and he stops, his face white and shocked.

Poor kid – he can't be more than eighteen.

Patch up those we can, carry or support them round the shoulder of the hill, into the next ravine. Distinct feeling of relief once there's high ground between us and the shelling.

Hand the wounded over to the stretcher-bearers.

This attack had better bring us victory before it's too late.

Germany may be 'rich in heroes' blood' as the song says, but it's been flowing in torrents for a year and a half.

*

Max was back at the bottom of the ravine.

The Brûle Ravine's not far. I just have to go round the hill and west a bit, and I'll be there. Maybe there are still traces of our positions. That would be interesting.

But the day's well advanced, and it'll take quite a while to get back to town with my single horsepower. I really don't want to have to find my way in the dark.

I'm not scared of the ghosts, of course – it's just that we won't be able to see where we're going, and the roads are bad.

The single horsepower was very pleased with the apple, and nuzzled Max's neck with apparent affection.

"You only love me for the treats," he said. "Let's go home."

And, of course, the heroes' blood started to run out, he thought on the way down the hill into Verdun.

By the end of the war, we were sending youths to the Front, skinny boys who hadn't seen a decent meal for years. Anyone who claims we weren't defeated in the field is talking out of his arse.

He tried a different restaurant. There was the usual slight reserve at his accent, but he had the feeling that money mattered more.

Let's hope the chef doesn't spit in my soup – though that wouldn't be as bad as some of the things I ingested back then…

Strange to be sitting here in comfort, eating good hot food off fine china set on a tablecloth. Frenchies are still a bit keen on garlic, though.

He looked around as little as possible, but halfway through dinner he realised that three people across the other side of the room kept looking at him and talking to each other: two women and a man, all about his own age.

I'm sure I've never seen any of you before – except maybe one of the women, but I can only see half her face.

Probably here for the same purpose as me – why else would anyone come all the way to Verdun?

After about ten minutes, one of the women got up and approached him.

I have seen you before – at the Ossuary.

He stood up.

"I…" she began, and stopped.

"Please – sit down," he said.

"No, thank you. I don't want to disturb you."

You are disturbing me. You might as well do it thoroughly.

"I would like to apologise," she said, rather awkwardly. "I was rude at the Ossuary. You were just being kind."

"It doesn't matter. You have every reason to…"

Dislike me, he'd been about to say, but it suddenly seemed absurd. There was nothing to say that she did.

"That's exactly the point," she went on. "We have to stop being enemies, or what will become of our children?"

"I have two sons," he said. "And I would give anything to prevent them having to – to…"

He couldn't say, *to do what I did*. Not to her.

She smiled, still with reserve. "Yes. It's in our hands, isn't it? Now, I've disturbed you quite enough."

Is it in our hands? That's quite a thought.

It wasn't in our hands back in August '14 – or was it? Was there something we could have done to stop the war starting?

He sighed. There was no answer to that.

As he walked back to the hotel along the dark streets, he heard footsteps behind him.

He stopped.

So did they.

He carried on, and the boots accompanied him.

He turned swiftly – the street was empty apart from a young couple at the far end.

Axel.

Or maybe another of the boys we left here.

Whoever it was let him go on alone, back to the room that wasn't quite empty.

It was a very bad night. Every time he closed his eyes he was back in the wood, or the Hassoule Ravine with the shells slamming in.

He woke shaking yet again, switched on the light, and tried to read.

'Shouldn't have been here,' said the voice.

"No one chooses where he gets sent."

'It's our country. You invaded.'

No point trying to reason with you. Max turned back to his book.

He couldn't concentrate, and after about ten minutes he gave up, opened the curtains wide, and sat smoking and waiting for the dawn.

In the morning, he felt so jaded that it took two cups of strong coffee before he felt ready to go anywhere.

Maybe I should move to Damvillers or Billy or somewhere else in our old rear area. I'll have a look when I go to the cemetery.

I think I'll make that today – be a good idea to have a rest from the battlefield. Don't want to push my luck or I could end up completely bonkers.

He went to the cemetery first, and as he went through the gate he stopped, in astonishment and dismay.

Where are the beautiful gravestones that the Regimental masons made for our officers: the splendid, tall obelisks, with the man's name and an Iron Cross in a wreath of oak leaves carved into the stone?

They've all gone – the Frenchies must have taken them away. The bastards.

Axel never had one of those headstones, though – the Regiment had left Verdun by the time what remained of him was found.

He searched slowly and carefully along the rows of plain crosses. *Here's Chrobak – so full of enthusiasm he was, and so proud to go in first – and here's a pillar for Doctor Meyer, with the Star of David on it.*

Max paused for quite a while in front of the Doctor, his bare head bowed in respect and sadness.

Lovely man he was, and as brave as a lion. We all owed him so much, and his grave was always covered in flowers.

I don't know where those idiots who run the Jews down get their stupid ideas – my Jewish comrades were patriotic Germans, and a lot of them got killed.

But then all politicians are liars.

Here's poor little Jahnke. That really got to me, though of course I couldn't admit to it. It got to Kropp as well, and that took some doing.

Jahnke was only eighteen, but far braver and tougher than many men twice his age. And then he had to die in the field hospital, the way no one wants to go.

I hope they looked after him properly, but I know how busy they were.

No doubt Strecker told the usual lies: 'Peacefully' and 'You can be sure he didn't suffer'.

Moot point whether Jahnke's father believed that, when he was writing it himself every other day. Perhaps his mother did.

Max could see his comrades' faces, as clearly as if they were alive. *So strange to be left behind...*

But where's Axel?

He wandered along the rows of crosses. *Someone grieves for each of these men – and they're only a fraction of the total...*

Ah, here he is. Not with the others – I suppose that's because he was buried later. If it's him, of course. The bodies must have been well mixed up by the shelling.

There's probably just a small box or a tent quarter, containing some bones caught up in the tatters of a uniform. And more of them are in the Ossuary and in the wood.

All that's left of Axel and his life. Such a fucking waste.

Max sighed.

I've seen enough. I'll go to Loison and see if I can find the camp there, then to the camp north of Azannes where we went when they finally pulled us out.

Not that we knew it was final, though. We were in reserve for two weeks.

And of course we could hear the fighting and we expected to be sent in again at any moment, so it wasn't exactly relaxing.

*

13th June 1916, camp near Azannes

To our amazement, His Royal Highness the Crown Prince pays us a visit, to take the salute and hand out a few gongs.

The new boys have eyes like saucers. The old hands are sceptical.

"How does he know what the fuck's going on from forty kilometres behind the lines?"

"He doesn't make the decisions, anyway."

"Yeah – you just have to be born in the right place and they make you a general."

I suppose I should tell them to shut up, but part of me agrees.
Until the inspection.

Instead of the usual stiff ceremonial, he strolls along the ranks, chatting to the men and shaking hands.

"And how long have you been at Verdun, Leutnant Schelling?"

"I was here on the first day, Your Royal Highness."

His expression changes. "Well done. Very well done."

"Thank you, Your Royal Highness."

"No – it's for me to thank all of you."

And he obviously means it.

Well, bugger me. Maybe they should give you some real authority.

*

I'd already been in that camp, because that's where they took me – but that was the second deployment. I've already rambled ahead to the end of our time here.

Keep it chronological, Max...

To his surprise, the camp at Loison was very well preserved, and the officers' bathhouse was still standing.

Being clean was very nice while it lasted – which wasn't long. Funny how all the things you take for granted in a civilised life – showers, clean clothes, shaving, lavatories – cease to matter when your life is on the line.

I'd like a Mark for every time I had to crap on a spade – and then we all had the runs from drinking shell-hole water, and what came out was just liquid and flowed off the spade anyway.

All the things men don't write about when they publish their heroic memoirs.

People want to read stirring accounts of dashing advances, not about shitting yourself because the only water was putrid and there wasn't time to take your trousers down.

And that was almost all of us, not just the blokes who were literally scared shitless.

Enough of that...

We helped to build this camp when we arrived, because there wasn't any accommodation for us. That was a good start. We were the elite, brought here to smash down the door to Verdun, and our first job was as construction workers.

Add to that the long wait in the wet Stollen, and the double slog to the front line and back, and you do wonder what the effect on our fighting ability was.

You don't ask a racehorse to plough a field, or a top athlete to dig foundations...

That wood was a perfect killing ground, Max – it wouldn't have made any difference.

He moved on to Billy, but there was no trace of the camp they'd been sent to when the battle was postponed.

Can't blame the Frenchies for taking it down – all that building material would be very useful, and I don't suppose they want to be reminded of us any more than necessary.

The road from Billy to Azannes meandered gently. It was strangely peaceful, in sharp contrast to the last time he'd made the journey, and he had the luxury of riding rather than tramping along.

Rather like home, he thought as they passed the lake.

It is a bloody long way, though, and so many of the men never came back...

The ghosts were all around, and to cheer himself up he started to sing 'The Watch on the Rhine'.

They all joined in the chorus, their boots ringing in time.

"Fast stands and true the Watch, the Watch on the Rhine..."

Probably not the best choice of song, but there's no one about that I can see.

A couple of minutes after the last notes had faded into the trees, he heard a male voice.

"Allons, enfants de la Patrie, Le jour de gloire est arrivé!"

Prince tossed his head and arched his neck proudly.

Max laughed. *Maybe I should sing 'Deutschland, Deutschland, über alles' next. Or maybe not. Better leave it at one each.*

He's got a good voice, though.

"... L'étendard sanglant est levé..."

Prince's ears were forward, and he was almost prancing.

Max slapped the black neck affectionately.

"You like the 'Marseillaise', don't you?"

A thought struck him.

You were a military horse. Papa's horse knew his old regimental march, and our national anthem.

So here we are, two veterans together – though you had it easier than me. You're not scarred.

And how I wish my only scars were the physical ones...

Bloody hell, it is a long way to Azannes, and then a good kilometre to our jumping-off positions.

"You are a good fellow, Prince, carrying me all this way. Even if I do bribe you with carrots and apples."

When he handed the horse back that evening, he asked, "Was he cavalry?"

"No. Infantry colonel's horse."

"He knows the 'Marseillaise'."

The stable owner smiled for the first time. "Good French horse."

A good French horse who doesn't mind a Prussian rider, Max didn't say. *And who must be bored out of his fine equine skull in your stables. Quite apart from the fact that he hates you – and I suspect it's mutual.*

Prince's ears had flattened themselves against his head at the sight of his owner, as usual.

Shame you're stuck here with him...

Must have been a nice life, being a colonel's horse. They must have pampered you no end.

And no leading the regiment into battle, not after autumn '14, anyway.

Nowhere near the front line after that, not like those poor artillery horses, half-dead from exhaustion hauling the guns through the mud – and I'll never forget the team that got shelled and the way they screamed until the gunners shot them.

Poor, innocent, trusting horses, caught up in Man's war…

He shook his head. Best not thought about, like so much else.

Here's the river – oh, bugger it, I forgot to look for somewhere else to stay. But then I wouldn't be able to ride Prince, and I am getting rather fond of him.

And I'm buggered if I'm going to let that voice chase me away.

'Back again?' it asked when he turned the light out.

He didn't bother to answer.

It didn't like that at all. A few seconds later there was a loud knock, and a few seconds after that his bedside lamp fell over.

He set it upright again.

The air in the room was vibrating with hostility.

This is getting a bit much. How could I tell that the knock at the Ossuary was friendly, but this one was anything but?

That was far too complicated.

I wish Frieda were here – it would be so lovely to have her beautiful soft body against mine, and her voice in my ear.

Everything else disappears when I'm in her arms. It's the only time I actually feel safe.

XIV

Right, Max thought as he shaved. *Today is in two parts. First I'll go to the Brûle Ravine and the Caurières Wood, where we were in reserve – which just meant we were out of the front line. We still got shelled to buggery – and then up to the Eastern Turret at the Fort.*

As usual, he looked at himself as little as possible, but when he'd finished shaving he did a quick inspection.

Ugly bastard, aren't you? God alone knows why Frieda wants to look at a face like that.

I'm not thirty yet, but no one would believe that. Not with all those lines, and the grey hairs.

He met his own grey-blue eyes, and wished he hadn't.

And you're still a cold-blooded bastard.

'Yes, you are,' said the Frenchie officer, his breath icy on Max's neck. 'Why don't you cut your throat?'

Max shivered and turned round. The room was empty.

Bloody hell. I've just about had enough of this.

Breakfast and get going.

He went straight from the breakfast room to the grocer's, and then to the stables.

Prince nudged him impatiently and nuzzled his pockets.

"Tart! I'm spoiling you, aren't I?"

The liquid brown eyes gazed at him.

"All right," he said, and handed over a carrot.

It vanished in seconds.

Prince pushed his muzzle into Max's neck, and snorted softly.

"Your whiskers tickle even more when you do that. Come on, let's get going."

To save time, he rode from Bezonvaux into the Brûle Ravine. As they left the village behind, the sides of the valley began to close in until it was narrow and deep.

"This is where they put us after your Colonel's gunner mates shelled the crap out of us in the Hassoule Ravine," he told Prince.

God knows why I'm telling the horse. I suppose because there's no one else here.

No one else? That's not quite accurate...

*

29th February 1916, Brûle Ravine

The ravine is very narrow and steep-sided. There's no way the Frenchies can drop shells onto the reverse slope, even using high trajectory guns.

Thank fuck for that.

Dig ourselves holes. Teach the surviving new fellows what to do.

Nehring barely knows one end of a spade from the other.

"What were you in civilian life?"

"An apprentice bookbinder, Sergeant Major."

"Well, if you want to make master bookbinder, you'd better learn to dig!"

"Yes, Sergeant Major."

And to be fair, he does put his back into it.

"Where's the beer, then?" Lorenz asks Stadler.

"Ask the fucking staff – bet they've got barrels full!"

Can't really blame Stadler for not finding beer.

Celebrate his birthday with stew and coffee instead, and the rum ration.

Which we need – it's fucking cold on this side of the ravine. The slope faces north and gets no sun at all, and the snow's much deeper. Once we stop digging, we all freeze.

Nehring, Braun and Burchartz look quite pleased with themselves, having withstood their baptism of fire.

"So much they know," Kropp says to me.

"They'll find out soon enough," says Otten. He sighs and lights another fag.

No one knows where Richter is. He and Otten are good mates. Maybe that should be 'were'.

What a fucking shit business this is, when your friends get mutilated in front of you or just disappear. Strong, healthy young men, who should have had a future, but who will lie here forever.

We'll be fighting again soon, no doubt, and the numbers of the dead will increase still further.

*

Prince walked on, the steep reverse slope towering over them, casting a brooding shadow.

There must be traces of our positions – we dug enough holes, after all.

He dismounted, left the road, and climbed part way up the hill.

Here's a piece of metal, folded in half.

And a deep hole in the hillside – and another.

And a post for wire, and wire itself. And more holed and twisted metal fragments.

Is all this stuff just going to lie here for eternity, like the men who put it here?

He shook his head and made his way back to Prince, who was standing waiting for him. He remounted, and they carried on towards the end of the ravine.

There was more debris scattered around.

And no doubt there are bones, too.

"This battlefield is one of the saddest places in the world."

He realised he'd spoken out loud again. *Better stop this now.*

"You don't care, do you?" he said, and reached forward and pulled one of the black ears affectionately. "Don't suppose you understand a single word."

The other ear swivelled back to listen.

I wonder what you do make of speech. You must understand some of it – you don't respond to German commands, but you would to French ones. And you understand my tone.

You must think people horribly noisy, talking all the bloody time.

Horses have their own language – on the farm, we all knew what ours meant when they whinnied or snorted, and they communicate with each other, like all herd animals.

If you ask me, they're much more intelligent than dogs. And as for cats!

Better not get into that one with my sisters.

You're rambling, Max.

The Caurières Wood was on the other, south-facing, side of the ravine. It was a collection of splintered, amputated stumps in a frozen sea of shell-holes, their edges blurred by a haze of green.

There were more pieces of folded metal, and a screw picket, twisted back on itself twice into a grotesque hairpin.

Max shuddered slightly, imagining the violence needed to bend metal like putty, remembering how it threw men as if they were rag dolls, and ripped bodies apart.

And then there would be that horrible rain of earth and stones and metal, mixed with parts of bodies and litres of blood.

If I had a Mark for every time I got covered in flesh and blood, I'd be a wealthy man.

It's a miracle we didn't all turn into gibbering wrecks – but no one who fought here is really sane.

He sighed.

And now it's time to go to the Eastern Turret. What a place that was.

If I carry on to the western end of this ravine, I can pick up the Bowling Alley and follow it south to the Fort.

"The Turret was an extension of the Fort," he told Prince. "It was supposed to hold one of those fucking horrible 7.5s, but the buggers never finished it. There was an observation tower and an underground chamber…"

They turned left onto the Bowling Alley, which still ran arrow-straight towards Fort Douaumont. The Fort itself was hidden until they reached the top of the hill – and then there it was. The Coffin-Lid, flat and dark, crowning the highest point.

Between them and it was a wilderness of craters, breaking the line of the road, and Prince picked his way carefully.

The terrain rose steadily. They were alone, and Max realised that he could hear nothing. No birdsong, no rustling in the grass, no signs of life apart from the two of them.

The atmosphere thickened as they neared the Fort.

Someone was behind them.

Prince stopped, his ears twitching back and forwards. Max looked round, but no one was there.

No one living, anyway. The dead are still here.

"Come on, boy."

Prince moved reluctantly forward, shivering.

"They won't hurt us. They can't hurt anyone, not now." *Who am I trying to convince?*

How many thousands of men died here?

Let's just get to the fucking Turret.

All that remained of it was a stone stump. The shells had destroyed everything else.

Jesus...

*

29th February 1916, Brûle Ravine

The First Battalion gets sent up to Fort Douaumont.

Although we have the Fort, we hold little of the ground around it, so it sits in its very own salient, vulnerable to attack from every direction except the north.

Not a comfortable situation.

So the generals want the salient flattened out, and our comrades are supposed to take the ground to the south-east of the Fort.

It turns out, once again, that the key words are 'supposed to'.

Three days later, it's our turn.

We move up in the night, in single file through the barrage. The new fellows are learning quickly when they need to hit the ground.

Most of us make it.

We relieve a Platoon of the Third Company – except that it *is* the Third Company, and they've made no progress forward.

"Jesus," says Kropp.

They've lost all their machine guns as well, and their flamethrowers.

"Good luck, boys," says their surviving Sergeant Major drily.

"Cheers, mate," I reply.

Bet you were pleased to see us...

We're in a trench about two hundred metres in front of the Turret.

Its tower gives our artillery observers a fine view of the French positions, while the underground chamber becomes home to the Battalion staff and the medical orderlies.

In front of us the ground falls away. We can see down into the Caillette Wood about three hundred metres down the hill.

Between us and the wood is a belt of dead ground, full of Frenchies. Far too close for comfort, and no doubt up to no good.

Naturally the Frenchies don't like us using their tower to direct our guns against them, and are determined to blow it and us to smithereens. And of course their guns have the exact range and bearing. This is their fortified zone, after all – they know just where everything is.

The shells land with horrible accuracy.

"The machine guns are to be kept in the underground room during daylight," says Strecker.

"So what the fuck happens when the bastards attack?" Weidner says after he's gone.

"The crews run like fuck to the entrance and get them out again," says Messner.

That'll be fun.

The entrance is under continuous shellfire. Every few seconds a heavy lands in front of it, with the most appalling detonation.

The racket inside must be quite something. Never mind the fear of being buried.

"And Doctor Meyer is with the medics in the underground room, so anyone who gets hit goes there."

That's if they can get in without being blown to fragments.

Good old Meyer. Solid gold, our Battalion Doctor.

He's always right up with us, however dangerous it is, armed with his medical bag and not seeming to give a shit about himself.

He's got a pistol, of course, but I can never imagine him actually using it. Presumably he would if he had to, but plenty of us would die to save him.

The French artillery is fucking horrible. All the next morning they shell the crap out of us.

Warn my boys to be ready for the attack.

"Hope to Christ the new buggers can shoot straight," says Kropp.

Obviously they passed their training, but they weren't shaking then.

Poor Braun's almost as bad as last time.

Horrible, being that scared. Fighting's one matter – the adrenaline gets going – but sitting there, hoping you're not going to be blown to pieces, is a far harder test of nerve. Especially when the evidence is all around you...

There are bodies and parts of bodies lying everywhere. Just as well it's cold.

Get hold of Weidner.

"Braun's petrified," I say into his ear.

"Yes, I'd noticed. I'll stay next to him."

"Thanks."

Weidner gives Braun a fag and some encouraging words, and he looks just a fraction less terrified.

The Frenchies don't attack.

So Gneist decides we should try to push down the hill.

Start to move forward.

Noise like an express train.

"GET DOWN!" yells Messner.

I'm already on the ground.

SHATTERING BLINDING THUNDER

Rain of earth, steel shards, flesh, blood.

And another. And another.

And 7.5s and shrapnel and medium shells.

Tornado of fire and steel.

Jesus, how can anything live in this?

Screams.

"MEDICS!"

You'll be lucky.

No one dares move.

Crouch there for at least a month.

Shelling eases, back to the usual steady rhythm.

Lift my head. Sit up.

"Be ready, boys!"

The old hands already have their rifles levelled, waiting.

The new boys look dazed.

Shake them, shout.

A piercing shriek, from about ten metres in front.

A grey shape twists up out of the ground and tries to crawl towards us, then falls back and screams again.

It's Jahnke.

God knows where he's hit, but the poor little bugger's in agony.

Another sharp cry.

"Poor little bastard," says Pieper.

Before I can stop him, he calls out, "It's all right, sir – I'll get you," and leaps up.

But the shelling hasn't stopped, and a splinter takes half his head off.

Motion to my boys to stay put. There's no sense getting even more casualties.

Take stock.

Of my lot, two are dead and five injured, Burchartz badly.

Lorenz patches him up as best he can, between the shells slamming in.

Make my way to Messner. Almost don't get there.

"What now, sir?"

"Strecker's sent a runner to Gneist. I'll let you know when I hear."

Let's hope it's off, then – I can't see much chance of our succeeding.

Now I understand why the First Battalion got nowhere. With this weight of artillery fire, we'll be lucky to get out at all.

Jahnke stays silent. Every now and again, I seem to see a grey shoulder where I think he is. I don't know whether he's conscious the rest of the time or not – but he's bloody tough, I'll give him that.

Messner manages to reach me, bent double.

"Strecker's runner didn't come back. Mine hasn't either."

"Fuck."

Send Bauer to the Turret.

He comes back after half an hour, looking rather shaken.

"The attack's off, Sergeant Major."

"Thanks. Well done."

He pulls a face. "It's fucking horrible in there – full of smashed-up blokes. Doctor Meyer's working his arse off."

"Let's hope the place doesn't get a direct hit, then."

"Let's hope we don't either!"

Crawl to Messner and back. That's another three of my lives gone – but at least we're staying put.

"Guess what's for dinner," Kropp says to me.

Pretend to ponder. "Er… Iron rations?"

"Go to the top of the class."

"Your eyebrow gave it away."

"What?"

"Never mind."

The boys pull a face over the lack of hot food but don't grumble, nor about our precarious situation.

Good blokes.

The new fellows are learning fast. If they survive, they'll be bloody useful.

Eventually it gets dark.

Go with Stadler and Tannwitz to Jahnke.

He's conscious and in a lot of pain, his hands clawing at the earth.

"Sorry – about – Pieper…"

"Wasn't your fault," I say.

"But…" He can't finish the sentence.

"But nothing. You did bloody well, lying there all this time and not making a sound."

"That's for sure," says Stadler.

"Too right," says Tannwitz at the same time.

Wonder whether I'd be able to do it. Don't want to find out.

Tannwitz rips Jahnke's tunic open.

That's a mess. At least the blood's clotted.

"Sorry, Officer Cadet, sir, this is going to hurt."

Poor Jahnke screams his head off, and then passes out.

Just as well, really.

We get him back to the trench – or rather what's left of it – and the stretcher-bearers take him up the hill to the Turret, still out cold.

"Brave lad," says Kropp.

"You're not joking," I reply. "Right mess."

It's an ill wind, though, as the saying goes. Hutten will be in command of that Platoon – for a few days, anyway, and who can look further ahead than that?

The next day is rather worse.

The machine guns get smashed to pieces, and so do the medium mortars.

Their crews look as if they've lost a close friend.

"Look at the state of that!" says one of the machine gunners, pointing dolefully at the twisted barrel. "Looked after that like my own wife, I did."

"Bugger that," says Stadler. "We were counting on you lot to repel the fucking Frenchies."

"Well, we'll just have to do that ourselves," says Messner.

Fortunately we don't have to. Far from attacking, the Frenchies are wiring busily.

"Don't like the look of that," Kropp says, his eyebrow signalling its disapproval.

"Nor do I." Can't help but smile.

Kropp gives me a very sideways look. "I do wish you'd tell me what's so bloody funny."

"It's your eyebrow."

"What?" He looks completely blank. "What's wrong with my eyebrow?"

"Nothing at all…" I can't find a way of explaining. "I'll buy you a beer when we get into rest."

"And then you can tell me what the fuck you mean."

"Deal… But I wish we could stop the Frenchies wiring."

"Yes."

It's going to make their positions harder to take, of course, and neither of us wants to say that the bastards have obviously got their arses well into gear.

Starting with their fucking artillery – the harassing fire is continuous, and every few hours it swells into a proper bombardment that has us digging ourselves further into the earth.

But they don't attack.

The bombardment does enough, though. There are dead lying everywhere, and the shelling dismembers them into ever smaller pieces. These were our friends and our comrades, and there's no way of giving them a decent burial.

Pick up a hand lying beside me, scrape a hole and inter it, knowing it won't stay there.

Is this what happened to Axel's body?

Far worse is the torment of the wounded – we can't take them to the Turret in daylight, so the poor bastards lie in agony until it gets dark. If we can get to them we patch them up, but what use are field dressings when the man needs morphine and surgery? All too often we can't even stop the bleeding.

Many die who could have lived...

The men don't grouse. We're sitting in freezing holes, without hot food, surrounded by death and pain and shelled non-stop, we know our chances of getting out aren't good, and there's not one word of complaint.

Good blokes. Best in the world.

The following night we're relieved, and what's left of us trudges back to the remains of the Caurières Wood.

What the fuck was the point of that?

We've lost a load more blokes for absolutely bugger all.

On the plus side, the new boys know what to do when they're being shelled now, and are quite a bit steadier.

How well they'd have done if there'd been an attack is another matter. If only we could have a few days out of the line to get them trained up. If only we could get some experienced fellows to fill the gaps.

We get more raw reinforcements.

Strecker gives them his usual welcome, but I catch sight of his face as he turns away and he's not pleased.

We're back up to full strength, in numbers alone.

"What the fuck are we supposed to do with this lot?" Kropp says to me.

"Divide them up among the experienced men, as usual," I reply.

"What experienced men?"

Give him a very straight look. "And teach them as fast as we can."

"Yes, Sergeant Major."

God help us next time we're in the front line, I can hear him thinking, and I can't disagree. I'll be trusting them with my life as well, and it's not a pleasant thought.

But on the plus side, we get Sergeant Henke back, healed up after Serbia and just as belligerent as ever.

"Surely they'll have to give us a few days out, just to get these boys trained up," he says.

They don't. We stay in reserve. The shelling is continuous, and from what we can hear, the front line is getting hammered.

XV

Max was sitting on the ground next to the ruins of the Turret.
FUCK!
He dived quickly into the nearest shell-hole, shaking.
What the fuck was I doing, sitting in the open like that? And how the fuck did the buggers miss me?
Minutes passed and nothing happened.
Why is it so quiet?
He crouched in the hole, listening.
There was no bombardment – no shells screaming overhead or slamming in, no stupefying concussions, no fountains of earth and metal.
No small-arms fire, no grenades.
The sun shone from a silent sky.
And where are my comrades? Surely they can't all be dead.
Maybe I'm the one who's dead. Maybe this is my punishment for killing – being stuck here in some kind of limbo.
You had to kill them, Max. Even the ones when you were a sniper. They were all there to kill you and your mates.
A black horse looked down at him, its ears pointed forward.
'What are you doing in that hole?'
The question was as clear as if the animal had spoken.
This is getting really strange. Why is there a horse here?
He sat up and lit a cigarette.
Think, Max. Think.

You're not in uniform, are you? You're wearing civvies, which you've made rather mucky.

Slowly his mind cleared – and he realised with horror that he had, again, lost all track of present reality.

Fucking hell.

It's almost as frightening as being in the war – in a way, it's worse. When you're dead, that's that – and in the moment when you know you're going to die, all fear goes.

Being trapped in my own mental hell would be truly terrifying. How would I get out again? Or would I spend the rest of my life thinking that I was fighting here?

I shouldn't have come. I'd better go home.

At least if I get taken to the nuthouse there, it'll be a German one. I don't want to know what the Frenchies would do with a mad Boche.

As he rode away from the Turret, he tried to concentrate on what he saw and heard around him, in an attempt to hold on to reality.

But I have two realities, and each is just as vivid as the other.

The horse is real in the Now. Then I was a humble foot-slogger, carrying everything on my back. Now I'm sitting here on a colonel's horse, when Leutnant was the highest rank I ever held.

Even our Oberstleutnant Jagenow wasn't riding by the time this lot kicked off.

He ran his hand over Prince's neck, feeling the warm life beneath the smooth coat. One ear twitched back to listen, and when he said nothing it pointed forward again.

The horse is real in the Now.

They were halfway to town before he realised that his mind had cleared.

I'll stay here as planned. I didn't run away then and I'm not going to run away now.

He thought back to the Turret.

We should have realised then that the tide had turned. The easy victories of the first few days were already over. If we'd gone over to the defensive then…

It wouldn't have worked. The Frenchies would have shelled the crap out of every position we held, until it was completely flattened, and us with it.

The whole offensive was a ghastly mistake, and the responsibility rests with Falkenhayn. I don't know how he lived with himself.

Maybe he didn't. Maybe that was what finished him off.

Max handed Prince back reluctantly.

How will I know it's Now if I don't have him to touch? And I have to go back to that room with the voice…

The stable owner gave him a strange look. So did the receptionist.

I must look just as crazy as I feel – ah. The mud.

"Fell over," he said. "Can I borrow a brush?"

"Of course, sir."

He let himself into his room and took his dirty clothes off.

The voice laughed.

'Now you really are a filthy Boche!' it said gleefully.

He didn't respond, because that would acknowledge that it existed. At the same time, he knew it wouldn't like being ignored. And it didn't.

The window blew open in a sudden gust of cold wind, even though it was a still, warm evening.

I've just about had enough of this. I'm haunted enough and I don't need whatever's going on here.

But I'm not going to let it win.

Later, he lay wide awake, staring at the ceiling, thinking.

*

8th March 1916, Caurières Wood

I actually feel sorry for the new boys, but of course I can't show it.

Of all the shit-awful places to have your baptism of fire – probably even worse than mine.

Wonder how many of them will survive it.

Spend as much time training them as I can – partly because being in reserve gives me too much time to think.

When we were small boys, Axel and I played soldiers together, with our other cousins. When we grow up, we said, we'll be in the same regiment and we'll fight together. We'll beat the Frenchies and the Russkis and win an Iron Cross each, and one day we'll be generals like Uncle Ferdi.

All Axel ever wanted was to be an officer, like his uncle and his father and grandfathers and so on back. He went off to cadet school at ten, with Cousin Friedrich. I was a year younger, and by the time I was ten I had other ideas.

Too many of my mother's Junker family had died on the battlefield, and I wanted to live past twenty. And science was my favourite subject at primary school, so I didn't follow Axel but went to the Gymnasium instead, and on to university.

And then the war came, and of course I volunteered. Axel was an officer cadet by then, like Friedrich, and we joked about how I was going to have to stand to attention and call them 'sir'.

But there were too many volunteers and we got sent to the new regiment instead, and all too soon into action at Diksmuide, where most of us got slaughtered and where I learned to kill. Not an accomplishment I'd ever wanted.

And then I became a sniper.

Unfortunately, I was rather good at it – unfortunately for the men who found themselves in my sight, and also for me, because it turned me into the cold-blooded bastard that I am now. I've lost hope of ever being anything else, even if I survive this mess.

Friedrich was commissioned after a couple of weeks at war, and dead a couple of weeks after that.

I finally made it to this regiment, but I'd only been here a month when I got that splinter across my stomach.

"I'll visit you in hospital," Axel said as they carried me away – but I got put straight on the train home, and then I was in the barracks when he got sent to Serbia.

Two months' garrison duty I had while I was getting fit again, and in the middle of that I had leave, and Aunt Hilda wanted Friedrich's body back and asked me to fetch it from France.

That's something I don't agree with. The man has been laid to rest with his true brothers, and there he should stay. I can understand a mother wanting her son close by – she gave birth to him, after all – but no civilian will ever understand how strong the bond is between men who fight together.

But how could I say no to her?

It was a horrible job. The rough pine coffin was disintegrating, and so was he. And it was a warm day.

I'd seen plenty of rotting corpses, but this was different.

And now Axel's dead as well, and I have no idea where he is – except that he's here every morning.

'Don't forget me, Max.'

Swear as my cigarette burns my fingers. Stub it out and order a kit inspection.

The new boys don't realise how easily a rifle gets clogged with mud, or how quickly death comes if you don't keep your weapons in order.

Better a bawling out from Feldwebel Schelling than one from the fellow with the scythe.

*

Max lit another fag.

I wish I could sleep – but God knows what will come for me if I do.

Especially as today I have to go to Vaux…

I really would prefer not to think about that accursed village. Each time I ride past the ruins, the boys call out to me.

And now it's their turn.

He got up as soon as it was light, and sat writing up his diary of the trip – partly to make sure he didn't forget anything, but more in the hope that it would help him to stay in the Now.

He almost forgot Prince's carrots and apple.

"You'd have been really pissed off with me, wouldn't you?" he said, stroking the warm black neck.

The horse snorted softly into Max's ear.

He laughed. "God, you do like to tickle! Better get going."

Do I really want to do this?

No. But I must.

Remember – the horse is real. If things start to blur, stroke his neck.

That will work fine if I'm on the horse…

Down into the darkness in the bottom of the valley. Past the ruins of Vaux. On to Bezonvaux.

I'll take the route over the Hardaumont Ridge, just as we did then.

That's a long climb up from Bezonvaux, and my leg's grumbling this morning. Too much walking all in one go.

I'll ride up to the Bezonvaux strongpoint, leave Prince there – no, that won't do. There's no water up there. He'll be better off by the stream in the village.

My leg will just have to shut up and get on with it…

Prince whinnied softly as Max left him, his ears twitching uneasily.

"Don't worry, boy – I'll come back."

Am I trying to convince you or me?

He started climbing up the hill towards the strongpoint.

It had trenches and a wall round it, and when you went inside there was a courtyard with two vaulted concrete rooms used by the medics. One was the operating room, and the other was the waiting room.

The rest of it was a store for rations and materiel, and – in theory anyway – those going to or from the front line could rest for a few minutes.

Normally that meant in the trenches outside. The waiting room was usually overflowing, and who wanted to see and hear the poor sods?

He carried on up, the past intruding…

*

9th March 1916, Caurières Wood

"Our boys have taken Fort Vaux!"

"Bollocks, Tiemann – you'll be saying we've won the fucking war next!" Stadler retorts.

But it's official.

"Thank fuck for that," says Hutten.

He's still in command of the Third Platoon. Poor little Jahnke died in the field hospital, and there was no replacement officer in the reinforcements.

"Indeed," says Kropp.

There's a palpable sense of relief – we seem to be moving forward again. Maybe the Frenchies are on the back foot, maybe we'll be in Verdun soon.

But as we all know, there are yet more forts between Vaux and the city, plus all the strongpoints between the forts.

Why in God's name did the High Command decide to attack

the Frenchies' most heavily fortified region? It must have made sense to someone...

Strecker gathers the Platoon and Group Commanders, and gives us our new orders.

We look at each other.

"They want us to do *what?*" asks Messner, before he can stop himself.

Strecker looks at him. "Do I have to say it all again?"

"No, sir."

Messner and I say nothing as we head back to the Platoon.

"Right, boys," Messner says, spreading out the map. "As you've heard, Fort Vaux is in German hands – and so's the eastern part of Vaux village. The Battalion's to roll up the village, then go up the hill, past the Fort, along the top and storm the battery there."

Meet Messner's eyes.

You did well to say all that, and with a straight face. What stupid cunt dreamed that up? I know no plan survives – but they could try a plan that might work.

What is it about this fucking place? The plan gets fucked quicker here than anywhere else – but maybe that's just this whole fucking war.

The new boys' faces show excitement and apprehension. The old hands stare at their fingernails.

Kropp's eyebrow expresses its opinion, which is just the same as mine.

With the old Battalion, we might have had a chance of doing some of it, but even then it would have been quite a task. How we're supposed to do all that with the boys we've got now is beyond me.

You can see when we fall in that the other three companies are just like the Seventh.

Get on with it. That's all we can do.

Set off in the incandescent, thunderous night, picking our way in single file between the craters. It's been snowing again, and the ground is white.

Up and up.

Sweat under the weight of my pack and equipment.

Gradient starts to slacken.

The temperature is frigid. My sweat starts to freeze.

"Bet they won't get hot food to us again," Dachwitz says to Stadler.

He's probably right.

"Best not thought about," says Stadler. "We are soldiers, after all, and you know what Soldat stands for!"

Soll ohne langes Denken alles tun...

"Should do everything, without thinking for long!" they say together.

And it's true – the last thing any soldier needs to do is think. About anything other than getting the job done, that is.

The barrage is just ahead – you'd think we'd all be used to this by now.

Do you ever get used to someone trying to kill you?

7.5s, heavies, shrapnel – the bastards mean this, all right.

The boys we got right after the wood know what they're doing now. Nehring grabs the youth beside him and throws him to the ground, just as I do the same to another.

*

You almost started to wonder why you bothered hitting the ground and throwing the new boys down. It just delayed the inevitable.

Where the fuck is the strongpoint?

There's no sign – ah.

Rubble. Blocks of stone and concrete, and a narrow path between them.

He followed it out of curiosity – and in front of him was what remained of the southern room. Most of the arched roof was still standing and he could see into the chamber. The rest of the strongpoint had been thoroughly destroyed. Blocks lay everywhere, some of them enormous, and there were deep holes in the ground.

Quite staggering, the power of heavy artillery. These blocks weigh how much? And they've just been thrown like toys.

Max shook his head, and walked back out onto the main path that led through the wasteland of shell-holes to the Hardaumont Ridge.

*

9th March 1916, Hardaumont Ridge

Most of us make it through the barrage – we leave only a few lying on the icy ground, dead or mutilated. At least it's not far for the wounded to go back to the Bezonvaux fortification.

Here's the Hardaumont complex – four strongpoints, all linked by a maze of trenches and surrounded by belts of barbed wire, in what was once a wood.

The Frenchies don't like us being here.

Not one bit.

There's plenty of cover, though – for those who know how to use it. The quicker the rest learn, the longer they're likely to live.

Even in the intermittent light, it's obvious that the strongpoints have taken a real battering, and it's continuing.

We pass the last of them, into the open at the top of the hill—

And come under a hideous weight of fire.

Throw ourselves to the ground, into shell-holes, wherever we can.

A couple of the new boys are still upright.

"GET DOWN!" Kropp and I shout together.

It's too late for one of them. A huge chunk of metal slices right through him and his body falls left and right at the same time.

Where the fuck is this coming from?

Raise my head cautiously above the rim of the hole.

Opposite, across the valley, is the Fort Vaux ridge, and it's alive with brilliant flashes. The guns at the Fort are firing at us, along with those at the batteries further west of it.

Their thunder reaches us between the scream and burst of the shells, redoubled by the racket from our batteries a few hundred metres away.

Fort Vaux in German hands? You could have fooled me.
So now what?

The ground between the tree stumps is white with snow. We must look like ants on a tablecloth.

No one in his right mind wants to go anywhere in this, which makes me stark staring crazy – but I need to talk to Messner, or Strecker.

"Stay here, boys."

Not that they should need telling.

Messner's face is eloquent as I drop down beside him.

"Strecker's sent a runner to Gneist," he shouts in my ear.

I nod. *Stay in cover and wait for orders, then. Let's hope this runner gets back.*

Leap up run like fuck loud shriek drop into a hole.

DEAFENING BANG

Fountain of earth metal flesh bone blood.

"MEDICS!"

Screams.

How the fuck did that miss me?

Somehow make it to Kropp.

"Must be Bavarians," he says, pointing at Fort Vaux.

We both laugh.

Light his fag and mine.

"Wait for orders, then?" he asks.

"Got it in one."

"Why don't you send a runner next time?" he says.

Shrug, but he's got a point. Trouble is, I want to hear direct from Messner, not get someone's interpretation of what he said.

Leap up run like fuck reach Henke.

He's worked it out too. So have Weidner and the old hands.

Manage to get round all the new boys, try to teach them how to read the shellfire.

We'd better get off here before daylight…

After a couple of unpleasant hours someone runs, bent almost double, and drops into the hole beside me.

"Orders from Oberleutnant Strecker, Sergeant Major."

"Go on."

"Move down the hill into the Zig-Zag Trench."

That sounds promising. A trench instead of shell-holes. Should provide better cover, anyway.

XVI

Max sat on the Hardaumont Ridge, looking across the valley to Fort Vaux.

It's no distance. This whole area, from here down the slope to the village, is dominated by that ridge opposite. It's what? A kilometre and a half away?

No distance at all for artillery. And the Caillette Wood off to the right is even closer and it was full of machine guns.

Moving down into the Zig-Zag Trench sounded like a good idea…

*

10th March 1916, Zig-Zag Trench

The sketch map shows the trench about two hundred metres in front of us, just a bit down the hill.

That's if the map is accurate and if the trench hasn't been obliterated. Hopefully it's deep, because it's very exposed.

We lose a few more blokes getting there, and that's only the start of our troubles.

We're in the worst position imaginable – on the bare forward slope in the snow, well within range of the Frenchies opposite. As if that weren't enough, there's machine gun fire from the Caillette Wood on our right.

To add to all that, the 'trench' is only waist-deep.

It gets light.

We are on a platter for the Frenchies, and they duly swat at us and keep on swatting.

The shells rain down incessantly, in front and behind, and far too close.

Make ourselves as small as possible in the inadequate cover.

What the fuck am I doing here? Why in God's name have they put us in such a fuck-awful position?

Stadler's praying again. I can hear him quite clearly in the brief gaps between the detonations.

Well, maybe it does some good. He's still alive, after all.

God knows how many of us will be after this.

Strecker's runner manages to squeeze along the trench, summons me to a meeting.

Lose another life getting there.

"The Seventh is to roll up Vaux village," Strecker says.

As easy as that.

The village is in the bottom of the valley. The Frenchies hold the high ground in an arc of over 180 degrees.

This could be real fun.

"We're going in at 3pm, straight after the bombardment…" he continues.

The Fifth and Sixth will be on our right, and another regiment on our left.

Down that white slope in broad fucking daylight? That's just suicide.

And who ordered it? Not our Oberstleutnant Jagenow, that's for sure. He's got his head screwed on. No doubt it's someone a long way behind the lines.

I'll keep that to myself – the boys have quite enough to think about.

And I don't want to think about it either. I'll be very lucky to see tomorrow.

Don't think, Max. Just do your fucking job.

A few minutes after I get back, a heavy slams in just in front of the trench, about twenty metres to my right.

Force my way there.

We've been very lucky. Most of the blokes got down low. There are only two dead, a few with minor injuries – but one man has caught it badly. He's out cold, blood pouring down his face, and I can't tell who he is.

Weldt and Ullmann, both new fellows, are patching him up. Grab Weldt by the shoulder and shout into his ear.

"LEAVE HIM AND HELP THEM!" Point to the men with slight wounds.

He stares at me.

Shake him.

"GO ON!"

It doesn't take two to patch the fellow up – and he won't fight again, while the others will. You were told all that in training – at least I hope you were.

Three of the others have a cut or two. They'll be able to stay with us and they want to fight.

The other four will have to wait until dark to go back.

"I can still fight, Sergeant Major," Frischler insists as I bandage him.

He has a long cut on his right arm, and blood is dripping from his fingers.

I shake my head. He has no idea how brutal the fighting will be. A man needs two good arms.

"No. Go back when it's dark."

And be thankful for a few more days of life…

Turn back to the serious case.

He's still out cold. The trench is crammed full and there's no room in the bottom. He'll get stepped on.

The bombardment steps up again.

"Put the wounded man in the hole!" I shout, pointing to a shell-hole behind the trench.

The new boys look at me as if I'm some sort of monster.

"GET HIM INTO THE HOLE!"

Henzen and Ullmann start to pick him up.

Scream of shell.

They duck and drop him. Just as well the poor bugger's unconscious.

The shell misses by quite a way.

"COME ON!"

Get my hands under his armpits. The other two take a leg each.

Lift and push him out of the trench onto the earth beside it, keeping low.

Roll up and out of the trench, start to push the man into the shell-hole.

The other two straighten up—

CRACKCRACKCRACK

Shove Ullmann back into the trench.

Henzen is slow to get down and his legs go from under him. He collapses half in the shell-hole, half in the trench.

He's got it in the stomach.

Pull him right into the hole and patch him up as best I can, which is bloody difficult when I have to keep so low. Leave him there with the other man.

Slide back into the trench beside Ullmann, who looks quite green with terror.

Poor little fucker. What's he going to be like when we go in?

Down this fucking bare slope with the Frenchies throwing everything they can at us. We'll be lucky if anyone makes it to the sodding village.

The snow is red. As I watch, the heat of the blood melts it, and then slowly it starts to freeze again into a red and white slick, with lumps of flesh embedded in it.

Vanilla ice cream with strawberry sauce, anyone?
I'll never see a sundae with the same eyes again.
Laugh at myself.
When in God's name am I ever going to see a sundae? Even if I get out of here, there's no ice cream in Germany.
There might be in Paris, though.
Jesus, I'm cold. What the fuck is the temperature?
Stamp my feet and slap my arms, in a vain effort to stay warm.
It's 2pm. We have another hour of sitting here being shelled, before we climb out and go down the hill.
And that will be the last thing many of us do.
I have a sudden, horrible self-doubt. *I can't do this – the weight of metal in the air is impressive, and it'll be even worse when they see us moving. I won't get fifty metres.*
What the fuck am I doing here?
You have to do it, Max. The others are relying on you to lead them – and God knows they need a leader.
Don't think.
Just don't think – we all have to die sometime.
For Brandenburg, for Prussia.
It's a good way to go, a fine soldier's death. As long as it's quick. I don't want to lie out there like—
Stop. Or you'll be no good for anything.
Kropp squirms along the trench.
"Attack's postponed," he shouts. "Six fifteen."

*

Without even thinking, Max had moved down the hill into the remains of the Zig-Zag Trench. It still ran quite clearly along the hillside.

I can't even say its name. It just gets stuck. I was more frightened here than almost anywhere else.

Almost. There are some impressive challengers for that title.

In front of him, the ground fell away steeply to the bottom of the valley.

Thank fuck they postponed the attack, or we'd all have been killed.

Just like the Third Battalion. They did try it in broad daylight and were reduced to one hundred men.

One hundred, out of over six times that number.

*

10th March 1916, Zig-Zag Trench

It'll be sunset soon after six fifteen. The valley will be in deep shade. We might have a chance after all.

How slowly the time passes. I swear I've never been as scared in my life as I am here, in this pathetic cover with the shells raining down.

It's fucking terrifying.

For the boys' sakes, I pretend not to care – and I've had plenty of practice at that.

Talk to each of them in turn, spend time rehearsing what they're going to do, teaching them how to read the flight of the shells and the sound of small-arms fire.

Weidner, Henke and Kropp are doing the same.

Meet and smoke a fag, pass my hip flask round.

All the old hands are looking as nonchalant as they can. In Tiemann's case, that's very.

He cracks a joke, and the boys beside him laugh.

Good old Tiemann.

Strecker comes round, smoking his pipe like a man on a stroll, chats to everyone, leaves a sort of wake of reassurance.

Wonder what's beneath that calm act. Genuine serenity? Or is he like a swan – calm on the surface and paddling like fuck underneath?

Our artillery starts up. Shells fly over our heads and smash into the ridge opposite and burst in the valley.

Hopefully it'll leave the French positions ripe for the assault.

That's what they said about the bombardment on the first day – you'll be able to march into Verdun.

And we're nowhere near.

Four o'clock. Five.

Braun, who was so terrified at the Turret, is reassuring Ullmann.

You either learn fast or you die.

Five thirty.

Messner's coming towards me. Squeeze along the packed trench towards him.

Everyone gets down low as another heavy arrives.

Thankfully it misses.

"Attack's postponed," he says.

"Till when, sir?"

"Don't know yet – the boys on our left can't get here."

Oh, bloody fantastic.

"Fucking hell," says Dachwitz when I tell them.

You mean we have to sit here having the crap shelled out of us for God knows how long? No one says it, but it's in all their eyes.

Be grateful for a bit more life…

Not that we can even be sure of that. Every hour that passes robs us of more men.

We heave the dead out of the trench, bandage the wounded and put them in the shell-holes, where they lie groaning and calling out for water, which we can't give them.

We don't know when we'll get any more ourselves, and we have to fight.

The new boys are beginning to realise what war is.

Our bombardment stops just after six, as planned.

So now there's nothing to keep the French artillerymen's heads down, and they step up their shelling.

There'd better be another bombardment before we go in – we want their infantry's heads down as well, or the reception will be rather too enthusiastic.

But how will our gunners know when we're going to attack?

The sun slides slowly below the hills, and it gets dark. This should mean that we get shot at less – but of course the Frenchies know just where we are.

Flashes light up the night, almost incessant. Parachute flares hang in the sky, lighting the snow to brilliance, like stage lights. Each one makes my skin crawl.

"Quite a firework display," says Stadler.

"Better enjoy New Year while we can!" says Tiemann.

"But it's not—" Bolkow begins.

Tiemann grins at him. "We'll all be lucky to see the next one!"

That doesn't seem to be what Bolkow wants to hear.

"You'll be fine," Lorenz assures him.

It's crap, of course, but he seems a bit happier.

Which is more than I am – I just want to get stuck in, and there's still no sign of anything happening.

Time drags. And drags.

For fuck's sake, where are those useless bastards? It's been dark for hours.

It's fucking cold and I'm fucking hungry. Try to keep the boys' spirits up, but the strain is starting to tell on them.

The sooner we go in, the better – then at least we'll be doing something.

Summons to Strecker.

Almost don't make it. Arrive covered in yet more muck and blood.

"Our comrades are in place on our left – so we attack at eleven. Move down to the jumping-off positions."

"Yes, sir."

Mix of fear and relief. See the same in the others' faces when they hear the news.

We're to go down the hill to the light railway line just north of the village. The houses at the eastern end are in German hands – at least I hope they are. That's what they said about the Fort.

If only our artillery would start up again…

*

Max climbed out of the remains of the Zig-Zag Trench and started down the hill.

Even on that quiet, peaceful morning, his hair stood on end and part of him expected to be shot.

There was debris lying everywhere, and he realised the clean-up teams hadn't finished here.

Better be careful, then. Don't want to get blown up here now.

I wonder if there's still any sign of the light railway, or our positions.

The slope got steeper as he descended, and it was hard to keep his footing in the loose earth.

His leg stabbed him sharply and he had to stop for a moment – but there, in front of him, was the light railway line on its embankment.

All around him the men made their way down the hill, in the banging, flashing night.

*

10th March 1916, above the village of Vaux

Messner wisely sends the Platoon down in Groups.

We go first.

"Move between the flashes, boys."

I have more sense than to be out in front – and Huber gets the bullet that would have been for me.

That makes the point about not leading. I'll think about Huber later.

It's quite likely I won't be thinking about anything.

Most of us get to the railway line. It's on a slight embankment. Creep quietly into the shell-holes and wait.

And wait.

Our artillery is silent. No support, then.

I can only hope that the Frenchies have decided we're not coming.

These last few minutes always take forever…

Eleven o'clock.

Signal to the boys to follow.

Out of the holes in silence, into the village.

*

What's that saying about frying pans and fires? Max thought as he crossed over the railway line. *It was seldom more apt than here.*

The ruins of the village lay slightly below him. Ahead, the steep Fort Vaux ridge blotted out the sky and much of the daylight, and the Hardaumont Ridge sloped up behind him.

The stream still ran through the bottom of the narrow valley, past the wrecked houses.

'You're here, then,' said the men. 'Coming to visit us?'

The atmosphere was so brooding that Max hesitated.

Suppose I have another turn? My mind might get stuck here forever.

He shuddered.

I've seen the village. Maybe it would be more sensible to go back up the hill.

'You weren't so yellow back then,' one of them said. 'We're lying here with the Frenchies, and it's not exactly comfortable.'

All right, then.

He steadied himself and walked down the slope, through the mud, towards the broken fragments of walls.

*

10th March 1916, village of Vaux

The village is pitch-dark, lit only by the shelling and the flares.

Fully expect to be shot from behind – but the eastern part really is in German hands.

Something's gone right, then.

Stay in the shadows of the ruined houses.

Almost bump into a man, half-seen – knife in my hand—

"This is as far as we got," he whispers almost soundlessly.

"You nearly got yourself killed," I reply in the same faint tone.

Beckon my boys to move towards the next house.

There's a gap in the shadows.

Run across in ones and twos—

CRACKCRACKCRACK

CRACK

Dirt and snow spurt in front of me.

Hit the ground, wriggle forward.

The Frenchies have reinforced the cellar, and it's full of riflemen and at least one machine gun.

But one of my boys has made it to the wall, and he drops a grenade into the cellar.

And another.

Blinding flashes from the cellar opening two loud explosions.

Leap up run into the shadows.

Leave three lying in the snow.

There are no more shots from that cellar. Just from the others nearby.

Run like fuck to the next patch of shadow.

Crack whine round my ears.

Someone yells. Another goes down.

Get to the next house.

Grenades into the ground floor.

Debris flies as they explode.

Frenchie runs out of the door, straight into one of mine who stabs him.

Through the door.

Ground floor full of dead and mutilated Frenchies.

Officer coming down the stairs, pistol in hand.

Shoot him.

Run upstairs.

Empty rooms.

Disarm the survivors.

On to the next house.

There are Frenchies in the ground floor and the cellar, and they're not pleased to see us.

Take cover and return fire.

They can see us better than we can see them – in the flashes I can just make out a shadow at the window.

Oh, for my Zeiss four-power...

"Machine gun here!"

There is no machine gun crew within earshot.

The Frenchies send up flares calling for artillery support.

So do we.

This is about to get very interesting.

*

The ground in the village was very marshy, and Max slipped a couple of times but stayed upright.

The atmosphere had thickened and was becoming hostile, as if someone were saying, 'Go away.'

Hardly surprising when so many men died here.

The Frenchies were brave men, I'll give them that. They died very hard indeed.

He sat on a tree stump.

This has been so battered since we were here that I can't recognise anything. Is that the remains of the church over there?

The scene in front of him shimmered slightly.

It's the light reflecting off the stream, he told himself. *That's all.*

Just pause a bit longer to remember, and to honour the dead, and then get back to Bezonvaux.

Leave while you're still in the Now.

XVII

11th March 1916, village of Vaux

It would get interesting if our artillery actually *did* anything, that is. The buggers seem to be asleep.

The Frenchies start bombarding the slope above us even harder, but only a few shells land in the village.

I wish our artillery would fucking well wake up. We could do with some support.

Two of our boys try to get close enough to the house to throw grenades in.

One goes down but the other succeeds.

The grenade flies out again, followed by the Frenchies' own contributions.

Duck down low. Explosions. Whirring fragments.

"MACHINE GUN HERE!"

This time they hear me and in the light of the flares I see them wave.

There's no way they can drag the gun across the road – they'd be riddled before halfway. But at least I've got their attention.

Move to the edge of the shadows, point to the house, get another wave.

Frenchies just miss me as I scuttle back.

The machine gunners set up.

The first burst smashes through the ground floor.

"AFTER ME!"

Run forward doubled over hit the ground.

The next move will have us close enough to storm the house.

There are ten of us. That will have to be enough.

Second burst.

Flat out to the side of the house.

Tiemann smashes a hole in the door with the butt of his rifle, Braun throws in a grenade.

Flatten ourselves against the outside wall, feel it shake to the explosion.

Second one to be sure.

Boot the door in, cloud of acrid smoke comes out. Duck through it.

Can't see a fucking thing in here – almost can't breathe either.

Move cautiously, almost fall over the bodies. House is full of dead and dying Frenchies.

Groans but no resistance.

Open the cellar door.

"COME OUT!"

No reply.

"COME OUT!"

FLASHCRACKBANG

Hit the wall beside the door.

Thank fuck he missed.

Dachwitz throws a grenade down.

Burst of flame ear-splitting bang.

And another for good measure.

Better make sure no one is alive down there.

Start down the steps.

Shot behind me, in the ground floor, startlingly loud.

Fuck—

"Fucking bastard!"

Choking gurgle. No more shots.

Cellar stinks of blood and shit. Shine my pocket torch round. Dead Frenchies. Quite a mess.

Back up the stairs.

"French are coming!" shouts Tiemann.

Line the windowsills.

Frenchies running out of the shadows, black against the snow in the light of the flares.

This time we have the better view.

Shoot several, rest flee – but they'll be in the next house.

"One of those fuckers tried to shoot me," Nehring complains.

"Didn't like the knife much, did he?!" Braun says with a grin.

You're learning. Good.

Out of the house. Stay in the shadows.

Pause to take stock.

There are eight of us.

Messner and his boys are on the other side of the narrow road.

Start to run towards the next house—

Brilliant blaze of yellow light all around.

CRACKCRACKCRACKWHISTLEWHINE

Hit the ground.

In the open, on the stark white snow. Like being on a fucking stage.

One of the houses is on fire. The village is lit like daylight.

Messner and his boys are caught between houses.

The Frenchies let rip at them, from in front and slightly left.

Three go down.

The others run for cover, dragging one with them.

Two lie where they fell.

Can't stay here. Won't last two minutes.

Wriggle back into the shadows, fast as I can, singing metal just above me.

"Thought they'd got you, Sergeant Major," says Lorenz.

"Not yet!"

God knows how. So now what?

Half my boys are by this house, half by the one next to it.

If we move, the Frenchies will let us have it properly – but there's only a narrow strip of shadow on this side.

Messner's side of the road seems safer – or rather less fucking dangerous.

Creep along the wall to the nearest men.

"Get to that side two minutes from now. We'll cover. Then cover us two minutes after that."

Take a deep breath and run like fuck to the other group. Dirt and snow kick up around me.

Brief them.

Two minutes takes forever.

I can just make out Messner's boys in the shadows.

Let's hope they don't think we're Frenchies…

Open fire on the nearest houses.

All but one of the first group make it to cover.

Another eternal two minutes.

Then it's our turn.

Leap up run like fuck Tiemann goes down grab his collar drag him with me.

Into the shadows.

"Fucking hell," says someone. And that rather sums it up.

Tiemann's got it in both legs, luckily just through the muscle.

Messner is lying beside the wall of the house. The snow around him is dark.

"Sir. SIR."

No reply.

Turn him onto his back. Blood is soaking through his tunic.

Rip it open.

There's a hole in his chest, with blood bubbling from it, and bloody froth round his mouth.

Shit.

Patch him up as best I can, and prop him against the wall.

He needs to be taken back now, but it's impossible.

Henke and I confer.

Between us, we have twenty fit blokes and five wounded. Two of the latter can still fire rifles and throw grenades.

Kropp is somewhere in the village, as are Scheumann's and Hutten's Platoons. Strecker won't be far away.

But how to make contact with them?

The fire must burn out soon…

It doesn't.

The house next door must have caught as well.

Someone waves to us from a house across the road, and attracts several kilos of lead.

We're truly stuck. The only consolation is that the bastards can't counterattack without us shooting them to pieces.

Four o'clock – it will soon be dawn.

"What d'you reckon – do we get into this house or is it safer out here?" I ask Henke.

He thinks for a moment.

"If we're in there and it burns, we're stuffed. Plus we'd have to clear out the Frenchies…"

And they're not all dead. Some of them are groaning.

"…While if we're out here, we can run if we have to," I finish. *But…* "But when it gets light, we'll be visible to everyone."

"There is that," he agrees.

"Get into the house, then. We'll put blokes at all the windows."

Go round all the fellows and tell them.

Half of us go into the house.

Tip the dead Frenchies into the cellar.

The injured ones gaze at us in fear, except for one who looks defiant.

Wish I could speak French as well as Kropp.

"Don't be scared – we don't hurt you," is all I can manage.

There are five of them. Three can walk.

Make sure they're disarmed.

"Sit there."

"Filthy Boche," mutters the defiant one.

"Take his belt and tie his hands," I say to Dachwitz.

Not really the way to treat a wounded prisoner, but I can't take any chances.

Lay their comrades beside them. Patch them up as best we can, but they too need to be taken back.

"He needs treatment," says the defiant one, pointing at a corporal.

"We send you back."

They jabber excitedly. The only word I catch is *Non*.

"Shut up, all of you."

Monsieur Defiant glares at me, but shuts up like his friends.

Check the upstairs. It's empty, but there are blankets and clothes which will do for warmth.

Beckon to the others to come in.

They bring our wounded with them.

Messner has come round, and whimpers as they sit him against the wall.

Daren't give him water – God knows where it would end up.

Tiemann can just about hobble, but is clearly in a lot of pain.

"I can shoot," he insists.

"All right." *Good bloke, Tiemann.*

Henke and I position our little force at the windows. Whichever way the bastards come, we'll give them a nice warm welcome.

There's a gleam of violet outside. Slowly, the dawn starts to outshine the fires, and the snow gets brighter.

An hour later, it's full daylight.

Across the road I can see a couple of field grey shapes by one of the houses, and shadowy figures at the windows.

So who is that?

Pick up a shirt, write 'Schelling' on it, and hold it up at the window.

A few minutes later, I see something white in the house opposite.

"May I borrow your opera glasses, sir?"

Messner nods. He's a horrible colour and his breathing's bad.

The sign says 'KROPP'.

Good. Wave and get an answer.

"Dachwitz."

"Sergeant Major?"

"Have a look at our wounded, would you?"

A few minutes later, he stands beside me.

"Herr Leutnant's not too good," he murmurs.

I had guessed that and didn't really want to hear it.

"And the others?"

"Braun's not that good either. Tiemann and the others should all make it."

That rather depends on how long we have to stay here…

Our job is to roll the village up, not to stay in this house.

Maybe we can get to the next one, make some progress through this fucking shit-heap.

I need to talk to Kropp.

"Henke."

"Sergeant Major?"

"I'm going to visit our friends across the road. You're in charge."

His opinion of this idea is written across his face.

Go to the door.

Take a deep breath, heart pounding.

Open the door run like fuck across the road.

Frenchies take a moment to get into gear.

But boy, do they.

Throw myself down by the house wall, gasping for breath.

How the fuck did they miss me?
Kropp opens the door a crack and I dive in.
"Welcome," he says, but his eyebrow says, 'fucking idiot'.
Burst out laughing.
He looks very hurt.
"Sorry, Kropp."
Lorenz is there, and Wredow, and Zeitler, Rausch…
Most of them are in one piece.
"Will you tell me what's so bloody funny?" Kropp demands.
"If you've got schnapps."
He hands me his hip flask.
Take a swig and hand it back.
"Ever play cards?" I ask.
He gives me a blank look. "Gave up – I always lost."
"Ever wonder why?"
'Get to the point,' says the eyebrow.
"Your right eyebrow," I say. "It speaks when you don't."
"Is that it?"
"'Fraid so. Now, what d'you reckon to a bit of fire and movement, try to get one or two houses forward?"
"Could give it a go," he says with a very un-Kropp-like lack of enthusiasm.
We're quite likely to get a shedload of casualties for no return, he doesn't need to say.
A few minutes later, we have a plan.
"Half an hour from now," I say.
All I have to do next is get back to Henke and the others.
Run like fuck back across the road.
Air fills with singing metal.
Tugs at my sleeve and my boot.
Throw myself through the window.
"That's not how your ma taught you to cross the road!" Henke says.

*

Max sighed. The dead were as vivid as if they were still alive.

We found out later that it was one of our own flamethrowers that set the house on fire.

We were in Alsace by then, and Kropp and Lorenz had to be restrained from giving the surviving flamethrower man a hiding.

"You think I did that on fucking purpose?" he demanded indignantly. "My oppo copped it as well."

Yes – he'd have been the first man the Frenchies shot. They always were.

Max lit a fag, trying not to look at the flame.

*

11th March 1916, village of Vaux

Explain the plan to Henke and the boys.

Henke's expression is similar to Kropp's, and having regard to the reception I got in those few seconds, maybe they have a point.

But the job's not done yet, and we have to try.

There's a long rip in my sleeve and another in my boot, but no blood.

"Dachwitz, you stay here and guard the prisoners, keep an eye on the wounded."

He looks relieved. Very relieved. Can't say I blame him.

"Right – how many grenades have we got…?"

Get ready to move.

In five minutes, Kropp and his boys will open fire.

"THE FRENCHIES!" yells Ullmann.

Run back to the window.

Half a platoon of Frenchies is running towards our house, bayonets fixed.

"FIRE!"

One – two – three – four – five – reload.

And again.

And again.

The snow is soon covered in Frenchmen. The others turn and run back, leaving dead and wounded alike lying there.

What price my plan now?

If we try to move we'll meet exactly the same fate, for fuck all result.

Dead men can't fight. Best save my boys for the next plan. Hopefully one that involves the artillery...

Pick up the shirt I wrote on earlier, turn it over.

'STAY PUT,' I write.

Hold it up at the window.

Kropp waves his acknowledgement.

Turn back to my fellows. "Attack's off, boys."

Undisguised relief in all their faces – and probably in mine too.

The injured Frenchies start calling for help.

Poor bastards – no one's going to go out there. And we don't have room for any more in here, anyway.

Messner is slumped against the wall, gurgling quietly.

Wipe the froth from his mouth with my filthy handkerchief.

He looks at me with dazed eyes. His face is grey and his lips blue.

Take a chance and give him some water and a mouthful of schnapps, put an extra blanket round him.

He tries to say something, but I can't make it out.

Squeeze his hand. "You'll be fine, sir."

Which is true, one way or the other.

The French corporal is going downhill as well. Give him another blanket and some schnapps.

"We'll get you in the end," says Monsieur Defiant.

At least I think that's what he said – not that I could give a shit.

Braun is unconscious, and I hope he stays that way.

The day drags on.

It's fucking freezing in the house. The shutters are smashed, and the icy wind blows in.

We're almost out of water. We could make a fire and melt some snow, but the smoke would show and some bloody artillery observer would see it – whether ours or theirs is irrelevant.

We're all fucking hungry as well and it makes us even colder. It feels as if the fire inside me has died right down.

Take rations from the dead Frenchies, share them out.

More cold garlicky stew and beans, stale bread – but at least it's fuel.

The fire inside me starts to glow a little brighter.

Bloody hell, I've had enough of this fucking place.

The Frenchies don't counterattack again, but their artillery shells the crap out of the slope up to Hardaumont.

Getting out of here will be real fun...

Laugh at myself.

Max, what in God's name makes you think you'll ever leave? Hundreds of men will stay here forever...

Fucking hell, I'm frozen. Oh, for a plate of hot stew and a mug of coffee.

We sit and wait and wait.

Nothing happens.

It gets dark.

The boys don't need reminding to be doubly alert.

Maybe we can do something now...

Just as I'm about to run across to Kropp again, Nehring calls out, "Runner approaching, Sergeant Major!"

The man darts from one house to another, the Frenchies chasing him on his way.

Reaches us. God knows how.

Brave bloke.

"Orders from Battalion, Sergeant Major."
"Go on."
"Relief is at 4am."
Thank fuck for that.
"Until then, hold the current position."
Double thank fuck.
So all we have to do is repel any more French counterattacks, and then we're out of here.

As easy as that... the barrage between us and Hardaumont is impressive, and the entire ridge lights up as the shells slam in.

The racket reverberates through the valley.

*

There's nothing more to see here, Max. Just get going.

I wonder which house we were in that day – it looks so different now, and most of them are just heaps of rubble. The boys we left behind must still be here, and the Frenchies in the cellars...

How far did we get, anyway?

He wandered further through the village, picking his way between the mounds of rubble, trying in vain to recognise any of the buildings.

'GO AWAY.'

He stopped.

They were watching him. He could feel their eyes gazing from the wrecked houses.

'YOU HEARD. YOU'RE NOT WANTED HERE.'

Someone was behind him, cold breath on his neck—

He turned quickly, but no one was there.

Slowly, he scanned the empty ruins. There were no signs of life. There was just the powerful feeling of hostility.

This must have been the Frenchies' part of the village.

Leave now, Max. Before you stay.

XVIII

He walked slowly back into the part they'd occupied, the hostility diminishing.

Getting back out was almost as bad as getting in – but then it often is.

*

11th March 1916, village of Vaux

Strecker reaches us just before midnight.

"Well done, Schelling."

"Thank you, sir."

Can't think why he said well done – we've made bugger all progress.

"How's Leutnant Messner?"

"Not too good, sir – he's by the wall there."

Strecker makes time to talk to everyone, then trots across the road to Kropp.

The Frenchies shoot like fuck but miss him.

He must have powerful connections, either upstairs or down.

Probably the latter. As the song says, soldiers ride up to Heaven on white horses, while the Devil fetches the officers.

Wonder if that includes NCOs.

You're a Sergeant Major, Max. Where do you think the men

want you sent? And you'd be bored rigid in Heaven when all your mates are in Hell.

Yes, it's Hell all right – and God help the devils when we get there.

Footsteps right behind me.

Turn but there's nobody close by.

No *body* close.

Axel?

No reply.

Or maybe Messner's croaked.

He's still gurgling, but unconscious and ashen grey.

Hope he lasts until the relief. And that's just the start. We have to get him to the Bezonvaux strongpoint alive.

If we're alive to carry him, of course.

But it has gone rather quiet – for now, anyway.

Everyone is frozen and fed up. Strecker's allowed us iron rations, but of course they're cold. No one is stupid enough to suggest making a fire. It would light us up like Christmas.

Jesus, I'm fucked. All I want to do is sleep. And sleep.

It feels like forever since we left the Caurières Wood.

Post sentries so the rest of us can get a few minutes' kip.

Lie down, but it's so fucking cold that I'm awake again in no time. And it's not just the cold. I'm well aware that our situation is not good, and I'm too keyed up to sleep.

It will have to wait until we're out of here.

The night drags on. All we can do is wait – for the Frenchies to attack, and for the relief.

Every time someone thinks he sees a movement, we're all at the windows. But the French leave us alone. They're probably just as battered as we are.

How much longer before the relief gets here?

Time creeps.

Messner groans quietly. He's a lot weaker.

If the relief doesn't come soon, he'll die – and he's not alone.

Where the fuck are the bastards? We need to get up the hill before dawn, or we'll be on that fucking forward slope on the snow in the daylight... And going up will be a lot slower than coming down.

"Relief's here," Strecker murmurs.

Thank fuck for that.

"Get your chaps off up the ravine. Rendezvous Middle Hardaumont."

"Sir."

Beckon to Henke.

"Sergeant Major?"

"Get the boys ready to move out."

"Right away." In the flashes, I see him grin.

There aren't enough stretcher-bearers to take all the badly wounded up the hill. In two hours it will be light, and movement on the slope will be impossible.

We'll have to carry them up.

Every unwounded man volunteers instantly. No one would want to be left here.

I go to Messner.

"Sir."

No response. Shake him.

He rolls limply.

"*Sir.*"

Shake him harder.

"SIR."

There is no pulse in his neck and the gurgling has stopped.

He stays here. We can't carry a corpse back.

We can't carry the wounded prisoners either. They will have to wait.

Climb out of the village. Stand by the railway, and point the boys towards the ravine. It should give them some cover.

Tiemann is lying against a splintered tree in the snow.

"I couldn't go any further, Sergeant Major," he says apologetically.

You did well to get this far – your legs must be fucking hurting by now.

"Don't worry – I'll take you up, soon as the rest of the Platoon's under way."

"Thanks."

Shadowy figures disappear into the night, supporting others or carrying them. The remnants of the Company.

"All gone, Sergeant Major," Henke reports. There's a man over his shoulder, I can't see who.

"Off you go, then."

Pull Tiemann to his feet and get him onto my shoulder.

"Hold on tight."

His hands clutch the straps of my pack.

Fuck me but he's heavy. Big lad, Tiemann.

Start up the hill.

Boots slip in the loose earth, frozen lumps break away, scrabble up gasping for breath with the extra weight, sweat pouring down me in spite of the cold.

Progress is so slow. We're all fucked, and the effort of carrying our comrades is almost too much.

The ravine shelters us from the machine guns in the Caillette Wood and the Quarry. But not from the Fort or the batteries on the ridge.

The fuckers know we're here and step up their shelling.

The ravine is incandescent, the noise shattering. My eyes dazzle, my ears deaden.

Sink to the ground, into freezing water.

Screams, cries for help.

It will be death to stay here.

Get up.

"KEEP MOVING!"

How the fuck are they going to hear me?

In the gap between the detonations, I shout again.

"MOVE!"

After an eternity, the men in front of me resume their trudge.

"All right, Tiemann?"

"Yes."

Lorenz and Tropfke are sitting on bare earth by a smoking crater. Between them is a man wrapped in a tent quarter tied to a pole.

"Keep going, boys."

Tropfke points to his arm.

"Can you still carry him?" I shout into his ear.

He nods.

I wait while Lorenz patches him up. *Jesus, I'm cold.* My sweat is starting to freeze.

Point at the tent quarter. "Who is it?"

"Gefreiter Weidner, Sergeant Major," Lorenz shouts back.

They put the pole on their shoulders and carry on up the hill, Weidner swaying between them. I follow with Tiemann.

We can't get out of here fast enough, but all we can do is plod.

The slope gets mercilessly steeper.

Ten steps.

Pause, gasping for breath.

*

Max stopped, out of breath, his leg aching viciously.

The hillside was so steep it was almost in his face.

How the fuck did I carry anyone up here? I was only eight years younger, but I must have been a lot fitter. And of course I had two good legs.

*

12th March 1916, between the village of Vaux and Hardaumont

Ten steps…
  Pause.
  Ten steps…
  More shells.
  The flashes reveal horrors.
  A body ripped in half, stark naked. An arm. A head. What look like intestines hanging in a splintered tree, but I have no wish to look more closely.
  Broken discarded rifles and packs litter the ground. Trip, almost drop Tiemann.
  "Sorry, Tiemann. All right?"
  "Yes."
  Plod on.
  The gradient starts to ease.
  The top will be the worst part, when we leave the ravine.
  And it is.
  Tropfke goes down, Weidner screams as he's dropped.
  Fuck.
  The top of Tropfke's skull is missing, his brains spread over his shoulder.
  "*You all right?*" I ask Lorenz.
  He nods.
  Pick up the other end of the pole, put it on my left shoulder. Stagger under the double load. Thank God we're on the flat.
  How much further to Middle Hardaumont?
  My boots are full of water and coated in mud. They slip on the ice and sink into the ground with every step, and the effort of lifting them out gets greater and greater. Just like one of those nightmares.

I've stopped caring about the bombardment. I'm too fucked to care about anything.

This is truly Hell, a freezing pitch-dark moonscape of smoking craters, lit by explosions and flashes and flares and searchlights, full of the cries of the damned and tormented.

Catch my foot on a leg attached to part of a torso.

Someone is howling close by, but I can't tell where.

Stumble on, shoulders back legs aching, mind numb, hands numb, clothes turning to ice. Can't feel my feet.

I just want to stop.

It must be over soon.

On and fucking on.

"Password!"

Thank fuck.

"Prenzlau."

"Pass, friends."

The howling is still with us, and I realise it's Weidner. Put him down carefully.

"Well done, Lorenz."

He's too knackered to answer.

Lower Tiemann gently to the ground. He's crying with relief, actually crying.

"Thank you," he says, clutching my hand. "Thank you."

"No need."

Report to Strecker.

*

You can't tell now which is Middle Hardaumont and which are the others, Max thought. *There are just wrecked blockhouses, deep holes, and hundreds of trenches with rusting wire. Not that it matters.*

All around him a dismal procession of men made their way along the path, filthy, ragged and bloodstained, the whole supporting or carrying the injured, all weary almost beyond endurance.

Funny – you get to the point when you're completely fucked and you can't go any further, and you still keep on going and going.

Wonder where that comes from, that extra bit that you don't know you have.

Tiemann was so absurdly grateful to me that night – but there was nothing else I could do. He was my responsibility and I had to get him out of the village.

I just hope we didn't leave anyone living behind. Bad enough that we couldn't bury the dead, and far worse that there were so many missing.

*

12th March 1916, Hardaumont Ridge

We still have to get to the Bezonvaux strongpoint. More men have been hit, two of the stretcher-bearers are dead, and we're going to have to carry the wounded again.

"Schwarz – run on ahead and fetch more stretcher-bearers," Strecker says.

"Yes, sir."

Put Tiemann over my shoulder again. Lorenz and I pick up Weidner, just like before.

I swear they've doubled in weight.

At least it's mostly flat now. And the shelling's not as bad – though we still take casualties. As if we haven't lost enough blokes.

Trudge on and on. I want to stop for a rest, but if I do then I don't think I'll ever get going again.

Turn your brain off, Max. One foot and then the other.

Stumble and almost drop Weidner.

Jesus Christ, how much further is it? I've fucking had it…

The extra stretcher-bearers reach us after half a century. Lorenz and I hand Weidner over with relief.

There still aren't enough of them to carry everyone. I'm at the end of my strength and I still have Tiemann on my back.

I can't do it…

One foot and then the other. It's slightly downhill now. Just keep going.

It's getting lighter and lighter. At least we're not on that fucking forward slope any more.

And here, finally, is the Bezonvaux strongpoint.

There's a big queue of wounded waiting for treatment at the dressing station. Most of them are in one of the concrete shelters, but dozens more are lying in the snow.

Hand our blokes over to the medical orderlies.

Tiemann hugs me and doesn't want to let go.

"Thank you, thank you." He starts crying again.

"No need. Get a grip, man. You'll be fine now."

Carry on down to the village of Bezonvaux. By the time we get there, it's broad fucking daylight.

*

Max walked down into the village and along where the main street had been, between the piles of rubble.

It's unrecognisable. What was left of us assembled somewhere here, but I don't know where.

These villages all look the same now. At least this one doesn't have the awful brooding feeling that Vaux has.

*

12th March 1916, Bezonvaux

Join the group shivering around Strecker.

The remains of the Seventh.

"Number." His voice is expressionless.

"One…"

"Two…"

"…Seventy."

Silence. No one says, "Seventy-one."

A hundred and sixty of us left the Caurières Wood three days ago.

"Roll call in the evening." His tone is flat and empty.

You can't really hope that stragglers will come in. We brought everyone with us.

Would I want to accept that my company has been smashed to pieces for the third time in three weeks?

An officer's first duty is to his men… But what can you do when the orders are impossible?

Get what's left of Messner's Platoon settled in a ruined house. Find my own billet with Hutten and Kropp.

Take my boots off and pour icy water out of them.

"Better check our feet," says Hutten.

"And get everyone to check theirs after roll call," adds Kropp.

Lie down and sink instantly into blackness, despite the appalling cold.

When I wake, the sounds of battle are loud. Someone else is copping it thoroughly.

No doubt they'll reinforce us and send us back in again – the battering ram of the Brandenburg Corps still has a job to do.

Assemble for roll call. The faces are strained, the eyes bleak.

No one else has arrived. We can only hope that we got everyone living out of the village.

"We're to go back to Billy tonight," says Strecker. "We leave at ten, so get some more rest."

At least it should be quiet there.

"Let's hope they don't shell the crap out of us on the way," Hutten mutters to me as we fall out.

"Quite."

"Maybe we can ride on the railway," says Nehring.

The rest of us laugh.

"We're infantry," says Lorenz. "*Foot* soldiers – means what it says."

"Foot inspection, boys," Kropp and I say, almost in unison.

Scheumann, Hutten and I send seven men to the medics with frozen feet.

"Surprising it wasn't more, really," says Kropp.

I'm surprised I haven't got frostbite – part of my right foot is still numb.

But the cookers are in Bezonvaux, so we get hot food and coffee.

Amazing what a difference it makes. Shovel the stew down, wrap my hands around the mug, and feel the blood start to trudge through my veins again.

And what's even better is that we get double portions.

Which is just as well, because the slog back to Billy is anything but fun. It's a fucking long way – and, to stop us getting bored, the fucking Frenchies send us some shells.

Sixty-one cold and exhausted men finally tramp into Billy, carrying two more wounded.

*

I'm not going back to Billy today, Max thought. *There's no trace of our camp now.*

But God, were we fucked when we got there that day in March. And then there was a problem with the accommodation.

13th March 1916, Billy

"*Well, you can damn well sort it out!*" Strecker's voice would cut through steel. It's matched by the look in his eyes.

"Don't take that tone with me, Oberleutnant," says the Hauptmann.

Strecker looks at him, with all the contempt of the front-line soldier for the base-hog.

"Who's in command here, *sir*?" His tone hasn't altered.

The Captain flushes angrily. "Major Pirchner."

"And where might I find him?"

"In the Mairie."

Strecker stomps off. The Captain hesitates a moment, then follows him.

Scheumann, Hutten and I look at each other.

Ten minutes later, Strecker returns alone.

"We've got three huts," he says.

"Wish I'd been a fly on the wall," Hutten says to me.

Sleep the clock round.

Our big packs arrive, and we get a bath and fresh uniforms. Someone has moved Heaven and Earth for us.

Strecker actually has a hint of a smile. "Well, boys – we're going to Alsace tomorrow."

No one dares look at anyone else. We've been reprieved – unless the bastards change their minds.

"Parade at nine, then march to Longuyon to entrain," he says.

Don't sleep that night. Every time I shut my eyes, I'm back in the fucking village. Every time I jolt awake, it's to the sound of shelling.

And I see the dead.

Axel, Messner, Jahnke… and all the bloody good blokes in my Group who've gone. Their faces are so clear it's as if they're here.

Morning comes, get as smart as possible, fall in.

Where is everybody?

"Where's the rest of the Battalion?" Kropp asks.

The other three Company Commanders each have a group about the size of ours.

"I think this is it," says Scheumann.

Jesus.

Between us, we're about one peacetime company.

A short distance away is a similar collection of remnants.

"Isn't that Hauptmann Piatkowski?" asks Hutten.

If it is then that's the First Battalion.

So where's the Third Battalion?

There's a group of about a hundred men on the other side of us – with one Company Commander and a Hauptmann whose name escapes me.

They must be it.

I don't want to believe what I must be seeing.

Nine o'clock is approaching, and no one else joins us.

The entire Regiment numbers about six hundred men, instead of three thousand. And that's after repeated reinforcement.

I look at the Seventh, count the men who were in my Platoon when we arrived at Verdun.

Twelve.

The General has come to see us. He climbs out of his car slightly stiffly, takes his place beside the road.

What's left of the bands plays our slow march, the 'Preobazhensky'. It rings solemn through the icy air.

The colours are blood red against the wintry sky. The cold wind blows through me and chills my bones.

We pushed the front line from Azannes to Vaux. The battering ram has smashed open the door to Verdun – but the cost.

Jesus, the cost.

Immense pride and profound sorrow fill my soul, tighten my throat. The raw aftermath of extreme violence intensifies the emotions until I can hardly breathe.

Axel. Messner. Jahnke…

Silence.

'The Glory of Prussia'.

It sounds so different today, heavily overlaid with death. So few of the men who sang on the first day are still here.

And now we have to march past the General. I could do without the parade march today – my back and legs are aching from the trudge up the ravine.

We're all bloody knackered. But we're the elite.

Strecker's order carries clearly.

The sound of the boots changes – but we are so few.

My eyes meet the General's briefly.

His too are filled with pride and sorrow.

Wonder how you live with sending men to their deaths. Maybe you don't.

Afterwards, they want photographs of each company.

Strecker, Scheumann, Hutten and I sit on a bench, the others gather round us.

Let's get this over with so we can get on the fucking train.

I just want to get pissed. Completely fucking hammered – because that's the only way I'll be able to sleep. The dead are haunting me, and the fighting repeats itself.

As we march to the station, someone starts to sing, "And when our Regiment was young…"

We join in, but many of the voices choke. We have all lost too many friends.

Head up, and sing with pride to honour their memory.

XIX

What I really don't understand is how I survived, Max thought as he rode back to Verdun. *Or why I survived.*

If there is a why, of course. And my mind is open on that one.

Maybe it was to bear witness, so my comrades won't be forgotten. Though there are times when I would very much like to forget – especially in the middle of the night, when they all come back.

At least I didn't lose track of reality today...

That thought turned out to be premature.

Everything seemed fine – he handed Prince back, wishing he could call Frieda.

I'll send her a cable.

What to put? There's so much I want to say...

I don't suppose I'll be here much longer. The second deployment won't take long – we got absolutely bloody nowhere.

He thought a bit more, then wrote, 'Miss you home in a couple of days Max x'.

And that will have to do for now. I miss her so much. Her and our boys.

I just hope she can keep on loving me, he thought as he walked back to the hotel after dinner. *It can't be easy.*

The voice was waiting for him. He felt it as soon as he entered his room.

'So how many of us did you kill?' it asked in the darkness.

No more than I had to. And for fuck's sake – I've never kept count.

Suddenly he was back in the village, in that suffocating atmosphere of hostility and dread. All the dead Frenchmen were in the room, surrounding him—

Max sat bolt upright, sweating, and put the light on.

They retreated into the corners of the room, and stood there watching him with their empty sockets.

Jesus fucking Christ.

He lit a cigarette and leaned back against the headboard.

That was the end of any hope of sleep, and he sat smoking and waiting for the dawn. The village kept intruding with ghastly clarity.

He was in the open on the snow, in the blinding light of the fire, with Messner getting shot just a few metres away…

If I burn myself with this cigarette, then I'll know I'm here in this room and not there.

Or will I?

That's a fucking stupid idea, anyway. It'll hurt.

And then he realised that physical pain would be preferable.

Still a fucking stupid idea.

He put the cigarette on the edge of the ashtray.

No point lying here staring at the ceiling.

He got up and wrote up his diary, in the hope that it might help him keep hold of reality.

Maybe I should have a break from the whole business today, he thought over breakfast. *Go sightseeing or something – there must be other things to see here besides that appalling wasteland.*

But the sooner I get it finished, the sooner I can go home.

I need to lie in Frieda's arms again, and I want to get out of this fucking hotel before I go completely insane.

So – today it's the second deployment. That means the Casemate Ravine and the Caillette Wood – and that's another place whose name I can't say.

Prince seemed genuinely pleased to see him, and was more

than usually affectionate, even though the ration of carrots remained the same.

I'll miss you when I go home, you and your tickly whiskers…

Now, where do I leave you? I suppose the best thing would be to leave you at the Ossuary. I can walk from there to Fort Douaumont and down the hill.

It isn't far after all – and that's the thing that really gets me every day. That so many lives were thrown away in such a small area.

No wonder it stank so badly.

That's what we couldn't believe when we got back from Alsace – that the front line hadn't moved.

*

16th March 1916, Alsace

Alsace is beautiful – green with the spring, and far warmer than that freezing Hell. And almost untouched by war.

Unlike us.

We've been here five minutes when Scheumann gets into a bust-up with an officer from the 24th. He says later that the fellow was shouting the odds about having taken Fort Douaumont, as if he'd done it personally, and he wasn't inclined to listen.

"So I said, 'Where the fuck were you in the wood? Never ready to go in, were you?' and 'You never took the bloody Knochgraben like you were supposed to.'"

Hutten and I start laughing.

"Don't suppose he liked that much!" I say.

Scheumann laughs. "That's for sure."

"So what happened, sir?" asks Hutten.

"He wanted to call me out, but his friend reminded him that duelling's banned for the duration. Then it all got a bit physical."

That's where you got the shiner, then.

"And the bastard gave me this, but I gave him a good whack back."

Hutten and I look at each other and laugh harder.

"And then Strecker turned up."

"Shit!" says Hutten.

"Yes... He wasn't best pleased. And even less so when the fellow's Company Commander made a formal complaint."

"That's a bit rich," I say.

"Quite. I got summoned to Gneist, and his sense of humour was rather lacking. Gave me a whopping great bollocking, said I was lucky not to be demoted or whatever. Said I was only being let off because of the circumstances, and if I couldn't drink without getting into trouble then I'd better not drink at all."

Not drink at all? How in God's name is anyone supposed to cope with all this without booze?

"So from now on, I'm just drinking with our own fellows."

Our superiors have the same idea. Jagenow issues an order stating that drink is only to be taken in establishments approved by the Regiment. No doubt our friends have the same restriction.

The next day the Brigade gets spread out, and we move to a different village. It's very peaceful, and hopefully we'll start to recover.

God knows we need to – everyone's nerves are still very strung out. I managed one good night's sleep through sheer fucking exhaustion, but every night since then has been full of the fighting.

I'm not alone in that. Every night, men shout in their sleep, and everyone still looks haggard.

A fortnight after we arrive, I get a surprise.

"Schelling, you're wanted in the Company office," says Scheumann.

Wonder what I've done.

Have to smile at that – how I can still feel like a schoolboy summoned to the headmaster is quite beyond me.

Strecker has a hint of a smile in his eyes.

"Do sit down, Schelling."

"Thank you, sir."

"I've got a package for you."

The smile is more than a hint now, and has spread into his face. He hands me a thick envelope, face down.

"Thank you, sir."

"Why not open it?"

I have a suspicion what it might be.

There's a rather impressive letter – and a set of gleaming epaulettes.

Strecker's smile has spread to my face as well. God knows why – this is my ticket for the Eternity Express, and we both know it.

"Congratulations, Leutnant Schelling," he says warmly, and shakes my hand.

"Thank you, sir."

Hope I'm allowed to stay with my fellows…

"And you're to stay in charge of 2nd Platoon."

Thank God for that.

For some reason, my boys seem pleased as well.

"I'll sew those on for you, sir," says Stadler.

"Thanks."

And I have to say they look good – if rather too shiny. They'll need a good coating of mud before they go into the front line.

I would rather not have got command through Messner dying. He was a good bloke, was Messner – I liked him as well as respecting him. And he was bloody good at the job, and now he's lying in that fucking village.

I gave Messner's tag, Army book and wallet to Strecker, but I kept the opera glasses – I reckoned they'd be more use to me than to his family.

We're reinforced yet again, and this time we get back a few of the fellows who copped it in Serbia, and in the first days at Verdun.

"Good, that," says Scheumann. "Doesn't always happen."

Hutten is less pleased, though. He's replaced as Platoon Commander by Leutnant Vossberg, who got whacked badly in Serbia and isn't quite right yet.

"Don't worry," Henke says to Hutten with a grin. "You'll get your command before long!"

Vossberg's a decent sort of fellow, Regular officer, knows his stuff. None of us know him well, though – he was Sixth Company before.

He knew Axel, of course.

"Good bloke," he said. "Real shame… Thought a lot of you."

And I thought a lot of him.

"Oh, right," is all I say. "We were cousins."

"So Gneist says."

He starts to get up, winces, and stops for a moment.

They've sent you back a bit too soon – but that's what happens after heavy casualties. With a bit of luck, you'll be fine before we leave here.

Most of the reinforcements are boys fresh from the homeland, but at least we've got time to finish their training. They look at us as if we've come back from the Moon.

The Seventh is on the way to being what it was again – or it will be, if the new fellows can get experience of the Front without being slaughtered.

If they'd send us to a quiet sector for a while, we'd be there.

*

Max made sure Prince had food and water, and set off towards Fort Douaumont.

I've been lucky with the weather. It's only drizzled a bit, and today's my last day of wandering about here. At least I hope it is.

Our reprieve in Alsace was lovely while it lasted…

*

20th April 1916, Alsace

A fortnight after my promotion, the Seventh falls in for Strecker to talk to us.

The new boys are starting to look like soldiers. Let's hope there's substance to go with the appearance.

Strecker's face is very serious. I never like that look.

"Well, boys… we've got fresh orders."

His eyes skate over our faces. He doesn't want to look at us.

Shit. Please God, or fate, or whatever, let me be wrong.

"We're going back to Verdun."

Fuck.

Cold runs down my back.

I won't come back this time. God alone knows how I survived the first deployment.

After we fall out, Scheumann lights my fag and his.

Our eyes meet. Neither of us says a word, but I know he's thinking the same as me.

"I should have married her," he says after a minute or so.

There's nothing I can say to that.

Vossberg looks at us both. I can see him thinking that we don't look happy.

There really isn't anything either of us can say. Our expressions plus the casualties should say it all.

Go back to my billet. Stadler and I pack in silence.

As we march to the station, some of the new boys start to sing, "I saw a ship go sailing, Captain and Lieutenant…"

Join in. Might as well.

"Soldiers, comrades, Take the girl take the girl, By the hand…"

Quite some fairy story – fine wine, good food, and every soldier gets a girl and then rides up to Heaven on a white horse.

Never saw one of those on any battlefield. Never found a willing girl after fighting, either. Only tarts.

Never find a willing girl again. Should have tried harder to get my leg over Frieda. Pretty girl… Beautiful eyes. Lovely arse. Really lovely arse.

And the way her skirt swings when she walks…

Pity she wouldn't drop her knickers.

Forget her, Max. It's over. It's just a matter of when.

As we board the train, I see the same thought in the eyes of everyone who survived the first deployment.

Get off the train in Longuyon. Familiar sound of distant bombardment as we fall in and start marching.

French aircraft welcome us by dropping 'Easter Eggs' – their aim is terrible, but the new boys jump half out of their skins.

Wish we didn't have so many of them. We've done our best to train them up, but the fact is they haven't fought before. They've never been shit-scared, and a lot of them will die before they become soldiers.

The lack of experienced NCOs is the worst thing – we got a handful back, but that was all.

There are too many men now who need to be told what to do.

*

Max had reached the Fort.

Now, what's the best way of doing this? I suppose I could walk down to the Casemate Ravine and then back up, and then down into the Caillette Wood and back up.

If I went straight from the Ravine to the Wood, that would be a lot shorter, but I'd like to retrace part of the journey I made.

Though not the part up the Bowling Alley…

So here we were, back at sodding Verdun again – and then they didn't want us for over two weeks. We were stuck in the camp in Billy, with fuck all happening.

We could hear the fighting only too clearly, and of course the Frenchies didn't leave us in peace. Billy was well within range of their heavies.

*

29th April 1916, Billy

"If you ask me, this is worse than being in the front line," Kropp grumbles to me as we clear up another wrecked hut.

The dead and wounded have been taken away, but the place stinks of blood and shit in the late April warmth.

"Yes, I know what you mean."

Being shelled without being able to fight is very hard on the nerves – as is not knowing when you'll be going in.

There are plans for an offensive, but no one knows when it will be.

Keep the men occupied, so they don't have too much time to think.

I could do with less time to think myself. When we do go in, I'm dead. It's as simple as that.

Sit on my bed, wishing with all my heart that I were somewhere else, that the war had never started, and wondering where I'm going to find the guts to do it all again.

And I have to lead the others.

You will, Max. Once it all kicks off, you'll be fine. You know how it is – you'll have far too much to do to be scared.

Just enjoy these extra days of life…
The delay means we get back some more of the old fellows. Tiemann comes back, with just a slight limp.
"Tiemann! Good to see you back."
"Thank you, Herr Leutnant. It's good to be back!"
We both laugh at that.
"How are your legs? Healed up?"
"Yes, thank you, Herr Leutnant."
Suddenly he realises what he's been saying quite automatically, and his face cracks into a huge grin.
"Congratulations, Herr Leutnant!" he says with real warmth, and holds out his hand.
"Thank you, Tiemann." Shake his hand with the same genuine feeling.

It's good to have another of the experienced men back – and Tiemann is reliable. I'd trust him with my life any day.

We get Bachmann as well, who copped it on the very first day, and Tischert.

Bachmann was lucky, and knows it. He didn't even get to the bottom of the hill, so he was picked up very quickly – and because he was likely to heal up and fight again, he was at the front of the queue for treatment.

But now he's back here, and you have to wonder just how lucky that is. Maybe it would have been better to lose a foot or something…

That's no way to think, Max. Deep in his heart, everyone wants a Heimatschuss, but as your gran used to say, you can have too much of a good thing.

*

Max sighed.
That really underlines the inhumanity of the business. Those

who'll fight again get treated first, then those who'll recover – and the poor bastards who are likely to die just get left.

Literally left, if there are a lot of casualties. I'll never forget, when I got hit in summer '15, seeing all those poor sods lying behind the dressing station, crying out for water and help, and the orderlies ignoring them.

Never mind the ones who never got taken to the dressing station in the first place...

That brought the first days of Verdun to mind, and he pushed the memory away.

I really don't want to think about that.

But once the image was there, it wouldn't leave him and kept coming back, far too vividly.

I'd rather think about the Casemate Ravine – though we were really in the bottom half, the part we called the British Ravine.

God knows why we named it after the Tommies when they weren't even here – but then we had a Russki Ravine as well.

The old path still led from below the Turret down through the cratered ground into the ravine. It was battered, like the remnants of trenches beside it, but enough was left for Max to follow it.

This part was in our hands. We were trying to push the Frenchies down into the bottom of the valley, to trap them between us and the fellows trying to roll up Vaux village.

Impossible to believe that Vaux village still hadn't been taken, two months after our attempt.

But it was obvious by early May that the Frenchies were gaining the upper hand. They had more artillery, more shells, more men, more aircraft – more fucking everything except courage.

We matched them in that – oh God, did our boys have courage. But what use was it against guns and machine guns and mortars and... and... and...?

The Allies had unlimited reserves of men and materiel, and Germany was slowly going under. And all our courage served only to delay defeat.

This ground is soaked with the blood of the brave...

He missed his footing in the craterscape, steadied himself, and stood looking at the blasted ground.

We must all have been insane, us and the Frenchies. What in God's name makes men do what we did?

I've never known the answer to that.

On the other side of the ravine was the old French battery position, and he crossed the valley bottom and climbed up to it.

I never saw this properly before – the ravine was always full of smoke, and I wasn't here long.

The guns had stood on a platform of reinforced concrete, first the French guns and then the German ones. Now the concrete was broken and the steel rods stuck out, twisted into spaghetti.

Jesus. Hardly surprising, the damage done to men's bodies...

He crossed back over and carried on down.

I suppose we were about here.

The path clung to the steep side of the ravine. Beside it, the ground dropped away, the gradient almost sheer.

Max tripped over a scrap of metal and almost lost his footing.

Be a bit much to end up down there again.

XX

Getting here was bad enough, Max thought, *over Hardaumont and along the fucking Zig-Zag Trench.*

That wasn't any better than in March. Fort Vaux was still in French hands, and they were still shelling the crap out of the slope. And that was apart from the barrage.

We had to move up at night, towards the incandescent fury of the Front. And long before we got to Hardaumont, we could smell the battlefield.

The main odour was rotting flesh.

No one wanted to mention it. We all pretended it wasn't there, as if mentioning it would somehow make it more real, as if ignoring it increased our personal chances of not adding to it.

We all just kept smoking, until we got near the top of the ridge, where it was fags out.

*

4th May 1916, Hardaumont Ridge

"Abandon all hope ye who enter here," Scheumann mutters to me as we pick ourselves up yet again.

"Indeed."

*

Not all the Company finished the journey to the Casemate Ravine, Max thought sadly.

And of course that was just the start.

The 'front line' was nothing of the sort – just a mass of shell-holes with wire here and there, and odd bits of 'trench' dug between them. The holes were nowhere near deep enough, and we found out very quickly why that was.

Every night, we dug deeper holes and deeper trenches – and every day, the French artillery filled it all in again. It was just like the Greek fellow who had to keep shoving the rock up the hill, only for it to roll right back down to the bottom every time.

We were trying to push the Frenchies down the hill, and they were trying to push us up. Shell-hole to shell-hole, the nastiest fighting imaginable, and with shells raining down all the time.

*

6th May 1916, Casemate Ravine

And then the fucking 7.5s join the heavies, firing shell after shell, three a minute from each gun, getting nearer and nearer.

No gun should be able to fire that fast—

BLAST FLAME

Flying.

What – where—?

Ears ringing head thick. Groggy. Could just fall asleep.

Open my eyes with an effort.

There's a face beside me, in profile, the mouth open.

Blink, try to focus.

The face is black with decay.

There isn't much left of the rest of him.

I'm in the bottom of a shell-hole in the depths of the ravine, next to a very dead corpse.

It's a deep hole. The Frenchies are still shelling. If I stay here I'll be buried.

Force myself to sit up.

Head spins.

Don't fall back, Max. Get out of this fucking hole.

Hands scrabble in the loose earth, boots slip—

Something soft. Fingers sink into it.

Rotten flesh.

Arm hand thigh black putrid rotting glutinous—

Scrabble frantically in the stinking pit, fragments of bodies fall out fingers sink in again and again—

Thigh bone stinking slime guts ribs—

I'm out, on my hands and knees.

Covered in filth, taste of death in my mouth.

Vomit.

Jesus fucking Christ.

Where the fuck are my boys?

Crawl on all fours up the side of the ravine.

Shells smoke grenades. Machine guns. Rifle fire.

Hit the ground again and again.

Land on something soft. Eruption of decay.

Vomit.

Can't see a fucking thing.

Smoke clears a little.

"Over here, sir!"

Stadler and Tiemann, waving.

Fall into the hole they're in.

"We thought you were a goner, sir," says Stadler.

"So did I."

"There was a colossal bang and you'd gone," he continues.

Wonder how long ago that was.

"What's the situation?"

"We managed to take this hole, sir," Tiemann says proudly.

"Well done."

"Sir, you're bleeding," says Stadler.

"Am I?"

"Left side of your head."

Put my hand to my head and it comes away bloody. And my helmet's gone.

Frenchies step up the shelling. Press ourselves into the hole. Bombardment eases abruptly.

"It'll have to wait," I say.

We are all ready, and the French attack is bloodily repulsed. That's the fourth today, and each time we shoot and bomb them to pieces.

We have to kill them before they kill us.

And of course they feel just the same. Every time we attack, we're met by a wall of metal. Two shell-holes in a day count as good progress.

Each one costs litres and litres of blood to take and yet more to hold, as the Frenchies counterattack with grenades and knives…

In a brief breathing space, Stadler bandages my head.

"It's a bit of a mess, sir," he says.

"Never mind."

What I do mind is that my head is now stark white. They can probably see it from the ridge opposite.

Simple arithmetic: white head plus epaulettes equals prime target for sniper.

Pick up a handful of stinking mud and smear it on the bandage. It might give me an infection, but the whiteness will definitely get my skull emptied.

"Does that show now?"

"No, sir."

I would like a helmet – mine must be somewhere near the bottom of the ravine.

There's one lying on the edge of the shell-hole. It probably won't go over the bandage, but it's worth a try.

Pick it up, the weight surprising.

Turn it over.

"Oh, fuck!"

Drop it in disgust – half its owner's head is still inside it.

It probably wouldn't have fitted, anyway…

The day goes on. Try to take their shell-holes, try to stop them taking ours or retaking the ones we've just taken from them.

More lives, more blood.

It's hard to know who's dying faster – them or us.

Every shell-burst unearths more stinking fragments of what were once men. We are surrounded by the dead in every stage of decomposition and dismemberment. Bones lie everywhere, putrid flesh still attached.

Somehow we cling to life and manage to fight.

*

Max's foot brushed against something hard, and he stopped dead.

Fuck. I hope that's not an unexploded shell.

He bent down.

Something greyish-white, more than half-buried.

A shoulder blade – or rather part of one.

Yours or ours?

Not that it matters.

What do I do with this? It should go in the Ossuary with the others. There must be a collection point somewhere.

Maybe I should put it with the shells I saw, near the top of the ravine.

Or maybe I should just leave it here. Presumably more of its owner is here somewhere.

He brushed some more earth off the shoulder blade.

What should I do, Axel?

'Mark the spot and tell the clean-up teams. They'll look for the rest of him.'

Thanks.

Close to the point where the ravine forks, on the western side. That'll do as a description.

I wonder where we were that day. Somewhere near here.

He shuddered at the memory of scrabbling out of the shell-hole, could almost feel his fingers sinking into rotten flesh, and taste the smell of death.

I've never been able to touch anything rotten since. Not even fruit. Frieda's father laughed at me until I said "Verdun" – and then he went very quiet.

*

6th May 1916, Casemate Ravine

After dark, Strecker makes his tour of our 'positions'. Make my report.

"Hm. And what's happened to you, Schelling?"

"Shell-burst, sir. Just a cut."

He looks at me carefully. "Need to go back?"

"No, sir."

No one in our lot would go back just because of a cut. Strecker knows that as well as I do.

"Carry on, then."

In the early hours, my head is throbbing and I'm being sick again.

There are two Stadlers, and I can't understand what either of them is saying.

Strecker pays us another visit.

"How's it going, Schelling?"

I hear words coming from my mouth, but I can't get them in the right order.

He looks at me closely. "It's time you went back. You're not making sense."

"Sorry, sir. I'll all be… right all… I – er…"

He puts a hand on my shoulder.

"Go and see Doctor Meyer and then go up to the Fort," he says. "And I don't want to see you back until that's healed."

"No, sir."

I stumble and almost fall.

"Here – take this." He hands me his stick.

"Thank you, sir."

"Not at all. Now be off with you."

Doctor Meyer is right up with us, as he always is. I don't know where he finds the courage. The thought of being here armed with a medical bag scares me half to death.

And he's so calm. You'd think you were in his consulting room in Berlin.

I flinch as he turns his torch on.

"Is the light painful?"

"No, Doctor…"

I don't want to say, *it's a fire magnet*.

"No other way of seeing what I'm doing," he says, and I hear the smile in his voice.

He is careful to shade the light, though.

You know perfectly well how dangerous it is, I think as he examines my head. *We'll just have to hope it doesn't get you killed.*

"Best get yourself up to the Fort," he says. "This needs a better clean than I can do here, and it'll need stitching."

He writes out a label and fastens it to my tunic, tears off one red strip and thinks for a moment.

"How long were you out for?"

"Don't know... all right walk."

He tears off the second strip. "Don't go by yourself – wait until there are half a dozen of you."

"Thank you, Doctor."

"That's what I'm for." Again, the smile in his voice.

There are a lot of wounded, and every man gets the same quiet, kind attention.

Balls of steel, our doctor. Good fellow to have with you in a bad situation.

Half an hour later, we set off up the ravine, quite a few walkers plus three stretcher cases.

The Frenchies take care to wish us 'Bon voyage'.

*

Max started back up the ravine.

I'm not sorry to get out of here – and that went double last time. Though of course getting out was easier said than done.

*

7th May 1916, Casemate Ravine

Their greetings are getting too friendly, the shells landing closer...

One of the stretcher-bearers drops like a sack. The casualty falls off the stretcher and screams.

Everyone hits the ground.

Give it a minute, and crawl very carefully to the stretcher-bearer. There's a single hole in the back of his tunic and he's stone dead.

What kind of murdering fucking bastard does that? When I was a sniper I never shot a medic, and I wouldn't now.

"STAY DOWN! SNIPER!"

Hope they heard me.

Up ahead, the ravine curves to the left. Once we're round that we should be safe. From him, anyway.

We'll have to use the shell-holes as cover until we get that far.

At least the fog in my head has cleared a bit.

Somehow we have to get the stretcher case into the next hole. It takes two of us plus the surviving medic, and then we're so fucked we can't move.

My head's throbbing from the effort, but the others are just as bad as me.

And on it goes, up the hill, from hole to hole. The poor fellow screams as we push and pull him, but what can we do?

A century later, we round the bend in the ravine.

Stretcher-bearers and reinforcements are coming down towards us.

Must stop them – open my mouth – no words come out—

"HALT!" shouts the Sergeant with the broken arm. "SNIPER!"

The NCO leading the reinforcements halts them, right in front of us.

"Cheers, Sarge," he says.

"Thank you, Sergeant," I manage to say. My face doesn't belong to me.

"That's all right, sir."

We make our slow, painful way round them, and on up the hill towards the Fort.

We know where it is because French shells are slamming into the top of it in massive bursts of orange flame. The detonations shake the ground.

It's like a volcanic eruption.

Jesus. How the fuck are we going to get in there?

Stop for a breather. We're all fucked.

The fellow we've been manhandling has gone very quiet. One of the surviving stretcher-bearers examines him.

"Dead."

Relief.

We don't have to drag him along any more.

What are you thinking, Max? If the poor fucker had been carried then he might still be alive.

No time to worry about that. Need to get all the living ones into the Fort – and my head's getting bad.

We have to use the north-east entrance… at least I think we do… which the fuck way is that?

We're heading north now, aren't we? Or are we?

My thoughts swirl in fog, run away as I try to catch them.

"Sergeant."

"Sir?"

Concentrate, Max.

"Might need… you… to take charge," I say slowly but coherently.

"Of course, sir. Whenever you like."

"Think now."

He takes my arm.

I gesture to another man, who can hardly stand.

"Help him."

Stagger along, leaning heavily on Strecker's stick.

More French greetings.

Hit the ground. Shattering bang.

Not everyone gets up again.

Head is really throbbing now. Dizzy.

Can't keep up.

In the flashes, I see the remains of the group pulling ahead of me: the two stretcher cases, the Sergeant and five other walking wounded.

Try to go faster but my legs won't.

No point shouting – no one will hear.

Scream of shell – *oh Jesus that's going to be close and it's big—*

Throw myself into a hole, press against the earth.

SHATTERING BLINDING THUNDER. Flame, smoke, metal shards, earth, rotting fragments fly up rain down.

I'm half-buried.

Dig myself out, sit up.

Head spins, ears ring.

No idea where the fuck I am… Where are the boys?

Head clears slowly.

On your way up to Fort Douaumont, Max.

Oh, yes.

Think I'll rest here for a bit.

No, you won't. There'll be more shells.

Struggle to my feet and get moving.

The others will have had to stop as well. Maybe I'll be able to catch them up.

There's no sign of them.

The flashes show me a large, smoking crater. At its edge is half a scorched stretcher.

An arm, attached to part of a torso, wearing a red cross armband. Bodies and parts of bodies all around.

The Sergeant's legs have been blown off, and he dies as I bend over him.

Someone waves feebly.

It's one of the stretcher-bearers. He's skewered with steel fragments, and I don't know how he's still alive.

There is absolutely nothing I can do for him, and he knows it.

His lips move. Put my ear next to his mouth.

"Give – my wife – my ring…"

"Of course."

Take his wedding ring from his hand, put it on my finger for safekeeping.

"I'll get your book out of your pocket."

"Thanks."

It's not a pleasant job, and the book is covered in blood. I'll have to take his tag, but I don't want to do that until he's dead.

One filthy, bloody hand reaches for mine.

Take hold of it and sit beside him.

This is for Axel, and for all the men I've seen die but couldn't help...

It doesn't take long.

Break off his tag, put it in my pocket with the book, force myself to my feet.

None of the others are alive. If I hadn't lagged behind, it would have got me as well.

*

On such small hinges turn life and death, Max thought as he trudged up the ravine.

There's no sign now of that crater – it's been shelled into oblivion.

I did feel bad about the stretcher-bearers. They were bloody brave blokes and no threat to anyone, and I never killed one in the whole time I was at war.

I suppose you could argue that they – and all the medics – were fair game, as they were saving men to fight again, but I never saw it that way.

Jesus, this is a steep climb – and I'm in reasonable health now. How the fuck did I do it with my head cut open?

What I've never known about that day was how much blood I lost, or how long I was unconscious for.

I do know, though, that it saved my life. At the time, though, it was far from certain that it would.

*

7th May 1916, below Fort Douaumont

Exhaustion starts to claim me. There's an endless line of men coming down from the Fort towards the front line, and I move aside again and again.

And I hit the ground again and again as the shells slam in.

Getting up is a bit harder each time.

I trudge on and on, but don't seem to get any nearer the Fort. It's like one of those nightmares where you walk on and on, but make no progress.

Stand leaning on Strecker's stick, trying to summon the energy for a few more steps.

"Need help, sir?"

"Thanks."

The man has an arm in a sling, but he's a lot fresher than me.

He puts his good arm round my waist, and I lay mine across his shoulders.

Amazing how much easier it is.

Maybe I have a chance…

The gradient slackens – but the volcano is ahead of us, spewing flame and smoke into the night.

The racket is unbelievable.

Need to stop.

"You… go… on," I shout. I don't want to put him in danger – more danger, that is.

"It's all right, sir – I could do with a breather."

Scream of shell.

Throw ourselves flat for the thousandth time.

Get up. Struggle on. Repeat…

Somehow we reach the Fort – but now we have to get into it.

Here's the huge shell-hole at the north-east corner of the ditch.

This is where we came back in February, when they intended us to be the new garrison.

We thought we'd soon be in Verdun…

Someone shakes me.

What – who—?

"Come on, sir – we can't stay out here!" My helper is pulling me to my feet.

"What? No… course not."

XXI

7th May 1916, Fort Douaumont

The shell-hole is full of men trying to get into the Fort. At the same time others are trying to get out. No one is going anywhere.

My helper and I hesitate. We don't want to get stuck in a crush like that.

An officer appears in the ditch and shouts. The men in the hole move aside as best they can, and the officer and his men run up out of the ditch and into the hole.

Scream of heavy shell.

Everyone hits the ground.

Thunder. Earthquake.

The officer and most of his fellows get up and run like hell away from the Fort. Some of those waiting to get in also run like fuck, into the ditch.

"What d'you reckon, sir? Give it a go?" he shouts into my ear.

"Yes – get bit closer," I reply.

We slide down into the crater on our arses and he pushes through the crowd. Most of them are uninjured, either reinforcements or just out of the line.

"Make way!" he shouts. "MAKE WAY!"

"Hey – don't shove!"

"We've both copped it, you twat!"

"Oh. Sorry, mate." He makes a gap and we squeeze past.

There's the door…

*

And here is the door.

Max stood in the ditch looking at it, surrounded by a crowd of soldiers even though he was alone.

I wonder if it'll open.

It was jammed shut.

I suppose they have to be careful about letting people into the Fort after the hammering it took. Parts of it must be pretty dodgy.

Wonder if I could go in, just for a few minutes.

He started to make his way along the ditch towards the south side of the Fort, and almost fell over a coil of rusting barbed wire.

You even have to be careful walking along here.

The ditch was half its original depth and full of debris, and the stone cladding of the outer wall had nearly all gone. Part of the original railings lay twisted and broken, their spikes pointing to the sky, and there was a cluster of bent screw pickets.

Thousands of craters bore witness to ten months of shattering violence.

The Fort was a refuge from that violence, which we were very glad to have.

*

7th May 1916, Fort Douaumont

Another shell.

Hit the ground by the door.

God, am I getting sick of this. My head hurts worse each time, and getting up's harder, even with my helper.

Jesus, I'm fucked. I wouldn't have got this far without him.

Get up.

Men run out. Men run in.

Another shell.

Hit the ground.

Could just stay here. It's too much effort to get up again...

"Come on, sir!"

He half pulls, half carries me, and we scuttle into the entrance.

Safety. We sink to the floor, lean against the cold stone wall.

Fucking hell. I didn't think we'd make it.

It's a while before I can speak.

"Thank you, Corporal. What's... your name?"

"Goldstein, sir."

I fumble in my pocket and give him all the fags I have.

He gives half of them back.

"Thank you, sir, but you'll need them later – and I was leaning on you as well!"

We both laugh, out of relief more than anything.

"Have one now," I say.

There's an almighty crash and the Fort shakes. My lighter goes out, the lights flicker, and dust cascades from the ceiling.

"Bloody hell," says Goldstein. "That was a heavy."

Get the fags lit. Rest against the wall, too fucked to move.

"Let's find... doctor," I say after a few minutes.

The Fort is a labyrinth of identical stone passages, all dripping water. The smell is indescribable.

"I thought it stank outside," he says, "but I swear this is worse."

He's not joking, either.

Wander along, past sleeping bodies and discarded equipment. God knows where we are.

"Fucking cold in here," Goldstein comments.

And I am starting to shiver. The air is bloody chilly.

Stop a fellow going the other way.

"Where medics?" God, but I can hardly speak.

"You need to go down, sir – take the next stairs."

"Thanks."

The smell gets worse – a horrible mixture of decay, piss, shit, and stale sweat. At least outside the wind brings a bit of fresh air.

As we near the infirmary, blood, iodine, disinfectant and chloroform get added to the cocktail.

It's hard to breathe.

The doctors are, of course, very busy. Anyone hit in the fighting east, south and west of the Fort comes here.

There's a long queue of casualties, and the air is full of groans and whimpers echoing in the stone corridor.

"Sorry, sir," an orderly says to me. "The doctors are operating almost non-stop. Can you and the Corporal dress each other, if I give you bandages and antiseptic?"

"Yes, of course."

"Sit over there, please. I'll just be a minute."

Sit on a couple of ammunition crates, wonder idly whether they're empty.

Goldstein leans back against the wall. "It's so good to stop."

"Yes."

Even if the place is a stinking warren echoing to blast after blast.

The orderly returns with what we need – and gives us each a bottle of water.

Clean, fresh water.

I have never tasted anything so wonderful. Realise how fucking thirsty I am, tip the last drops into my throat.

"Bloody hell," says Goldstein. "That was fucking good."

Too late to ask for another. The orderly's gone.

"I do you first," I say.

Cut the bandage, but it's stuck to his arm.

The only thing to do is pull it off quickly, but I'm not sure how much he'll bleed.

"What they say... when they... put this on?"
"Get it changed as soon as possible, sir."
"Right... Where... you from?"
Take a firm grip, hope I'm distracting him.
"Essen, sir—"
Pull sharply.
He yells good and loud.
"Fucking hell," he gasps after a moment or two.
There's a bullet hole through his upper arm, trickling blood. He grits his teeth hard as I douse it in antiseptic.
I'm not looking forward to him doing this to me.
Make as neat a job with the bandage as I can.
"All done."
"Thank you, sir... Do you mind waiting a few minutes?"
"No... Another fag?"
I'm putting it off, of course...
He picks up the scissors.
Oh, shit. I am not going to like this.
"Sorry, sir – this is well stuck."
"Get your... own back, then!" I reply, with an attempt at a grin.
My turn to grit my teeth. Yell. Almost throw up. And then there's the iodine.
Jesus.
"Sorry, sir – this is a bit awkward with one hand. Could you open the package, please?"
"Course... maybe we should... done me first."
"Don't think it would have made any difference, sir – my arm's been really stiff for hours... Could you hold the pad in place, please?... And now this end?"
Relief when it's done. Nausea subsides slowly.
"Sorry it's not very tidy, sir."
"'Sall right... yours isn't!"

Sag against the wall. Neither of us feels like moving, but more men are coming down to the hospital and we're in the way.

"Better move," I say. "Find somewhere... kip."

Climb back up the stairs, traipse wearily through the endless, crowded corridors. Every few minutes a heavy shell lands, the Fort shakes, there's a gust of stinking air, and the lights go out and then come back on.

Hope the place can take it...

Sit down for a rest, on boxes marked 'Hand Grenades'.

"Are these full?" Goldstein asks, and lifts the lid of the one beside him. "Bloody hell."

The box is packed to the top, stick grenades head to tail like sardines.

Wonder what else is lying around in here.

Sit gazing blankly at the wall.

How the fuck am I alive?

That was one near miss after another, especially that direct hit when we were climbing up the ravine...

But how do I know I'm alive?

My head hurts, and I'm fucking freezing.

My tattered uniform lets the cold right in, the sweat on my body chilling me to the core.

There's torment in Hell, though, isn't there?

If you believe all that.

We could all be ghosts.

Too complicated. Everything's too fucking complicated.

A hand shakes my shoulder.

"Come on, sir – there must be somewhere more comfortable than this. I'm bloody frozen. And I need a piss."

"Me too. Must be... latrine somewhere."

But the Frenchies actually managed to build a fort without latrines. Neither of us can believe it.

There are stinking buckets. Try not to breathe.

Eventually we find the barracks, well sandbagged against the shelling.

"Officers' accommodation this way, sir, NCOs' that way."

Turn to Goldstein, shake his hand warmly. Try to speak clearly. "Thank you very much indeed, Corporal."

"You helped me as well, sir."

"All same… hope they send you home."

"Thank you, sir."

*

I never found out whether they did, or what happened to him, Max thought. *I should try to find out – if he's still alive, I could send him a present. If he hadn't come along, my bones would be in the craters somewhere.*

Max walked out of the ditch and up to the south side of the Fort. The arches, which had once been the barracks windows, were blocked almost completely shut, and the façade had taken a massive battering.

There was a small entrance.

"May I come in?"

The man looked at Max, obviously displeased by his accent.

There was a pause.

"All right." The tone was very grudging, and the entry fee high.

Probably a special price for visiting Boche.

It took Max's eyes a moment to adjust to the dimness inside. The lighting was working, but without enthusiasm.

"Mind the hole," said the man. 'Why don't you fall down it?' said his tone.

There was a massive hole in the floor, going down at least two levels, and a narrow path around the side.

The air was cold and damp, and water ran down the walls

and dripped off the ceiling, just as it had then.

The barracks must be this way…

A series of rooms opened off the corridor.

He turned into one. At its far end was one of the arches, blocked with masonry apart from a few slits.

I wonder which of these rooms I was in.

*

7th May 1916, Fort Douaumont

The officers' room is crammed full, but at least that makes it warmer.

"There's a space over here," says a voice.

It's a young Leutnant in the 12th Grenadiers, clean-shaven and fresh-faced.

"Thanks."

He fails to hide his disgust as I sit next to him.

What's your problem? Oh, of course. I'm covered from head to foot in blood and stinking filth.

So will you be soon.

"Pretty lively out there," he says.

"That's for sure."

I would love a wash, just to get rid of the stench. My face is encrusted with something, and I don't want to think what it is.

"Is there somewhere… wash?"

He laughs. "No water for washing – goes with there being no latrines. Maybe the Frenchies don't piss and shit like other men!"

"Extraordinary…"

He gestures to my head. "Where'd you get that?"

I'm too fucked to talk. "Sorry… done in."

Wrap myself in a grubby blanket, lie down—

Wake to a shattering crash.

And another.

Sit up. Head spins and thumps.

The Fort's barracks once had windows facing south. Perfectly safe when the attack will come from the north, but complete shit when the Frenchies are south of us.

The windows are long gone, replaced with sandbags, but even those have been blown in.

Some of the others are making a barricade from a couple of wooden beds.

Go to help, rather unsteady on my feet.

One of the other Leutnants looks at my head.

"We can manage," he says. "Go and sit down."

I don't argue.

My watch says 8. am or pm?

There's light coming through the gaps between the sandbags, but at this time of year that's not much help.

They finish the barricade. The young Leutnant from the 12th Grenadiers comes and sits next to me.

"You were out for hours."

I do feel a lot better for it. "What time is it?"

"8.30pm. Fancy something to eat?"

"Definitely."

And I am fucking starving. It's hours since I ate anything, and that was iron rations.

"Why don't you stay here, and I'll bring some back for you," he says.

"Is it far?"

He gives me a cheerful grin. "I don't know yet!"

Bugger traipsing through the Fort in search of the cookhouse.
"Thanks, then."

"Coffee?"

"Please."

Lie down—

"Wake up. *Wake up.*"

It's the Grenadier Leutnant. He hands me a mess tin full of stew, and a mug of coffee, then pulls a chunk of Army bread out of his pocket.

"Thanks."

Feel much better after the food and a fag.

It's almost dark outside. I want to get out of here and on my way back.

Even in here, the Fort stinks. I want to get the smell of death off me, and I'm concerned about my head. It's throbbing more and more, and Doctor Meyer did say it needs cleaning out properly.

Time to leave.

*

Max realised he was still in the barrack room, staring into space.

I'll have a bit of a wander round, and then I'll get out into the sunlight.

It looks so different now, so empty. It was actually difficult to walk along the corridors then – there were so many men, and so much stuff lying about.

Too much fucking stuff, and no one knew what it was or took any control of it.

Negligence, really – but with the endless coming and going of thousands of men, it would have been very difficult to keep the place in order.

If only they had. No one will ever know how many men died…

He shivered as a cold drip went down his neck.

I've had enough of this place.

At the exit, the man said, "Of course you only took it through treachery."

Max stared at him. "What do you mean?"

"Disguising yourselves as Zouaves."

"Zouaves? I can assure you we didn't."

Disguise ourselves as North African soldiers? That's ridiculous!

Max left before the man could say another word. *Any more of that shit and I'll lose my rag.*

I really have heard everything now, he thought as he climbed up to the top of the Fort.

Then he remembered something.

In the wood, in the first couple of days, that French sentry thought we were Frenchies too – and when we put on one of their helmets we saw why. It was just like one of ours with the spike removed.

Maybe the Frenchies here made the same mistake. And all our faces were so covered in dirt that no one could see what colour they were.

Not that I give a shit. They should have defended their Fort better.

The view from the top of the Fort was incredible. The whole East Bank battlefield was laid out around him.

Fort Vaux was clearly visible on its ridge. So was the Hardaumont Ridge opposite it. And there was the wooden Ossuary, and the beginnings of the massive stone edifice to replace it.

To the south-east was the wreckage of the Caillette Wood.

He turned and faced north.

There's the wood where we were at first, where so many of my men lie.

And there's the Bowling Alley running ruler-straight until it curves near Azannes, how many kilometres away.

*

7th May 1916, Fort Douaumont

How the fuck do I find my way out of this labyrinth?

Tag onto a group heading for the front line. Judging by their faces, it's not their first time.

We all pause near the door.

Three men start to go through it.

There's a blinding flash and a thunderous detonation.

They stop and laugh, then make a run for it.

Wait for the next shell and then follow them.

Fresh air – well, everything's relative, as Professor Einstein says. Less stink, anyway.

The ditch is crammed with men, and I can hardly move. I need to get out of here.

Head towards the northern point. The smooth wall of the outer perimeter is a heap of rubble in places, the ditch partly filled with blocks of stone. Pieces of the iron fence lie everywhere, viciously sharp, mixed with barbed wire and twisted posts.

Hit the ground over and over as the shells slam in, feel the structure shake.

How much more can the Fort take?

Trip, almost fall. The flashes dazzle and then it's pitch-dark…

Join the slow procession of walking wounded and stretchers climbing the ramp out of the ditch. At the top, a group of stretcher cases is waiting for transport.

"Where are you going?" I ask one of the stretcher-bearers.

"Ornes, sir."

Ornes, where I heard that Axel was dead.

"But they're getting full up, sir, and so's Bezonvaux. You'd do better to go to Azannes."

Azannes. Where we started from in what's already another century.

"How do I get there?"

"Get onto the Bowling Alley – or rather, next to it – and carry on where it turns right after St André."

Where?

I must look totally blank, because he adds patiently, "St André's a ruined farm from before the war. After that the road bends towards Azannes."

"And past the Aid Post in the old front line."

"That's right, sir. Sure you can make it?"

I shrug. There's no other option and I don't feel too bad.

"You should go with them, sir," he says, pointing to a group of walking wounded.

"Going to Azannes?" I ask them.

"Yes, sir."

Set off alongside the Bowling Alley. In the bright flashes, I can see that it runs dead straight, downhill and then up.

XXII

8th May 1916, north of Fort Douaumont

The surface of the Bowling Alley is packed dirt between the craters, and it would be easier to walk on the road. No one dares do that. The French gunners know exactly where it is, and the craters multiply steadily.

Keep to the side, fall into the holes, clamber out, hit the ground when the shells arrive.

Get up, dazzled. Fall into a hole again.

Over and over.

The others are leaving me behind.

Down into the valley bottom, where the mud is deep. Fuck me, but it's hard work pulling my feet out.

Start up the hill. It gets steeper.

Another group passes me and I try to latch onto them, but only manage a few hundred metres.

Jesus, I'm fucked.

Keep going, Max. One foot and then the other.

On and on and fucking on.

Lean heavily on Strecker's stick.

Thank God he gave it to me. Hope I don't come across anyone needing help, because it's all I can do to drag myself along.

Stop for a rest. Light a fag.

Goldstein was right. I do need them later.

Bloody good bloke – hope he gets sent home. That arm was quite a mess.

Stadler said my head was a mess, and it's so hard to think straight.

You don't need to think. You just need to keep moving.

There are fewer shells falling now.

Move onto the road. If I get a direct hit then I'm dead anyway – and I'm almost too fucked to care.

Two fellows pass me, holding each other up.

No doubt they're hoping not to meet anyone needing help as well.

There's a faint gleam of light off to my right. As I stumble on it gets brighter, and slowly the ground ahead becomes visible in the grey dawn…

I can see properly now, and I wish I couldn't.

The road goes on endlessly into the distance, ruler-straight, climbing steadily.

Jesus, how far is it?

The sun comes up, and the temperature starts to rise.

Fuck me, but I'm thirsty.

On and fucking on.

There's no end to the fucking road, and the hill gets steeper with every step.

I'm fucked.

Stop for a rest, force myself to get going again.

I've walked and walked and made fuck all progress…

Don't look ahead. Just look at the ground in front of you.

Must be nearly there, surely.

What do the ruins look like, anyway?

Fuck me, it's a long way. I'm not going to make it.

Come on, Max – you have to make it. You can't just die.

One foot and then the other. On and fucking on.

Here's a bit of downhill.

God, that's so much easier.

But oh fuck now it's up again…

Don't think. Just remember some of the poor bastards and be thankful...

That was quite a whack on the head – wonder how long I was out for.

God, my head's swimming – it's like being drunk but not so much fun.

Good old Strecker, giving me his stick—

Shit, almost fell over again.

Wish everything would stop bloody moving – it's making me feel sick. Wonder how much blood I lost. And how infected it's getting now.

At least I'm out of the muddiest part – it's quite sandy up here.

Fuck – a bloody bramble. Arching over the path.

Evil fucking thing – and I'm going to have to walk under it.

Stop and peer at it more closely, try to focus.

There's a tatty pink rose at the end of the stem.

Shit – now I'm seeing things. How the fuck can there be a pink rose here?

Stare at it blankly, hoping it's real...

Because of the ruined farm – remember? Follow the Bowling Alley, go past the ruins of St André and turn right. They must have had roses in their garden.

At least it wasn't a bramble. I'll never be able to stand the sight of those things again.

Turn right.

Jesus, how much further?

I can't do it. And where are the others? There's no one else on this path.

Staying upright is getting rather difficult—

Shit, that goes down steeply, and there are rocks everywhere.

Almost go arse over tit. Knees almost give way.

Stop, look down the slope.

I'll never do it without falling – and I must have gone the wrong way – the Aid Post's on the ridge. I shouldn't have to go down.

Shit. I'll have to go back and find the right way. It's so far and I'm so fucking knackered...

I'll just sit on these stones for a bit, have a rest, then I'll go back.

Ah, that's better. And the view from up here! All the way to the north – might even be Germany in the distance.

The sun's lovely and warm, and so are the stones. I'm so fucking tired.

I'll just lie back for a bit, soak in the warmth. A rest will do me good.

It's so good to have stopped... I could just... fall asleep... now... It wouldn't... matter, would...

'Get up,' says a voice.

What?

'Sit up and then get up.'

But—

'If you fall asleep here, you'll die.'

Oh.

All right.

Such an effort to sit up. *How the fuck am I going to get down there?*

Boots and voices, coming along the path.

Thank fuck. I hope they're in better nick than me.

Two artillery privates. Uninjured.

"Boys..." God, my voice sounds so strange – cracked and hoarse and distant. "Can you help me?"

"Of course, sir!"

"It's just – the stope is sleep – I mean, the steep is – slope – er..."

A friendly grin. "The slope's steep, sir."

"That's it."

"Don't worry, sir," says the other. "We'll get you down."

They take an arm each and help me up. They feel so strong and solid.

"Going to Azannes, sir?"

"Yes. Think I – wrong way."

"We can take you as far as the bottom, sir, then we'll have to leave you. We've got to get to Division with a request for more shells."

"Why both…?"

"Battery Commander always sends two runners, sir," said the other.

Of course. That way, one might get through.

"Phone line's shot to bits again, sir."

"Ours too."

Even with their help, I can only just do it…

Here's the bottom and the wreckage of Soumazannes. Pity they can't take me all the way to the Aid Post.

"Thanks, boys. Here." Give them the last of my fags. "Sorry – no more."

"Thank you, sir."

"No, thank you."

If you hadn't come along, I'd probably still be there – or I'd have fallen down the fucking hill and broken my neck.

It's still a fucking long way. If I can just get to the Aid Post on the top…

Jesus, I'm fucked…

'Come on, Max,' says Axel. 'I'll go as far as the top with you. You'll be all right from there.'

"Thanks."

It's definitely easier with him beside me.

Start up the other side.

Fuck, it's a steep climb.

Head swimming, almost fall.

I can't do it.

'I've got you,' Axel says. 'Just keep going.'

Up to where we started from, back in February.

And how far have we got since then?

Here's the old front line, and the Aid Post.

"Thanks, Axel," I say – but he's not there.

So where is he?

The medic is giving me a curious look.

"Where – my cousin?" I ask.

"Who's that, sir?"

"Leutnant Axel Paetow – here just now."

His face changes. "Sit down here, sir. Let's have a look at you… Nasty gash, this. When did you get it?"

"Three days – I think."

He looks at my label. "Did they put this dressing on in the Fort?"

"Yes – one of the others. Medics were busy. I did his arm."

"Right… It needs cleaning out properly and stitching. Are you all right to go on to Azannes, sir?"

"Yes. Rest here?"

"Of course, sir. I won't change this now – it would just be a waste."

He ties the bandage back round my head.

"Coffee, sir?"

"Yes, please."

Something strikes me.

Axel's dead. Fell right at the beginning.

But he was with me just now.

Bang on the head, Max, that's all. Does strange things to the mind. Have a bit of a sleep and you'll feel a lot better.

'Don't do that,' Axel says, quite clearly. 'Drink your coffee and get going.'

"Was it you who told me not to fall asleep earlier?"

No reply.

Hope I didn't say that out loud.

"Thanks for coffee. I – go on."

"It's downhill from here, sir. Just take it steady – you'll be fine."

Not sure about fine… it's still a fucking long way. I can see the wrecked church tower of Azannes, below me in the distance.

It's too far.

It's downhill, Max – you can do it.

There's a dishevelled fellow shambling along the track, his ragged uniform caked with mud, blood, and filth. He's got a bandage round his head, one end dangling down to his left shoulder. From the way he's swaying, you'd think he was pissed—

Fucking hell. It's me – and here I am, above and behind me, watching me stumble along.

My head's throbbing now – I'm back. Not watching any more. Strange. Very strange.

Battered houses. Azannes. The main dressing station.

Ambulances, fellows like me, hell of a queue.

Medic standing by a table with a big bowl of water.

"Water, sir?"

"Thanks."

He hands me a tin mug.

Nectar. Hand it back for a refill, and another. My throat begins to stop sticking to itself.

"Whe…" Croak. Try again. "Where – wait?"

"Over there, sir – by the wall."

Sit at the end of the queue. Lovely warm wall. Safe. Lie down…

*

Azannes is a fucking long way from here, Max thought. *Must be the best part of eight kilometres.*

I wonder how close I was to not getting there at all.

Very strange, a lot of that day – Axel being there, and then watching myself from the outside.

Funny what a whack on the head does to the mind. And of course I had a fever by then.

But I've always felt there was more to it than that.

'There is, Max. Far more than you realise.'

Axel's voice was so clear that Max started.

Did you really help me that day?

No answer.

Does it matter? I got to Azannes, and got treated, and lived.

*

8th May 1916, Azannes

Wake with a jolt, reach for my pistol.

"It's all right, sir – it's your turn."

My turn for what? Oh, right.

The medic helps me to my feet, and takes me into the operating room. It stinks of blood and antiseptic and chloroform.

"Sit here," says the doctor.

Bandage has stuck. Try not to yell.

Doctor examines the gash.

Grit my teeth as he prods it.

"No bone damage, but it needs opening right up and cleaning out, then stitching and dressing. Buchwald, you can do that."

"Yes, sir." Buchwald turns to another man. "Kraft, can you hold Herr Leutnant's head?"

That sounds like it's going to fucking hurt.

And it does.

Jesus, does it.

Grit my teeth harder. Can't stop myself yelling.

Far from being alone in that.

Why does anyone think we should be able to stand this? Do soldiers not feel pain like other men?

"All done, sir."

The orderlies help me up—

This shell-hole's very comfortable. And why am I lying down? Where the fuck am I?

My eyelids are stuck together. Rub my eyes and open them slowly.

I'm on a straw mattress in a dim room. There are quite a few of us.

Someone is groaning.

Sit up. Room spins.

Lie down again, glad to be still.

Head's throbbing, and moving makes it worse.

Sunlight streams through the windows.

Kindly orderly gives me a bottle to piss in, and a mug of coffee, and breakfast.

Doctor comes round, picks out some fellows for transport to base hospitals – and to Germany.

Wonder if there's any chance of being sent home.

Brandenburg. The Uckermark. The villa by the lake, the water sparkling blue in the sunlight. Soft green rolling land…

Home. The most beautiful place in the world.

I've got fuck all chance of ever seeing it again.

My parents, my sisters. Frieda.

Ah, Frieda – with the beautiful eyes and the lovely arse and the gently swaying skirt.

You might as well be on the Moon, all of you.

"I'd prefer to keep you here another day or two," says the doctor. "But we need the bed, so you're going to the camp a few kilometres away. Come back in a week and we'll take the stitches out. And if you start to get a fever, come back anyway."

"Thanks."

There's a wedding ring on my right hand, shining gold amid the grime.

What the fuck is that doing there?

Some of my mind's a bit of a blur, but I'm sure I never got married.

An affair at university, quite a few girls in the park opposite the barracks, but no wife. Don't want one either...

Ah. The stretcher-bearer.

Get his bloodstained Army book and his tag out of my pocket, take the ring off my finger.

"Doctor – I took these from a stretcher-bearer when he died. Would you pass them on, please? He wanted the ring to go back to his wife."

"Yes, of course."

Hope the ring doesn't get nicked – but there's nothing I can do about that, short of delivering it by hand.

There is, thank God, a truck to take the assorted crocks to the camp.

"Thank fuck I don't have to walk any further," says another Leutnant.

After a few minutes of being jolted over the potholes, I'm not sure I agree.

"Fuck me," mutters an Oberleutnant, grimacing. He shifts his bandaged leg just as we hit another hole, and yells before he can stop himself.

"Hope it's not much further," says the Leutnant beside me.

"You and me both." My head's really throbbing, and I'm starting to feel sick.

We stop about twenty minutes later, to everyone's intense relief.

The driver lowers the back.

"Here we are, gentlemen. I'll just find someone to help you down and show you to your huts."

Someone has made a real effort to make the huts cosy. There are proper pictures on the walls, as well as the pin-ups.

I share a room with Leutnant Schwarzkopf from the Pioneers. He's got multiple cuts on his arms and legs, and dozens of stitches.

"Wire," he says. "Got blown into it."

"Shell splinter," I reply.

At least we're out of it, neither of us says.

After more sleep and a bit of a wash, I almost start to feel human again.

Almost.

The next night is full of the fighting in the ravine. Every time I close my eyes I'm there.

"Have I got a fever?" I ask Schwarzkopf in the morning. We're supposed to keep an eye on each other.

He puts his hand on my forehead.

"No. Have I?"

"No."

Just the aftermath of battle, then…

There's an officers' bathhouse. Schwarzkopf and I wander along there together.

Hot water. Soap. Shave.

Schwarzkopf stands in the concrete tub. I help him to wash round his bandages, and then to dry off and get dressed.

I sit in the bath and he washes my hair, carefully avoiding the left side of my head.

Lie back and soak.

Heaven.

Lovely fresh smell of soap, and not the battlefield.

A clean uniform, and the temporary absence of lice.

And no fighting.

Doesn't take much to make me happy these days.

"Terrible about Fort Douaumont," says Leutnant Schröder, a couple of days later. He's a recent arrival, with a broken wrist.

"What – have the Frenchies taken it back?" asks Oberleutnant Lindner.

"No, sir – I meant the explosion."

We all stare at him.

"We were in reserve in the Hassoule Ravine," Schröder says, "and men came pouring down the hill, blackened faces, singed all over, completely terrified. None of them made any sense, just kept babbling 'Douaumont – terrible' over and over. Then we got some sense out of one of the officers – said there'd been a huge explosion. They sent us up to the Fort and the mess was unbelievable – they reckon there are hundreds of dead."

"Jesus," says Schwarzkopf, echoed by Lindner and me.

"When was that?" I ask.

"Early hours of the 8th," he replies.

Think for a moment… I left at about 11pm on the 7th.

Another close shave.

Wonder how many lives front-line soldiers have. Hope it's more than nine.

"How did it happen?" asks Lindner.

"They don't know for sure, sir – but there was a Pioneer depot full of grenades and they went off—"

"Bloody hell."

"And then there was a massive bang – there was a dump of French heavy shells nearby, and they all went up."

"Jesus fucking Christ," says Lindner.

"Says a lot for the Fort that it didn't collapse," says Schwarzkopf.

"It did go up and down in the shelling," I say. Then I have a thought. "Which regiments?"

Schröder looks at me. "Nearly all Brandenburg, I'm afraid. The 24th, and the 12th Grenadiers for a start."

Shit. What a fucking stupid way to die.

That young officer in the 12th Grenadiers, the kind fellow in the barracks who fetched me food... Hope he's alive.

What for, Max? To die miserably in some fucking hole in the mud? If he got blown up in the Fort then at least it might have been quick.

Nothing you can do about it, anyway – just be thankful you left before it happened.

And make the most of this temporary reprieve...

The huts form a courtyard, and it's warm and sunny. Sit with a mug of coffee, half listening to the distant thunder and the conversation of the others.

The thunder rises to a crescendo. The ground shakes and the windows rattle even more.

We exchange glances.

Someone else is deep in the shit.

Hope it's not my boys. I should be there with them.

But I'm half-asleep in the warm sunshine, too lethargic even to finish my coffee. I'd be fuck all use to anyone, and I know it, but all the same...

"It's those fucking 7.5s that get me," says Leutnant Meisner.

"Fire far too bloody fast," Schwarzkopf agrees.

"And they've got far too many of them," adds Oberleutnant Pallenberg.

"Think they did get me," I say wryly.

At least we're here and not there, runs unspoken through the group.

Followed by, *we've earned a rest.*

And indeed we have – but all of us know we're not where we belong.

I hope Kropp's doing a good job... hope my boys aren't getting slaughtered...

Almost spill my coffee.

The conversation dies away. We're all dozing.

Finish my coffee, slide down further in my chair.

Close my eyes.

Might as well enjoy the rest – I'll be fighting again far too bloody soon.

And that'll be the end of me.

XXIII

Max ran a finger along the scar on the left side of his head. It was over ten centimetres long, and the hair had never really grown back.

By the time I'd recovered from this, the Seventh was in reserve again – what was left of it.

Hutten was back in temporary command of his Platoon. Leutnant Vossberg was missing.

That was one of the worst things – men disappeared and were never heard of again, and no one knew what had happened to them. Sometimes we guessed they'd been blown to fragments, or had fallen wounded into the bottom of a hole and died there.

But there were always stories of the enemy not taking prisoners, or of men being taken prisoner and not making it to the rear.

And the French medical service was notoriously awful – and of course everyone cares for their own men first, and prisoners second. That's only human nature, and you need your own fellows fit to fight again.

Max sighed. *Terrible for the families, not knowing whether the man was dead or alive, and hoping for evermore that he'd turn up.*

When I rejoined the Company, it was almost unrecognisable again. We'd been reinforced with yet more green boys straight from the Fatherland.

And the heaviest blow of all was that Doctor Meyer was dead, shot on the day of the explosion in the Fort.

If he'd been a bit less brave, he might have survived, and I've always felt that he died for us…

Max lit another fag, and looked around him at the cratered surface of the Fort.

So much blood this place cost. And for what? Yes, the Frenchies can boast that they saw us off, but really all they did was retake most of the ground we'd taken from them.

Was that really a victory worth all those dead Frenchmen?

The only victor here was Death.

He got up, and made his way back down to the road.

Time to leave here and go down to the Caillette Wood.

That was even worse than the Ravine.

We were just about to launch our own offensive, when the Frenchies decided they really did want their Fort back.

And they didn't ask nicely. Oh, no.

And so we had to traipse back through the fucking Zig-Zag Trench and the Casemate Ravine into the Caillette Wood, just below the Fort.

That was late May. The bastards had managed to get onto the top of the Fort and the fighting was the worst I've ever known – which is saying something, given the competition.

The Wood was a wilderness of shattered trunks and shell-holes, ruled over by Death.

*

23rd May 1916, Caillette Wood

Frenchies in the next hole, just a couple of metres away.

Throw grenades in, duck down, BANG BANG, showers of earth, fragments of metal.

Screams.

Scrabble out of our hole, boots slipping, leap into their hole.

Bludgeon, stab, shoot, fast as we can.

Frenchies all down and staying down. Take stock. Bettermann slight wound but he can fight, rest all right.

Ullmann patches Bettermann up, turns to me.

"Let's go for the next hole, sir," he says.

"You're on."

Repeat.

"How many grenades have we got?" I ask.

Heavy shell fifty metres away.

Deafening thunder. Fountain of earth, hot shards, fragments of fresh and rotten flesh, bones, shower of blood.

God, this business is disgusting. Someone should show the politicians the slaughterhouse they've created.

Screams.

"MEDICS!"

Too far away for us to help.

Another heavy behind us. Same result.

Let's hope the fucking 7.5s don't start up.

They do.

Press into the earth in the bottom of the hole.

Shit, those fucking things fire fast.

Keep missing, just keep missing. If we get a direct hit we're all fucking dead—

Taint in the smoke.

Gas.

"GAS, BOYS!"

Get my mask on – look round to check on the others—

Grenades—

Steel helmets—

"Frenchies are coming!"

Can't even hear myself.

"FRENCHIES!"

Grab Ullmann and Lorenz, shake them, point to the edge of the hole. In a flash they're there, ready.

Good blokes.

We're all fucking ready—

Yelling masked faces, knives clubs rifle butts—

Dachwitz goes down beside me.

Only seven of us left, five Frenchies, Bettermann stabs, I shoot point-blank, the rest scarper.

The 7.5's haven't let up, and we barely draw breath before the bastards attack again.

My eyepieces are steaming up and I can hardly see.

Dachwitz starts screaming, "Sir! SIR! HELP ME!" and he doesn't fucking stop.

I can't help him. The fucking Frenchies are on three sides of the hole.

"SIR! HELP ME!"

He writhes in agony, clutches at my leg.

"SIR! HELP ME!"

Over and bloody over.

"*SHUT IT!*"

Frenchies jump in. Club stab shoot—

No more attacking masked faces under steel helmets. Thank fuck.

Shelling dies down a little.

"Be ready, boys!"

Frenchies attack yet again. Shoot the officer, the rest turn and run back.

God knows where they find the courage to keep attacking. The ground's so covered with their casualties that there's almost nowhere to put their feet.

Their wounded cry out, but no one can go to help them.

The sun has moved across the sky.

The smoke and gas look thinner, though it's hard to tell. Lift my mask and take a cautious sniff.

Stink of explosive, blood, shit and decay but nothing else.

Take our masks off and breathe freely – as freely as you can in that miasma.

Heave the dead Frenchies out of the hole.

Take stock.

There are five of us. Bettermann's head is smashed in.

"How many grenades have we got?"

We count. Fifteen.

"Herbeck – get over to Company. Bring as many grenades as you can carry and get them to send more."

Water would be good as well, but there's not much chance of that. And more blokes, but we won't get those either.

Now at last I can have a look at Dachwitz – at least he went quiet.

He went quiet because he's dead.

God save me, I told him to shut up. And that was the last thing he heard from me. After the wood, the Turret, Vaux, the Ravine…

He was one of the best.

What the fuck else could I do? Get everyone else killed as well?

*

Max wandered through the maze of craters.

It's impossible to tell now where we were. It all looks the same.

The Frenchies meant it, all right. They attacked again and again, day and night, and their fucking artillery never stopped. Every calibre imaginable, high explosive, shrapnel, gas…

It was all we could do to hold them, never mind trying to advance.

*

24th May 1916, Caillette Wood

What…?

I'm lying in the bottom of the hole. Henke and Stadler are looking down at me with concern, turning to relief.

Why...?

Sit up, lean against the side of the hole. Dazed and rather groggy.

"You had us worried there, sir."

I can't move my right arm – oh. There's a shell splinter sticking out of the front of my shoulder. Not much blood, though – of mine, that is. So far as I can tell.

"Let me have a look, sir."

Henke starts trying to pull my tunic off and I almost yell out loud.

"Just rip the sleeve out!" My voice is harsh with pain.

He gets his hands into the rip in the cloth, and pulls tunic and shirt sleeves off together.

Grit my teeth, manage not to yell. God knows how.

There's a small, jagged piece of steel embedded in my flesh, near the joint.

Jesus, I was lucky. If that had been a bit bigger it would have taken my arm off, and I'd be bleeding to death.

Stadler is looking at it thoughtfully. There isn't time to think.

Fish one of my field dressings out of my pocket and hand it to him.

"Leave it in. Just bandage round it."

With a bit of luck, it'll keep the blood in and the Verdun muck out.

Bite back a yell as he snags the splinter. It's a couple of minutes before I can speak.

"Thanks... What's the situation?"

"They tried to take the hole, sir, but we changed their minds."

"Well done. How long was I out?"

"Only about a minute, sir."

Thank fuck for that.

"We thought you'd had it, sir."

"'Fraid you're stuck with me a bit longer!"

But only a bit.

My right arm is almost useless. I can't throw a grenade, or use a club or a knife. I can't put a rifle to my shoulder. I can probably fire my pistol.

I'm in the front line in the worst battle there's ever been, and I can't fight.

I can organise the defence, and if we attack I can lead – but that will be the last thing I ever do.

The next time they attack, I'm dead.

It's today, then.

I shan't see night fall. I shan't see the Uckermark again, or my family, or the lovely Frieda.

It's over.

Fear turns into calm finality.

It will be a good soldier's death.

For Brandenburg, for Prussia.

*

Strange how the fear goes when you know you're dead, Max thought.

I wrote myself off completely that day – and I've always had the feeling that part of me stayed written off, that I've never really managed to get back from the other side.

There's always a shadow, a feeling of being not quite connected.

Sometimes even when I'm with Frieda. And then I see her looking at me with that gentle concern in her eyes, and I have no way of explaining.

What was it that fellow wrote in the book about Douaumont? '…the dull memory of some place that may be found between death and life, or beyond both…'

Definitely beyond both. That place has nothing to do with either life or death, but with something much bigger and infinitely stranger.

*

24th May 1916, Caillette Wood

Abandon all hope ye who enter here, Scheumann said to me. And now I have.
    Wonder what happens.
    I'd like it to be quick.
    The French bombardment steps itself up again.
    Press into the earth in blind endurance.
    Can't breathe. Can't think or hear.
    There is only blinding thunder and obscene rain.
    Shelling stops.
    We're ready.
    Grenade. Stadler throws it back out again.
    Bearded Frenchmen, yelling and leaping out of their hole towards us.
    The boys open fire.
    I have a knife in my left hand and my pistol in my right.
    I will not die easy.
    Frenchies leap in—
    Tiemann pushes in front of me, collapses.
    Knife a Frenchie awkwardly. He climbs back out and staggers away.
    Stadler and Henke club stab—
    Brutal fighting all around but I'm detached. It's as if I were already dead.
    Frenchie raises his club, Stadler knifes him.
    Rest flee.

We are again in sole possession of our shell-hole.

Our comrades on either side have also seen the bastards off, for now, anyway.

Tiemann is lying in the bottom of the hole, soaked in blood. He took the knife for me.

What the fuck did he do that for? Jesus.

"Stadler, can you patch him up?"

"Course. Can you hold him, sir?"

Get my left arm round Tiemann's shoulders. Stadler rips his tunic open.

Fuck – it went in deep. Blood pours over Stadler's hands. Looks like Tiemann's lost quite a lot already.

I should be grateful. But I don't want anyone to die for me – especially not when he's under my command.

"What the fuck did you do that for?"

Tiemann looks up at me. "You carried me…"

I carried you so you would live, not for you to take a knife for me.

There's no point saying it.

He's only delayed the inevitable.

The Frenchies attack again, but someone has got a machine gun into position and it blasts the crap out of them.

Stadler and Henke throw grenades, but we don't have many left. Herbeck didn't come back. We don't have much ammunition left, either.

There's no way of getting anything. We are all cut off in our shell-holes.

The thirst is appalling. My throat is so stuck together I can barely speak.

Slowly the shadows get longer. There are only a handful of us left in the line of holes.

If the Frenchies really go for it, they'll have us all.

But they don't.

Their casualties are horrible – the ground is covered in pale blue, and the groans and cries for help are unceasing.

Tiemann is chalk white, barely conscious, and in obvious pain. There's nothing we can do for him.

We don't have any water and the sun is still hot.

The suffering all around is hideous. There's no point anyone calling for the medics – they can't leave their shell-holes either.

This appalling wasteland of death and agony is not where I imagined I would die.

I just want it to be quick. A direct hit would be good.

I don't mind being blown to pieces, but I don't want to suffer for hours like poor little Jahnke or those poor bastards in the wood at the beginning.

Don't think about them, Max – not now. It's far too late.

The sun sinks below the horizon and twilight creeps from the east. The explosions and bursts of machine gun fire are much brighter.

Maybe I have a chance…

Don't start to think like that. It's easier not to hope.

The bombardment of the Fort rises to deafening pitch as the French send over heavies. It's joined by intense machine gun fire, followed by grenades.

Forget it, Max. The bastards want their Fort back and you're in the way.

My shoulder is throbbing evilly.

The buggers attack again.

This time, I have a club in my left hand and my knife in my right, with my right elbow jammed into my side.

The pain has gone, wiped out by adrenaline as we repel them.

Almost collapse with relief, but the same time I'd like to get it over with. I'm fed up with waiting to die.

The long May twilight lingers.

I always loved this time of year – sitting watching the light change on the lake, listening to the birdsong.

It's a good time to go. I'll be back home soon and there'll be no more of this shit. Just peace and stillness…

Dusk creeps across the wrecked wood.

The French seem as exhausted as we are. They've left us alone for over an hour…

It's quite dark now. Dark enough to move.

Maybe, just maybe, I might get out of here…

"Henke."

"Sir."

"I'm leaving you in command."

"Yes, sir."

Go together round our 'positions'. The boys are in good spirits, but they are too few and they're short of everything.

Henke and I shake hands, possibly for ever.

Where the fuck is the Company Command Post?

Stumble between the shell-holes and shattered trees.

Hope the Frenchie snipers are asleep…

Strecker is as filthy as the rest of us, his face lined with fatigue.

"Sir."

"Ah, Schelling – caught it again, I see."

Hands me his hip flask, bless him.

"Thank you, sir."

Take a swig of schnapps, very awkwardly, and hand it back.

Ah, that's good.

"I've left Henke in command, sir. I'm very sorry, but my right arm's fucked."

He nods. Give him my report. He pulls a slight face.

"You go back. I'll see you once we're relieved."

"Sir."

Shake hands, again with that feeling of likely finality.

Go to the medics.

There is no kind Doctor Meyer, caring for the wounded in that calm way of his. That's one of the worst losses of all, and everyone feels it. Schlenk and Tannwitz are doing their best, but it's not the same.

"Can you pick up Musketier Tiemann? He's been knifed in the stomach."

"Yes, sir, soon as we can," says Schlenk. "Let's have a look at you, sir... That's well embedded."

And it's fucking well throbbing now, especially with you prodding it.

Fuck me, that hurts. Enough to make me feel sick.

He writes out the label, tears off both red strips and ties it through my buttonhole.

Tannwitz is giving one of the stretcher cases a drink of water. My throat is so dry I can hardly swallow, but I'll have to manage.

'I'll see you once we're relieved.' Two huge assumptions there, Strecker.

Hope Tiemann makes it...

The Fort is still impersonating a volcano, fire spewing from its top, the earth shaking as heavy after heavy crashes in. God help the poor bastards who are fighting up there.

I'll have to go east, back across that accursed fucking forward slope, then over Hardaumont and down to Bezonvaux.

Another fucking long trudge – but I don't feel as crap as last time. Maybe, just maybe...

*

Max gazed unseeing at the wreckage of the Caillette Wood.

Tiemann. I've always felt so bad about Tiemann.

He died. Too weak to stand being jolted over the craters. The stretcher-bearers put him down when they realised, and went back for another man.

He must lie somewhere between here and Hardaumont. No doubt his body got broken up in the incessant shelling. Maybe some of his bones are in the Ossuary.

He gave me my life, and my sons theirs, and I am forever in his debt.

Max got up to walk back up the hill towards the Fort, the dead all around him.

The only way I can honour what Tiemann did for me is to help the Archive to give a true account of what my brothers did, and of their magnificent courage.

And of the equal courage of the French, who attacked again and again, even though the ground was covered with their comrades, and they knew the same would happen to them.

The world must not forget what happened here.

God forbid that it should ever happen again.

That thought stopped him.

In the marketplace back home is the memorial to the fallen of 1870, with names from top to bottom on all four sides. The casualties here alone dwarf those from that war. Never mind all the millions who fell in the other battles, or in the day-to-day attrition of the trenches.

God forbid that my sons should ever have to do what I did. I would die a thousand times if it would prevent them having to fight.

He shook himself and carried on up the hill.

XIV

I won't retrace the route I took back through the Zig-Zag Trench and on to Bezonvaux, Max thought. *I've already been that way. I'll just walk from the Fort down to the Ossuary and ride back into town.*

That was a walk I'd rather forget, anyway.

*

24th May 1916, Caillette Wood

I might be out of the front line, but there's nothing to say I'll make it back.

I have to go through the Casemate Ravine into the Zig-Zag Trench, under shell and machine gun fire, then up to Hardaumont through the barrage.

Plus there are the snipers.

I never shot someone who'd been hit and was going back, but I knew plenty of fellows who didn't give a shit, and you could argue that they were right. Shoot the fellow and he won't heal up and come back...

If I'm not through the barrage before dawn, I'll be stuffed – but the night is short, and of course the boys going up have priority, as they should have. They and the supplies they carry are vital. Max Schelling getting back is not.

I lose another life or two getting through the Casemate Ravine.

The shells slam in, over and over. Hit the ground over and over, try not to land on my shoulder.

Here's the Zig-Zag Trench, and a carrying party coming the other way.

The Fort Vaux ridge opposite is incandescent with fury. *How the fuck can they have so many shells?*

Scream of shell, louder than the rest. Listen for a moment – throw myself into the nearest hole.

Blinding deafening crash rain of earth shards of metal.

And a leg. Bounces off my back and lands in front of me.

Screams.

"MEDICS!"

Raise myself slightly. There's half a rib cage, black and stinking, just where my head was.

This place is enough to drive any man insane.

The fellow is still screaming. Struggle to my feet. Luckily they don't need my help.

Carry on beside the trench – it's chock full now, and jammed solid by the casualties.

Everyone wants to get out of here.

Cacophony of shouting.

"CLEAR THE FUCKING WAY!"

"OUR MATE'S BEEN HIT!"

"GET HIM OUT OF THE FUCKING TRENCH!"

"*GET MOVING YOU STUPID CUNTS!!*"

Turn round and head back to the blockage.

I do not want to linger here…

Nor does anyone else, and they're all fucking stuck.

Stop by the casualties. Shake the nearest man's arm, point.

"*Get them out of the trench. And the rest of you.*"

"But—"

"MOVE IT."

In the flashes of light, the man's eyes meet mine. His expression changes.

God knows what I look like.

"Come on," he says to the others. "Do what Herr Leutnant said."

A few minutes later, the carrying parties and reinforcements start moving again.

"Thanks," says a Leutnant on his way up.

"No problem."

The French 7.5s start up. Dive into another fucking hole full of stinking filth. Better than being blown to fragments.

I hate those fucking things. Twenty shells a minute is just fucking rude.

More screams, shouts of "Medics!"

Get up, move on.

Have to get through the barrage…

"GAS!"

Fumble one-handed with my mask.

The men moving up must be new – they're slow, so slow to get their masks on.

Their Sergeant is screaming at them, so loud I can hear him in spite of his mask and the racket.

Grab one of the men, shake him, point to my mask, he gets his out, starts to put it on – grab another and shake him…

They trudge away from me – lose sight of them in the clouds of smoke and gas.

Keep going, Max, for fuck's sake! Don't stand there looking back! Get up the fucking hill!

Ahead of me is the barrage. The very Earth erupts in flaming smoking thunder, as far as I can see to left and right.

There's no alternative to going through, and no point pondering my chances.

Run like fuck into the inferno.

Blinding dazzling deafening smoke hot whirlwind metal fragments earth rotten flesh—

Run boots slipping stumbling gasping lungs burning—

Suddenly the shellfire is less intense.

The air looks clearer and I have a cautious sniff, then take my mask off with immense relief. The burning in my lungs eases.

Exertion, not gas. Thank fuck.

Somehow I've made it through the barrage, and here's the top of the hill.

Hardaumont.

The ruins of the strongpoints.

Middle was our rendezvous back in March, when what was left of us came up out of Vaux – but it's shelled to pieces now.

Its remains and the trenches give some cover, anyway...

Some. I'm on the crest of the ridge and it's horribly exposed.

Turn north towards the Bezonvaux strongpoint. At last, the ground starts to slope down.

Sit down. Light a fag. Nowhere near safe yet, but there's a chance.

Nowhere's safe in this poxy fucking place.

There's a stream of casualties heading for Bezonvaux. *Just like in March when I carried poor Tiemann. Hope he makes it, but that looked bad...*

In a curious reversal of the last time I walked back out, there's a fellow with a bandaged head who's barely staying upright.

"Need any help?"

"Thanks, mate."

My epaulettes are covered in muck and it's dark. 'Mate' and 'du' are fine for now.

Hold him up with my left arm and we stumble along together, trying not to fall into the craters.

"Sorry, mate," he says. "Need to stop for a bit."

"No problem. I had my head cut open a couple of weeks back."

"They send you home?" Hope in his voice.

"'Fraid not. But it was only a cut."

"Oh, well…"

Give him a fag and we carry on. He gets steadily heavier, and we have to keep stopping.

There's a massive queue of wounded at the Bezonvaux strongpoint. The waiting shelter is crammed full. Men are lying in the courtyard and beside the track.

"Sorry, sir," one of the medics says to me. "We're asking all the lightly wounded to go down to the village. There's a dressing station in the Chateau."

I can make it, but my companion's practically out on his feet.

"Can you put this fellow in the queue here?" I croak, my throat like dust.

The medic looks at the man.

"Yes, sir – that would be best."

Hand him over.

"Cheers, mate," he slurs.

"Any chance of a drink?" I ask.

"Yes, sir – there's water over there."

My shoulder's really throbbing now, and the splinter sends a sharp stab through me each time I move my arm.

A mug of water and another fag get the blood trudging round my veins. The pain's sickening as I set off again, but it's not much further and it's all downhill.

The early dawn light competes with the bombardment. At least I'm on the reverse slope now.

I never thought I'd get this far…

Down to the village, past the ruined houses in the twilight, along the gurgling stream.

The water must be filthy, but everyone drinks it. There's nothing else.

"Where's the Chateau?"

"At the end of the village, sir – just keep going."

And there it is, a bit battered but mostly intact.

There's a fucking long queue of casualties here as well.

Sit down to wait—

Wake with a yell. Leap to my feet.

"It's all right, sir, it's all right. You're next for the doctor."

Oh, right. Just like last time.

The orderlies must get this all the time – blokes jumping out of their skins when they wake them.

Down into the cellar.

Stink of blood and disinfectant. Cries of pain.

The doctor's apron is covered in blood. An orderly cuts the field dressing off me, and the doctor peers at the splinter.

"Easier to get at this if you lie down," he says. "Tunic and shirt off."

Drop the stinking, lousy rags on the ground, lie on the table.

"Hm." The doctor peers again, picks something up.

Forceps bright in the light—

Vicious stab of pain as they grip the splinter.

And slip. And grip again.

YELL. AND LOUDER.

Jesus fucking Christ.

"Want to keep it?"

Can't speak.

Iodine. Stitches.

Grit teeth harder. Try not to yell again. Fail.

"All done. Sit up."

Table spins. Throw up over my trousers.

Someone holds me up, lifts my right arm out to the side.

Table spins again.

My shoulder's bandaged and my arm's in a sling.

"This way, sir."

Lean on the orderly, trying not to be sick again as he takes me out of the room and up the stairs.

"Sit down here, sir."

Cool shade and a wall against my back.

He hands me my tunic and shirt, comes back after a few minutes with a water bottle and a mug of coffee, strong and sweet and steaming.

Coffee.

Up in the wood, I'd have sold my soul for coffee. Hope it stays down now. My shoulder is horribly painful, and I still feel sick.

Empty the water bottle, realise how desperately thirsty I am.
The boys in the front line have no water…

Take a cautious sip of coffee, lean back against the wall, and look round.

There's quite a group of us in this makeshift shelter. Everyone looks the same, pale and drawn and lined. Everyone is bandaged, stark white against the filth, red where the blood seeps through.

*

Max reached the Fort, and started down the slope towards the Ossuary.

'Don't go. Stay with us.'

He stopped. "I have a wife and two small sons. I have to go back to them."

'You belong with us.'

"I shall come back. I promise. Once we've told your story."

But I do belong with them, he thought as he walked on, *and nothing can ever change that.*

I should have died here.

*

25th May 1916, Bezonvaux

Start shivering with reaction.

"Want to put those on?" A Leutnant beside me, his head bandaged, blood caked down his unshaven face, wrapped in a blanket.

He helps me as far into my rags as the sling allows, then moves closer and puts his blanket over both of us. Feel warmth start to creep into me.

Nice bloke. "Thanks."

I offer him a fag, take one myself, and he lights them both.

No one says much. We're all exhausted – and what is there to say?

An orderly comes in with a list.

"Herr Major Schalk, Herr Hauptmann von Pritzkow, Herr Oberleutnant Schmidt, Herr Oberleutnant Zierdt, Herr Leutnant Finkel, Herr Leutnant Knospe. This way to the transport, please, gentlemen."

The Leutnant gets out of the blanket and shakes my left hand. "Good luck."

"And you."

He gets up with some difficulty. One of the others takes his arm, and they help each other out.

God, I'm fucked. But I got out. I was certain that was my last day, and here I am.

Strange. It feels so strange, as if I have to get used to being alive after all.

Maybe I shouldn't be. Maybe I'm supposed to be dead.

Tiemann took that knife for me…

Hope he makes it.

My head is resting on someone's shoulder. Sleep comes and goes.

The shoulder is still there.

Open my eyes.

A grubby epaulette. One star, two.

And I'm dribbling.

Shit.

Push myself upright.

"I do apologise, sir."

"No need." The Captain's voice is weary and strained.

Won't mention the dribble. You can't see it, anyway.

He shifts with an effort, pulls his blanket up to his chin, closes his eyes.

More men leave, more arrive.

Share my blanket again – the other fellow gives me a grateful look, too fucked to speak.

An orderly brings us stew. Standard Army fodder, but it's bloody wonderful.

The boys in the front line haven't seen hot food for days.

I'll feel all right after a good night's sleep. Then I can help – there must be something I can do.

Scream of shell, explosion—

"How many grenades have we got?"

"Three, sir."

Another shell—

Wake with a shout.

And they're running out of grenades and ammunition.

"Herr Hauptmann von Dorndorf, Herr Oberleutnant Necker, Herr Leutnant Kettner, Herr Leutnant Schelling – this way for the train, please, gentlemen."

My legs don't want to work. The Hauptmann helps me to my feet, grimaces before he can stop himself.

"Thank you, sir." *And for letting me use your shoulder as a pillow…*

"Not at all."

Wobble towards the little train.

Reach the orderly. "Where does the train go?"

"Back to the rear area, sir, near Loison."

If I go there, I'll just be sitting in the sun. Regimental HQ is here, isn't it?

"Get in, please, sir."

"I'd rather stay here."

He looks at me as if I've got two heads, and I don't blame him.

"We're just a dressing station, sir," he says very doubtfully.

"Yes, I know…"

I'm in their system.

"Can I see one of the doctors?"

Now he really does think I've lost my marbles.

Of course, I have to wait – they must be operating non-stop.

After an hour or so, a doctor appears and the orderly points to me.

It's the doctor who took the splinter out of my shoulder. He looks at me, surprised.

"What can I do for you?"

"It's pretty bad in the front line – I want to report to my Regiment and – there must be some way I can help."

"I'd say you've earned a rest."

"It's bad enough that I've left them. I can't just sit in the sun."

"No. I see… Blum! Take Herr Leutnant to his Regimental Command Post."

"Yes, sir."

"I'll send them the paperwork."

"Thank you, Doctor."

It isn't far, thank God.

The Orderly Officer is clean-shaven and smartly turned out. He looks up from his papers at the ragged, filthy apparition standing before him.

The front line has just walked – or rather stumbled – into his office, bringing its appalling stench with it.

But his nose doesn't wrinkle.

"Have a seat."

He opens a drawer, pulls out a bottle and an enamel mug, and hands me a generous brandy.

God, that's good. "Thanks."

"Don't mention it. What can I do for you?"

He opened and poured with his left hand.

His right is in a leather glove, which looks rather floppy.

I explain.

He nods.

"You can help organise carrying parties, act as a guide if you feel up to that. We'd be grateful."

He picks up a piece of paper, and then his pen, still with his left hand.

"You'll need a billet – and where's your luggage?"

"Somewhere in the rear."

"I'll get someone to find it."

He writes, awkwardly, and hands me the sheet.

"There should be a bed for you here. I'll get a message to Hauptmann Gneist."

"Thank you."

His writing is spidery and takes me a moment to read.

He smiles, and pulls the glove off his right hand. It's mangled and misshapen, all the fingers gone except two stumps. I can't tell which fingers they were.

"I wanted to be useful as well."

I feel a ghost of a smile cross my face.

"Get as much sleep as you need and report when you're ready."

We shake left hands, and I wobble out into the sunlight.

The billet is comfortable – a straw mattress on an old iron bedstead in a ruined house, with a rather grubby blanket.

I'm so fucked I could sleep in a nettle patch and not notice. And I have no right to call the blanket grubby.

When I surface, my luggage is beside my bed, and there's a bowl of hot water.

Get out of my filthy rags with some difficulty. My right shoulder has stiffened up and I can barely move my arm – plus it fucking hurts.

Wash and shave left-handed.

Cut myself a couple of times and swear, then laugh.

Such a fuss over a small cut or two.

Underpants, socks, shirt – ah. That's really awkward.

Get my right arm in but can't pull the shirt over the bandage.

Give up and put a vest on instead – and that takes a bit of doing. Sit for a minute to let the pain subside.

Can't get my tunic over the bandage either. Put my left arm into the sleeve, put my right arm back in the sling, and pull the right side of the tunic over my shoulder, where it doesn't want to stay.

Well, I'm mostly dressed. Hope some stuffy major doesn't give me a bollocking.

A polite cough.

"Can I help you, sir? Oh. You've managed."

"Yes, thanks – and you are?"

"Aue, sir. Leutnant Massow sent me to look after you."

Who the fuck is Massow – oh, maybe he's the Orderly Officer.

"Would you like coffee, sir? Dinner is at seven in the Officers' Mess."

"Yes, please." Hesitate. "Would it be possible to eat here?"

"Leutnant Massow said to tell you they're expecting you."

I want to get to work – but I'll work better once I'm refuelled.

The Officers' Mess is what you'd expect – a salvaged table and assorted chairs in a half-wrecked cottage.

"Feel a bit more human now?" asks the Orderly Officer with a grin.

"Yes, thanks."

"These gentlemen are Hauptmann Steinhaus, Third Battalion Commander, and Leutnant Watzdorf, Regimental Adjutant. I'm Massow, by the way. The Colonel won't be joining us – gone to Brigade."

Axel was our Battalion Adjutant... So long ago, now, and yet it's only three months.

Thank God Jagenow's not here to see me looking so untidy.

Hauptmann Steinhaus looks at me kindly. He reminds me of my Uncle Moritz.

"I do apologise for not being properly dressed, sir."

"Good God, man – don't worry about that! All credit to you for being here. You'd have every right to go back and have a good rest. Now, are you quite sure you feel up to it?"

It's rather embarrassing, but I'm saved by the arrival of dinner.

Massow's food and mine has been neatly cut up. *That's thoughtful of someone.*

"Cook takes care of me," he says with a smile. "And I took the liberty of telling him that we had another crock for dinner."

"Thanks."

Manage to eat without spilling it down myself, and start to feel better. A couple of glasses of red wine set me up nicely.

Massow and Watzdorf take me back to the light railway.

"This is where the supplies come in…"

The sun is sinking behind the hill, and men are gathering to collect their loads.

Everything imaginable has to be carried up over Hardaumont, through the Zig-Zag Trench and on to the Caillette Wood. Under fire most of the way.

We all know that a lot of it won't get there, and that many of the men won't make it back. It's almost as dangerous as being in the front line.

Boxes of grenades, anyone? Fuses? Ammunition?

Mortar shells? Blocks of explosives?

Fancy carrying those through the barrage?

Someone has to.

Water. Coffee. Iron rations.

Everything loaded onto men's backs as night falls.

The human packhorses trudge off towards the violence of the barrage, and the next lot load up.

I watch them go – but there isn't time to stare.

The work is unceasing. It's almost midnight.

"Right," says Watzdorf. "The next lot's for the Seventh."

"I can act as guide," I say.

"You sure?"

No. I don't feel too good – but I know how desperate the need is. "Yes."

XXV

What in God's name possessed me? Max thought. *I'd been fucking lucky to get out of there alive, and I let myself in for going twice more through the barrage and along the fucking Zig-Zag Trench.*

And my shoulder screamed at me every time I moved my arm. Not that I admitted that to anyone.

*

26th May 1916, Bezonvaux

Why the fuck am I doing this?

I know EXACTLY what it's going to be like.

So do the boys from the Eleventh. This is their third night of carrying supplies, and none of them looks enthusiastic. *Wonder how many they've lost so far.*

Leutnant Hoffmann, one of their Platoon Commanders, gives me a very straight look.

"I won't get in the way," I promise.

"That's not it. You know we won't be able to help you, if you run out of steam."

"Yes, I do – it's just position reports don't always seem to get through."

He laughs. "Don't I know it! Last time we were in the line, we missed out on a load of stuff. Never did find out where it ended up… Well, you come at your own risk."

"That's fine. I don't know what I can carry—"

"You're not carrying anything. Just show us where your boys are."

And that's final, he doesn't need to add.

It's nearly one in the morning before we set out. We want to be back through the barrage before first light – and that's going to be quite a task.

Reach the top of the Hardaumont Ridge. I'm leading with their Feldwebel Schwarz. Ahead, the barrage is bursting with undiminished rage.

And this time I can't run through it, and right behind me are men with boxes of ammunition and explosives.

Never did like being in a carrying party.

Make it through without anyone being blown sky-high. Lose a few dead and injured.

And on into the fucking Zig-Zag Trench.

I shall be very happy if I never come this way again – shut up, Max! The God of War might grant your wish...

This time we have right of way, and those coming back have to move aside.

Which is pretty bad when the poor bastards are injured – but then I've been on the other side of that equation twice within a month.

Shudder at the memory of that long slog up the Bowling Alley, when I nearly didn't make it.

Hope I make it back tonight.

The shelling is horrific.

Massive explosion some way behind me, blast knocks me over, manage not to land on my shoulder.

Schwartz and I get to our feet.

Turn.

There's a huge smoking crater with the usual hideous debris around it.

One of the crates of grenades must have taken a direct hit.

The unhurt pick themselves and their burdens up and we trudge on, leaving the medics to deal with the mess.

Suddenly the wasteland of craters littered with broken bodies and equipment is also studded with shattered tree stumps. We've reached the Caillette Wood.

The Company's here somewhere – but it's all the same vision of Hell, half-lit in the flashing smoke.

"Seventh?"

"No, sir… No, sir…"

This looks more like it…

There's Henke.

"Henke!"

"Sir! What – why…?"

"Where's Oberleutnant Strecker?"

"Nehring! Take Herr Leutnant to Company."

"Right away, Sarge."

Nehring looks at me as if I'm some kind of apparition.

"This way, sir."

And there, sitting in a shell-hole, is Strecker. Calmly smoking his pipe, as if he were sitting by the fire at home.

"Good morning, sir."

He stares at me. "Schelling, what the bloody hell are you doing here?"

"I wanted to make sure you got everything, sir – we've brought water and coffee, and iron rations, and grenades and ammunition."

For the first time ever, I see emotion in his face. He gets up and takes my left hand in both of his, squeezes so hard I almost wince.

"Good job. Bloody good job. Well done."

He hands me his hip flask. I take a sip.

"Take a decent swallow," he says.

"Thank you, sir."

The spirit settles inside me with a warm glow.

That'll help me get back…

Hand over the supplies – or most of them, anyway.

Hutten and Kropp thank me so profusely it's embarrassing.

"You'd do the same," I tell them.

"*Schelling! We're leaving!*"

"See you later," I say as nonchalantly as I can.

I hope I do.

The journey back is a race against the sun, and now we have to give way to those going up.

We're not going to make it.

We're in – or rather beside – the Zig-Zag Trench. The sky overhead is luminous violet and there's an unwelcome gleam of amber in the east.

"Go straight up to Hardaumont," Schwartz orders.

Hoffmann must have said the same thing, because the slope is covered in grey forms scrambling upwards.

And of course the Frenchies see us and the shells scream in.

Fucking bloody 7.5s, twenty a fucking minute from each gun, multiplied by fuck knows how many of the blasted things.

Dive into a hole and land on my shoulder.

The pain is atrocious and I almost throw up.

More explosions.

Screams.

Hope no one near me needs help because I can't give it. The pain is so bad I can't move.

Lie staring at the sky for a few minutes.

Come on, Max – get out of here.

Crawl out on my hand and knees.

Leap up and run into the barrage.

Shattering crash. Flying—

Land on my back with a thump that knocks the air out of me.

Scarlet jet, right beside me. And another.

Shit.

The man's knee is smashed, his lower leg hanging half off.

Blood's spurting out.

"MEDICS!"

Not that anyone's likely to hear.

Take my belt off one-handed.

"Hold this end. HOLD THIS END!"

But he can't.

Grip the end in my teeth, get the belt round his thigh with my left hand.

Blood spurts into my face.

Fucking hell.

Pull tight. The bleeding slows.

I have just enough grip in my right hand to tie the belt. Not tight enough to stop him bleeding, but almost. The jets are reduced to a pulsing trickle.

Patch him up as best I can, grab his arm with my left hand and start to pull him up the hill.

He screams his head off.

How the fuck am I going to get him to the top?

Ten steps. My strength is starting to go.

He's still screaming.

"MEDICS!"

Fury of the barrage all around, screams and cries. There's no way they can hear me.

I want to run but I can't leave him.

Drag him screaming and screaming up the hill, a few steps at a time.

Shells slam in all around, smoke's so thick I can hardly breathe.

Can't think for the concussions, head reeling.

No strength left – not going to make it.

Mind goes back to the first wood—
Don't think about that – not the same—
"MEDICS!"
Someone turns.
Wave frantically.
The man runs down towards me.
You're a fucking hero.
Take an arm each and pull the fellow up the hill as fast as we can. Thank fuck he's stopped screaming.
Get him into a trench on the top.
Sag against the side of it, gasping for breath, shoulder and head throbbing.
Thought my head was fully healed. Hope it hasn't reopened.
Side of my head is wet.
Blood.
Prod the scar, but it doesn't hurt.
"Your face is a mess, sir," says the other man.
"His blood."
"Nice."
Shout together, "MEDICS!"
This time they hear us.
Hand the fellow over to them, heave myself to my feet.
Jesus, I'm fucked.
But we're through the barrage, and its intensity hides us from the Frenchies. Doubt they want to give us a smokescreen, but they're succeeding.
By the time we get back to Bezonvaux, it's broad fucking daylight and I'm dead on my feet.
Wash the blood off my face and fall into bed.
Sun through the windows, lie dozing.
God, I'm sore. Not just my shoulder but all over, as if I've been in the ring with Jack Johnson.
"Coming to lunch?" says a friendly voice.

Open my eyes, peer blearily.

It's Massow.

"What time is it?"

"Half past twelve."

And I am fucking starving. Better enjoy having hot food while I can.

That was quite a night – and I'm going to have to do it all again tonight.

That's a horrible thought.

Aue makes me halfway presentable, which takes quite a bit of doing. There are blood and mud stains on my uniform, and the usual vile filth.

Head for the Mess.

Hauptmann Steinhaus looks at me with concern. "Very well done last night, Schelling."

"Thank you, sir." *I do wish people would stop saying that. I only did what anyone would do.*

"I'd like you to see the MO."

Look at him in surprise.

"I feel fine, sir."

He smiles, the corners of his moustache lifting. "I'm sure you do. See him after lunch."

That's an order, however kindly it's said.

The MO also looks at me with concern. "Let's have a look at your shoulder."

"It's fine, Doctor."

He smiles too, and starts removing the dressing.

A couple of minutes later, he frowns, and takes my temperature.

"Hm. Touch of infection. This needs cleaning out again, and then you're to rest. I'll see you again in a couple of days."

"Er… What counts as rest?"

He smiles again. "No traipsing up to the front line. You can help organise the carrying parties but that's all."

There's no point arguing. If I do, he'll just put me on the train to Loison.

Having my shoulder cleaned out again is fucking horrible, and it's a struggle to retain my lunch. All I want to do afterwards is lie down.

*

And I never came up to the front line here again, Max thought as he neared the Ossuary.

Sad loss, that.

The Seventh was relieved that night, so they didn't need me anyway.

What was left of the Seventh, that is. The Frenchies shelled the crap out of the position just before the relief arrived.

Strecker was untouched, but the Almighty – or the Devil, whichever it was – called in the debt the following year on the Chemin des Dames.

Scheumann got hit in the stomach and made it as far as the field hospital, but died the next day. Hutten came out in one piece, and was promoted to Acting Officer.

Kropp was killed outright by a splinter which half decapitated him. Hard to imagine that eloquent eyebrow still and silent in death. At least it was quick.

Henke was lucky to get out with a broken ankle. Unfortunately for him, it healed well.

Only half my Platoon made it out uninjured, and of those, Stadler and Lorenz were the only men who'd been there on the first day.

After that, they pulled the Regiment out completely and we went to the camp where His Royal Highness came to see us.

We were in reserve, and of course we expected to be sent back in at any moment, so it was hardly restful.

Not that I could rest, anyway. My mind was full of the battle – we could hear it quite clearly, and the dead were before me every day and especially every night.

Finally, the Regiment went to a quiet sector and I got sent home, and then I was in the barracks until I'd regained full use of my right arm.

*

16th June 1916, Uckermark region, Brandenburg

Brandenburg is unbelievably lovely in the early summer, like a vision of Heaven.

Sit by the window of the train as it puffs northward. The land is green and softly rolling, the lakes sparkle in the sunlight.

Home. The most beautiful place in the world.

Home, that I'd lost hope of ever seeing again.

Home, for which I've bled and nearly died.

Home, for which I shall have to fight again, for which I shall give my life when the time comes.

That is in the future. For now, I have a few weeks of guaranteed life. As soon as I can, I'll go home to the villa by the lake and see my parents and my sisters.

And with a bit of luck, I'll see Frieda of the beautiful eyes and the lovely arse and the gently swaying skirt.

Mustn't let the opportunity go by this time… I want a naked Frieda in my bed before I go back to the fucking Front, because I won't be coming home again.

Get off the train, start down the hill towards the barracks.

A squad of recruits is going the other way, to the exercise ground. I see respect in their eyes and something close to – I'm not sure I want to know.

God knows what I must look like. I'm properly turned out

in a new uniform, but with my arm in a sling and that look in my face…

Maybe they're wondering what does that to a man.

They'll find out – some of them, anyway.

As I continue into town, people move aside for me. At first, I think they're being careful not to bump my sling, but then I notice that each one glances at my face and then quickly away, without meeting my eyes.

I'm making them uncomfortable.

Hope I don't make Frieda uncomfortable as well.

Here's the barracks, looking just as it did in '14, as if nothing's changed.

An absurdly young sentry presents arms, with the same slightly awed expression as the recruits.

I wish people wouldn't look at me like that. It makes me feel like some sort of exhibit.

This is where I came to volunteer, nearly two years ago. This is where I saw Friedrich for the last time – well, it isn't, but it was the last time I saw him as a living man. I'd rather forget what he looked like when they dug him up. This is where Axel and I were last year…

So many men left here never to return. And there's no end in sight.

Hauptmann Richter hobbles from behind his desk and greets me warmly.

"Hauptmann Gneist gave you a very favourable report," he says with a smile.

"Thank you, sir."

His face clouds. "It's good to see someone back," he adds quietly.

I can't speak. The dead are all around me.

Richter is silent as well.

We both stare at the floor, and I have the feeling he can't trust his voice either.

Finally he says, "Go to the hospital – Doctor Michalowski is expecting you."

"Thank you, sir."

The hospital is across the road from the barracks.

"Doctor Michalowski is on the first floor, sir – up the stairs and turn left."

"Thanks."

Climb the stairs and turn left.

A man in a wheelchair is being pushed towards me. He's bone-thin, his face pale and drawn, and he's wearing blue and white hospital uniform with a blanket over his knees.

He stares blankly along the corridor.

"You left me for dead, you bastards," he says. "You left me for dead."

"Quiet," says the orderly pushing his chair.

But he will not be quiet. His eyes look through me.

"You left me for dead, you bastards. You left me for dead. You left me for dead in the wood."

In the—?

Cold runs down my back.

"You left me for dead, you bastards."

How many men did we leave in the woods?

"Be quiet. Don't talk to Herr Leutnant like that."

His voice rises. "*You left me for dead in the wood, you bastards.*"

"*Be quiet, Degenhardt.*"

Degenhardt?

Shit. We thought he was dead or we'd have taken him with us.

"*You left me—*"

"BE QUIET!"

"It's all right," I say to the orderly. "He's right. We did."

Crouch beside Degenhardt's chair and take his hand in mine.

"Degenhardt, I…" *What in God's name can I say to him?* "I

am so sorry. We thought you were dead. If we'd had any idea you were still alive, we'd never have left you there."

His eyes stare, unfocussed. *"You left me for dead in the wood."*

"Degenhardt, it's Schelling."

It isn't me he's seeing. *"You left me for dead in the wood, you bastards."*

"It's no use, sir," says the orderly. "He just says that over and over. I'm taking him back to bed."

"Yes. Of course."

I release Degenhardt's hand and stand up, feeling more than a bit sick.

Wonder how long it was before he was picked up. I'd never have recognised him, he's so pale and thin.

And the poor bastard's mind has gone.

Shiver as I knock on the doctor's door.

*

That shook me up far worse than I wanted to admit, Max thought as he walked down from the Fort, *and I've never been able to forget it. Goldenbaum couldn't find any sign of life, he said, so Degenhardt must have been a long way down – but, shit, to think we left him lying there like that. No wonder he went mad.*

And my own peace of mind's gone, probably for ever. I'm nowhere near as bad as Degenhardt, but no one could call me sane.

I wonder if anyone who fought here is really sane, on either side.

He'd walked along unseeing, and gone straight past the Ossuary.

So much of me is still here, and always will be.

Where – oh. I've gone too far.

He turned and went back.

Prince whinnied softly as he approached.

"You've been a good companion," he said, stroking the soft nose. "Shame I shan't see you tomorrow, but it's time to go home."

Home. Where is home?

Brandenburg with Frieda and my sons, or here with the boys?

He still didn't have an answer by the time they'd arrived at the stables.

He handed Prince back with mutual reluctance.

Pity for such a fine horse to be stuck in a place like this. And with an owner he doesn't like.

Quite a trip it's been. I need a beer after all that – or something stronger.

He went into the first bar he saw, sat down, and ordered a large beer.

XXVI

Max sat staring into his glass, seeing the dead, and barely noticed the bar filling up as men finished work.

"May I join you?"

He looked up. A Frenchman about his own age was standing in front of him.

"The other tables are all full," the man added.

"Yes, of course."

The man got out a cigarette and tried to light it. The lighter sparked but didn't catch.

"Do you have a light?"

'May I ask for a light, sir?'

Axel smiles at the formality and lights both our cigarettes…

The man was staring at him.

"Do you have a light?" he repeated with some emphasis.

"Sorry – yes, of course."

Max reached into his pocket for his lighter.

Shit. I really don't want him to see it.

He tried to hide the lighter in his hand as he lit the Frenchman's cigarette.

"Thanks… May I see that?"

Shit.

"Yes, of course."

Max handed the lighter over reluctantly. It was made from a rifle cartridge case, and dated from his time as a sniper.

If there's one thing worse than an enemy soldier, it's an enemy sniper… *But those lighters are really popular – lots of soldiers have them.*

The man examined the lighter and handed it back.

"Very nicely made."

"Thanks."

Please don't ask…

There was a long pause, and then the man said, "I saw you in Vaux, in the village."

The hairs on Max's neck stood on end.

"When?" He tried to sound casual.

"A couple of days ago… And maybe before."

"Before?"

"In March '16. By the light of the fire."

Shit.

But if you'd really seen me then, we wouldn't be having this conversation. Unless you missed, of course.

There was a wary silence. Both were careful to avoid eye contact.

By the light of the fire… I stayed in the shadows as much as I could.

"You did well to recognise me," Max said.

The Frenchman smiled slightly, and met Max's eyes. "Magnification."

"Ah."

"You run fast," the man added, as if excusing himself for missing.

Just as well. "I did then. And no one manages a hundred per cent."

"Indeed."

So we both did the same filthy job, if not at the same time. And each of us knows exactly how the other thinks.

Wonder what else we have in common. A lot of dead friends, for a start.

"Where are you from?" Max asked.

"Toulouse. You?"

"Brandenburg." *And if there's one thing worse than a German, it's a Prussian...*

Another faint smile.

"So we are here for the same reason, I think," said the man. "Jacques."

"Max."

They shook hands with reserve on both sides, and their eyes met again briefly.

The future is in our hands, the woman said. We must stop being enemies, for our children's sakes.

"Do you have children?" Max asked.

"A daughter. You?"

"Two sons. I don't want them to have to fight."

"And I don't want my daughter to mourn."

The wariness eased a little.

It's too soon. Max saw the same thought in Jacques's eyes. *Maybe in a few years' time, when it's all less raw.*

Jacques finished his beer and stood up.

So many fine men, on both sides.

"Yes, there were," Jacques said, and there was a hint of warmth in his voice.

Oh – I must have said it out loud. What else do I say and not realise it?

"I have a train to catch," Jacques said. "It's been interesting meeting you."

"And you."

We're just the same really, Max thought as they shook hands in farewell. *God alone knows why we were supposed to kill each other.*

No one's ever been able to tell me why the war started. Everyone believed his country was under attack and rushed to defend it – but where is the truth?

Buried with the dead.

I wish I could call Frieda. We haven't been apart like this since I got home in December '18, and I miss her so much.

He sent another cable. 'Home tomorrow miss you x'.

So few words, and they don't say what I really want.

I want to lie in your arms and make love to you, feel our bodies meld until there is no end or beginning to either of us, and then hold you tight in that sweet afterglow...

The only times I feel safe and whole.

'You can go home to your wife,' said the voice in the room. 'Someone else is fucking mine.'

You know, I've really had enough of you, carping on at me every night. You can fuck off.

The window slammed shut, and he had to get up to open it again.

'Don't tell me to fuck off, you filthy Boche. This is my country. And we made you fuck off in the end. Except the ones we kept, of course.

'To arms, citizens, until the furrows run with our enemies' blood...'

Stop singing the fucking Marseillaise.

The voice laughed and carried on.

Max sat up, sweating. He was surrounded by the dead, and he kept seeing Degenhardt.

I'll be bloody glad to get out of this sodding room.

Still, it can't get much worse...

And there he was wrong.

'I know what you did,' said the voice.

Oh, yes? When, exactly?

'In the wood, your second night in.'

Max started, cold running down his back.

How the fu—

I do not want to think about that. Ever since, I've tried to put it out of my mind.

"They were nearly all ours," he said out loud. "And if you know what I did then you know why I did it. And I'll bet you did the same at some point."

'I'm a good Catholic,' said the voice. 'Not a murderer.'

"If you saw a horse like that, you'd shoot it. There was no hope for them."

*

23rd February 1916, Herbebois

The wood rings with screams and cries of agony – the results of two days of carnage, lying where they fell, in appalling pain in the freezing cold.

No one is going to take them back. Not tonight, not tomorrow.

The rule is merciless – first treat those who will fight again, then those who have a chance of living.

The hopeless cases don't get treated. And they won't even get taken back until all the men in the first categories have been collected.

These will lie here until they die in torment.

A rib cage split open, his heart and lungs visible.

A shattered spine, pieces of vertebrae studding the torn flesh.

Half a face gone and part of his skull with it.

My comrades, beyond all help.

Almost. There is still one thing I can do for them.

The wood is dark. No one is near me, and no one can see more than a few metres. If I were in that state, I hope someone would do the same for me.

Six men, five German and one French. As far as I can tell, that is.

Their suffering is over. I have to make peace with myself.

*

Ever since, I have wanted to forget, have tried not to ask myself whether what I did was right or wrong. Every time my pistol was in my hand, it reminded me.

I come back to what I thought then – that if I were dying in agony, then I hope someone would put an end to it.

The voice is right, though. It was murder.

And Degenhardt survived, even though he must have lain there for days. Would they have lived?

It was a pointless question, but it wouldn't leave him.

He got up, dressed and packed, then sat smoking and looking out of the window.

After an eternity, the dawn came up.

As he was about to leave the room, he said, "I'm not just any sort of filthy Boche. I'm Prussian – so stick that up your arse."

He left the voice to contemplate – but then it probably knew.

It knew about – the thing I try not to remember.

He had breakfast, paid his bill, and went to the station.

As he passed the stables, there was a loud whinny.

He turned.

A pair of familiar brown eyes looked at him from a long black face.

"Not today, Prince."

He turned away.

Prince neighed loudly.

And again.

Max kept walking towards the station.

Loud neighing and stamping of hooves.

"Steady, boy!" shouted the stable owner.

Prince ignored him, reared up and slammed both front hooves into the ground, and neighed again.

Max turned round.

Prince looked at him and whinnied, softly but insistently.

Bugger me. Suppose I'd better say goodbye properly.

Prince calmed down as soon as Max approached him.

"Sorry, boy – no carrots today. No ride up to the old battlefield either. I have to go home."

And of course you don't understand a single word.

He stroked the long face and the soft nose.

Prince nuzzled Max's neck and snorted softly.

"You do tickle, you really do."

Max started to walk away, and Prince stamped and neighed again.

You couldn't say 'come back' more clearly if you could speak.

He stopped.

What you're really saying is 'don't leave me here'.

When I had that funny turn, you helped me get back to reality...

He turned back, put his bag down beside Prince and went to the stable owner's office.

"How much?" he asked.

"How many days more?"

"No – to buy him."

There was a sudden gleam in the stable owner's eye, and Max saw it before the man managed to hide it.

You don't want him, do you? He's quite a handful, not the sort of quiet beast you need.

The stable owner named a price.

Max offered him half.

The man refused.

Max made to leave.

"All right."

Bloody hell – you really don't want him. What were you planning to do with him, then?

That doesn't bear thinking about.

Max handed over the money, and the man untied Prince and gave Max the rope.

"Come on, boy. Let's go home."

I don't need a halter, Max thought as Prince walked beside him to the station, the rope slack in his hand. *You'd just follow me.*

Wonder what Frieda will say when I turn up with a horse.

"You can live in the barracks stables in Potsdam," he said. "You'll like it there – be just like old times for you. You'll just have to learn – our anthem instead of the 'Marseillaise.'"

'Our anthem' – Max had almost said 'Hail to Thee in the Victor's Laurels', but remembered just in time that the Kaiser had abdicated.

You'd think I'd be used to that by now. Will I ever be used to it, to the Prussia I fought for being rather different now?

Prince followed Max into the guard's van without hesitation.

"It really is 'whither thou goest I will go', isn't it?"

"Where will you be sitting, sir, in case there's a problem?" asked the guard.

"Right here."

The guard looked surprised for a moment, then smiled.

"He's beautiful," he said.

"Yes. I think so too."

They had to change trains twice, and each time Prince followed Max quietly, even through the hubbub of Berlin.

I wonder how much you know, how much you understand. Horses aren't stupid. You knew that man didn't like you, and you know I do. And you probably feel safe with me.

Nearly home… it does feel strange, going south-west from Berlin rather than north.

But home is wherever the lovely Frieda is. It could be a shack, or a caravan, or an igloo. It wouldn't matter.

He smiled to himself. *Quite a girl, my Frieda.*

*

16th June 1916, Uckermark, Brandenburg

Doctor Michalowski gives me two weeks' leave, bless him.

"Come back after that – I'll have a better idea how much muscle damage there is once the wound's fully healed."

"Thank you, Doctor."

I'll be glad to see my family again, but there's one thing – or rather one girl – on my mind.

As soon as is decent, I escape and call on her.

She's in the garden, her hair glowing reddish-brown in the summer sun, her skirt draped softly over that lovely arse.

I stop and look at her. And look.

I'd lost all hope of ever seeing you again. And you're even lovelier than I remembered.

It's like being reborn.

"Hello, Frieda."

She turns, and those beautiful eyes rest on my face, and she smiles.

"Max – what a lovely surprise!"

Then she notices the sling.

Her eyes fill with concern. "You're hurt."

"Just playing for sympathy!"

She laughs.

I am going to get your knickers off if it's the last thing I do...

But she won't drop them.

Days pass. She'll walk hand in hand with me, kiss me until my blood is on fire, but that's it.

Put my hand on that shapely round arse.

She takes hold of my hand, and puts it on her waist.

She does the same when I touch her breast, but not before I feel her nipple harden.

"Frieda – don't you want me?"

She looks at me.

"I'll be going back soon, and—" I don't want to say it out loud.

"Yes, I know…"

She leads me to the sofa, sits beside me, our hands linked.

"Max, I do want you, more than anything – but not until we're married."

Shit. What the fuck is the chance of my living that long?

And so on it goes. Her knickers stay in place.

"We're running out of time," I say.

"I want a husband and children."

Children? Whatever for? Why create more life to suffer?

"You'll have plenty of time after the war."

She shakes her head. "This is my only chance."

"Boll— nonsense." *Not in the field now, Max…*

"There won't be enough men to go round – and no one will want me if I'm second-hand goods."

I hadn't thought of that. I'd thought only that she has an 'after the war' and I don't…

My shoulder has healed. Dr Michalowski is happy with it, but I have a lot of work to do to regain the strength in my right arm.

And while I'm doing that, there are recruits to train.

Every time I look at them, I think of what's waiting for them, and that most of them won't last six months – or six weeks if they get sent to Verdun or the Somme.

That's too depressing for words. Try not to think about the war, because I'm so fucking haunted…

What I'd give for a proper night's sleep.

My arm is improving. I'll be fit for the Front soon, and Frieda still won't drop them, no matter how hard I try.

Maybe I should give up – but the more I see of her, the more

I realise that no other woman will do for me. I pick girls up in town, but it's meaningless physical contact and no more.

Walk into the park opposite the barracks, thinking of those beautiful eyes – and suddenly, without warning, *I actually feel happy.*

Stop dead. I'd forgotten what that's like.

Since Verdun, I've been cold inside, so fucking cold. I believed I would never feel anything again – but the thought of her brings a scrap of warmth and a gleam of light into the frozen darkness.

And if we could go to bed, how much better might I feel…? Maybe I should propose – but marriage. That's a big step. I don't know.

'I should have married her,' Scheumann said, just as if he were still alive.

But it was far too late. I wonder if he thought of her when he was dying…

I don't want to die with regret in my heart.

So, one fine August evening, I take Frieda's hand and kneel before her.

"Frieda, my darling… would you do me the honour of becoming my wife?"

Her face lights with joy.

Have I done that? Made her so happy?

She leans down, throws her arms round me, kisses me. "YES. Of course I will."

The surge of emotion takes me by surprise. *Frieda is going to be my wife.*

Get up and sit beside her, hold her, feel her arms around me, kiss her, gaze into those lovely eyes. I never thought I could feel like this.

Frieda is going to be my wife.

Do I tell her about the nightmares?

Don't be stupid, Max. Just marry her. She won't have to worry about those for long.

*

That wasn't the end of the matter, Max thought. *Her father wasn't best pleased, to put it mildly. The list of my deficiencies was a long one, starting at the beginning of my life and continuing on to just about everything I'd done.*

I was mere Leutnant Schelling, not good enough for Fräulein von Erhart. My mother was born Elise von Sternhagen, but of course that didn't count. And I was a war volunteer and not a career officer, so had no real prospect of promotion.

Max laughed to himself. *Given the rate officers were being killed, my prospects of survival were fuck all, never mind promotion – and you'd have thought the old bugger would have realised that, being as he was in the War Office.*

Or maybe he did realise it, because yet another objection was that he didn't want his daughter widowed before twenty-five.

*

20th August 1916, Uckermark, Brandenburg

"So I told him what I said to you," Frieda says, "that this is my only chance."

"And what did he say to that?"

She laughs. "That someone as beautiful as me will have no difficulty finding a suitable husband after the war."

"'Suitable' meaning with a 'von.'"

"And preferably a title as well. Apparently there are plenty of candidates on the Staff or in the War Office – as if I'd want a man like that, with water in his veins."

"Some of them have good reason to be there," I say, without conviction. *Bloody Staff.*

"That doesn't mean I'd want to marry them."

"Frieda – he has a point, you know. I'll be going back soon and—"

She lays a finger on my lips. "Let's not talk about that. I've made up my mind."

And when you've made up your mind, my love, there's no budging you – as I'm finding out.

"So will he give his blessing?"

She sighs. "He's cross that you proposed to me without asking him first. I told him that it's 1916 not 1816, and that it's my life."

Good for you. "And how did he take that?"

"Not very well. Said he had a good mind to cut me off without a penny."

"Do you believe him?"

"I don't know…"

"Do you care?" I ask cautiously.

"No. Not at all." But there's a shadow in her eyes.

"Are you sure?"

"Why do you ask?"

"Because something's bothering you," I say quietly.

She hesitates.

"Come on. Spit it out."

She looks very awkward.

Stroke her cheek. "Frieda, darling, we have to be honest with each other. Whatever it is, just tell me."

"You won't like it."

"I won't bite either. Come on."

"He said… he said the war's done things to you."

Ah. "What does he expect?"

"That's what I said. That you can't expect a man to fight and see men killed and not be affected by it, and there'd be something wrong with you if you weren't."

You've got a point there, my love. I hadn't thought of it like that.

"And I pointed out that it's a bit rich to call a man a hero because he's fought and bled for us, and then say he can't have the girl he wants."

"And what did he say to that?!"

"Nothing. What could he say?"

Direct hit, Frieda. Well done.

*

And that was just the first time I learned what Frieda is, Max thought. *A tough little thing who does what she puts her mind to, and won't let anything or anyone stop her.*

If she'd been a bloke, I'd have been more than happy to have her – him – in my Platoon. But then if she'd been a bloke I wouldn't have fallen for her – him.

You're rambling, Max.

Her father refused to give us his blessing, and we didn't know whether her parents would come to the wedding or not. We made all the arrangements without them, and then at the last minute he realised that he couldn't stop her, that he risked losing her completely, and he gave in.

I have never felt so proud as I did when we walked into our village church, Frieda's hand on my arm. The best, the finest girl of all was going to the altar with me, to tell the world she loved me.

And that night, she undressed in front of me, so beautiful that I could hardly breathe... All I wanted was to please her and to make her happy.

For the first time in my life, I understood that 'making love' means exactly that.

God alone knows what I had done to deserve such a reprieve.

XXVII

Max looked out of the window.

"Nearly there, Prince – and then you can meet Frieda and my sons."

Ah – Frieda, Frieda.

Frieda, who made life worth living again, who made me glad I'd survived Verdun instead of feeling I should be lying there with the boys.

Frieda, who saved my life at the Somme, though she doesn't know it.

The Tommies had broken in on our right rear after our neighbours pulled back, and we counterattacked to retake the lost ground and throw the buggers back to their own lines. And we did it. We got them properly on the run and chased them into No Man's Land.

*

24th October 1916, Somme

Massive detonation, fire, smoke, flying—
    Wet earth against my face.
    Quite soft and comfortable. Could go back to sleep.
    What's that noise? Like New Year's fireworks a long way off.
    Ground keeps shaking.
    Sinking. Can't breathe—

Push myself up out of the mud, gasping for air.

Fireworks are a lot louder. They must have got closer… Strange.

Cold. Wet.

How the fuck did I get here?

I'm in a shell-hole almost full of water. Must get out or I'll drown.

And the water's fucking cold. I'm shivering.

Start to crawl up the side.

Vicious stab of pain from my right leg. Hear myself yell.

Lean against the side of the hole, trying not to be sick.

Look reluctantly at my leg. Not sure I want to see it…

My trousers are wet with blood as well as muddy water, and my thigh looks all wrong.

Shit.

There's no one else alive in the hole. I'm alone.

I'll have to get myself back, but the Tommies sound rather pissed off with us.

Raise my head cautiously above the rim, lower it very quickly.

The air is full of singing metal. I'll have to wait until dark – and then hope I go the right way.

Come on, Max – get your arse into gear. Patch yourself up before you lose any more blood, and see if there's something you can use as a splint.

And try to keep your leg out of the filthy water.

There's a broken rifle not far away – that will do. Just need to reach it—

Fuck me, that hurt.

Lie still for a few minutes.

Get on with it.

Rip my trouser leg open. My thigh has a deep cut in the outside, and it's bent halfway along. The bone must be in two pieces.

At least it's not sticking out.

Never did want to see my own bones. Don't like seeing other men's, either – a fellow's bones should stay decently covered.

Get a field dressing out of my pocket.

Pause.

The splinter's still in there. This is going to fucking hurt.

It takes me three attempts, because the pain is atrocious and I daren't faint and fall into the water.

Finally the job is done, and I lie against the side of the hole, trying not to throw up. After a while, the pain diminishes to bearable.

Have a swig out of my hip flask – medicinal, of course.

Time creeps past. The fireworks continue, good and loud now.

Wonder where I am.

If the Tommies attack, I've had it.

I probably have, anyway. I'll have to crawl back…

Hope I've got the strength.

I really don't feel too good. The pain's getting worse and I feel sick and dizzy.

Jesus, I'm cold.

Curl up, wrap my arms round myself, shivering. Wish I had a coat, or a blanket.

God, how long can a day last? Why isn't it getting dark yet?

Why am I getting even wetter?

It's raining. Fine, soaking rain. As if I weren't wet and cold enough already.

Jesus, my leg hurts – but the light's a lot dimmer. I must have been asleep.

Reach for my hip flask.

No, don't. You have to stay awake, Max. Watch the shells going overhead or something.

Or prod your leg.

Don't even want to think about doing that.

Hope the light's dimmer because the sun's going down and not—

Don't think like that. You're still breathing, aren't you?

Finally it gets dark.

At last… But which way do I go?

Fish my compass out of my pocket.

The needle swings and swings, distracted by all the metal lying about.

Roughly east will do.

Start to crawl out of the hole.

Catch my foot.

Scream.

World spins black.

Try again.

Same thing.

And again. Throw up.

I'm not going to make it – I can't even get out of this fucking hole.

Get my breath back. Try again, harder.

Out of the hole – but in front of me are more and more of the fucking things.

Get onto my hands and left knee.

Left hand sinks into something slimy, stinking – don't want to look.

Just like fucking Verdun – keep going, Max. Don't think. Not about that place.

Crawl round the next hole, teeth gritted.

Catch my foot again.

Yell, but no one will hear me over all the others and the endless barrage.

Another few metres. Repeat.

Jesus, this is fucking horrible.

Throw up again.

Lie still for a few minutes.

There's a Tommy helmet, with a skull staring at me.

I'll be the same if I stay here.

Get up, crawl halfway round the next hole, collapse in agony.

It's too far. I can't do it.

If only there were someone to help me.

Degenhardt. I left Degenhardt in the wood, and now they've left me...

I'm going to die here.

Frieda. Oh, Frieda.

Your father was right – you're going to be a widow and you're only twenty.

See her lovely face in front of me, her beautiful eyes.

Ah, Frieda. How I love you, my darling...

Then get your fucking arse into gear, Max, and get back to her.

Just a few metres, then rest. And then do it again, and again, until you're there.

Crawl towards Frieda.

She smiles at me and moves away.

Follow.

"Frieda, wait!"

She moves away again.

"Wait for me!"

But she doesn't. She backs away, gazing at me with those lovely eyes, luminous in the dark.

The night is wearing on. I've crawled halfway to fucking China and I haven't reached our lines. My love is still in front of me, but I'm exhausted and I'll never reach her.

The pain is appalling. I can't move any further.

'Come on, Max,' Axel says.

'Keep going,' says Friedrich.

They take an arm each and pull me towards her.

She smiles.

'She's carrying your son,' says Axel.

'You have to live, for them,' Friedrich says. '*Move it. Move your fucking arse, you lazy bastard!*'

Not lazy—

'You fucking well act it. MOVE.'

Another few metres. Repeat… Repeat… Over and over… Endlessly…

Here's the wire. Hope it's German.

God, there's no way through.

Shit.

I'm done.

You heard what Friedrich said. You have to live.

Grab hold of a screw picket, shake it. The tins on the wire jingle faintly.

For fuck's sake, Max, no one's going to hear that.

Shake good and hard with what's left of my strength.

The tins jangle.

Voices.

"Who goes there?"

"German… Don't shoot…"

"Password!"

"Help me, please – Leutnant Schelling – leg—"

"We're coming, sir!" shouts someone. "Bring a tent quarter!"

Two shapes come through the wire.

"Where is he?"

"Here…"

"Where are you, sir?"

Can't speak. I am so fucking exhausted…

"There he is!"

Sinking…

"Stay awake, sir."

Someone is shaking me.

I want to sleep. Just sleep and sleep—

'Stay awake, Max,' Axel says.

Someone shakes me again, slaps my face. Strong arms lift me, hear myself scream as they move my leg.

Wide awake now.

"Here, drink this, sir."

A water bottle.

A slug of schnapps.

"Thanks…"

The man squeezes my hand. "You'll be fine now, sir."

Axel and Friedrich are standing next to him. 'You'll be fine now,' they echo.

Swaying in the tent quarter. Frieda smiles at me, her eyes full of love…

*

The surgeon told me later that it had been touch and go, Max thought. *First, whether I would survive, and second, whether I would keep my leg.*

"Amazing what men can do when they're determined to live," *he said.*

It would have sounded soppy to say that I was thinking of my wife – and I couldn't possibly talk about Axel and Friedrich.

And that was the really strange thing. I'd been in the base hospital for a month or so when I got that letter. It was the best Christmas present I've ever had.

*

22nd December 1916, German military hospital, Cambrai

Orderly brings the post round.

"Here you are, sir." Hands me a letter.

From Frieda. Always lovely to hear from my darling.
Open it and start reading…

"Oh!" I exclaim before I can stop myself.

Leutnant Wilke, in the next bed, looks at me sharply.

A huge, stupid grin is spreading across my face.

"Good news?" he asks.

"Yes. My wife's expecting."

"Congratulations!"

The orderly has turned round. "Good news, sir?"

"Yes. *My wife's expecting.*" Say it loud enough for half the ward to hear.

Chorus of "Congratulations!"

Doctor Zimmermann smiles and shakes my hand.

In the evening, he brings a bottle of brandy and splashes it into tin mugs for us all.

"Wet the baby's head," he says. "What are you going to call him or her?"

"We haven't decided yet."

Him. It's a boy. Axel said so.

*

And it was, Max thought. *I've never told anyone about that. It's just too strange.*

That was the end of my fighting, and I wasn't sorry. My leg took months to heal, and I was left with a pronounced limp and could only walk with a stick. Even with the shortage of officers, I was rated fit for garrison duties only.

I didn't want to stay in the barracks, though – not while the boys were up to their eyeballs in the crap. And my lovely Frieda understood, bless her.

Oberst Jagenow got me a post on the Divisional Staff – not where I'd ever wanted to be, but it proved very interesting indeed…

The train was slowing down.

Potsdam.

"Here we are, boy. Home. You'd better come and meet the family first."

He swung himself onto Prince's broad back, the halter rope loosely in his hand.

I never thought I'd be coming home on horseback. Have to get you some decent tack.

Haven't ridden bareback since I was a kid, out in the country.

"Here we are," he said again, as they reached his house.

He dismounted and opened the garden gate, the shadows already lengthening.

Prince followed him to the front door.

Frieda opened it.

"MAX!"

She flung herself into her husband's arms. Her face tilted up and his down, and their lips met softly and lingered.

I could take you straight upstairs, he thought, squeezing her tight against him.

Oh, I love it when you squeeze me, she thought. *Especially when we've got nothing on…*

She stepped back, looked at Prince and then at Max, and raised an eyebrow.

Kropp, and his eyebrow that spoke when he didn't.

Frieda saw the sudden shadow in Max's eyes.

I wish I knew what does that to you, she thought.

"And who is this?" she asked.

"This, my love, is Prince. I'll tell you the full—"

"PAPA! PAPA!"

The boys came running out of the house, and stopped dead when they saw the horse.

"Wow!" said Ernst.

"A horse!" said Peter.

Prince bent his huge head down and blew gently over the boys, and then pushed his muzzle into Frieda's neck.

She laughed. "Your whiskers tickle!"

"I keep telling him that... I'll tell you all about him over dinner."

"Where's he going to live?" asked Frieda.

"In the barracks stables. I'm sure they'll find a space for him." *Now that we barely have an Army...*

"I'd better take him straight there. He'll be hungry – we didn't get much to eat on the journey."

How on earth am I going to explain to him that I'm not abandoning him there?

Prince followed him to the barracks, his nose over Max's shoulder.

"Who have we here, sir?" asked Sergeant Jeismann.

"This is Prince. Or Prinz, if you prefer."

"Well named. Beautiful animal." He ran an appreciative hand over Prince's neck.

"He was a French colonel's horse," Max said.

"Booty of war, then, sir?"

"Not quite – I did pay for him! Can he stay here?"

"Of course, sir – be a pleasure. There's plenty of space. We can sort out the charge tomorrow."

"I'll come by later, make sure he's settling in." Max stroked Prince's face. "This is your new home. I'll come and see you every day, and we'll go out for a run."

The horse whinnied softly as Max walked away.

"Come on, boy," said Jeismann. "I've got oats for you, and hay, and you can meet your new friends..."

Prince stamped a hoof and neighed.

Oh bugger, thought Max, turning round. *He's not going to let me go.*

The sound of shouted orders came from the parade ground.

Prince turned an ear to listen, and then his head.

The band began to play. The horse snorted and shook his head, and then gave Jeismann a long look of inspection.

His ears went forward, and he went quietly with Jeismann into the stables.

You're back in the Army and you're at home, Max thought. *I wish I could be.*

But I have Frieda, with the beautiful eyes and the lovely arse, and her skirt still swings so captivatingly when she walks. I shall love her until I die, and maybe even after.

And our two boys. My sons.

"So how do you come to have a horse?" she asked over dinner.

"I hired him to get to the battlefield and back – it's some way north of the town – and got rather fond of him."

She smiled. "You mean you got rather fond of each other."

He smiled back. "That's about the size of it."

"Can I ride him?" asked Peter.

"He's a bit big for you, but you can sit on him and I'll lead him round."

"And me! And me!" said Ernst.

"Of course."

"Will he be gentle enough?" asked Frieda.

"Yes. Let's all go and see him after dinner, see how he's settling in."

Prince reserved his affection for Max, but greeted the others kindly.

You understand, Max thought, *that these are my 'mare' and my 'foals'.*

"How's he settling in?" he asked Jeismann.

"Oh, fine, sir. Just fine."

On the way home, Frieda linked her arm through his, and the boys ran on ahead.

"So how was it really, my love?" she asked quietly.

He sighed.

"I wish I could say… I'll tell you what I can over the next few days…"

"I do realise you can't talk about it," she said. "And even if you could, I wouldn't be able to picture it."

You don't want to…

The boys had to be persuaded to go to bed.

"You can have an extra story each," Max said, "but only if we go up now."

"Can we have a story about horses?" asked Peter.

"Of course. Come on."

He read them their stories, kissed them good night, and went back downstairs.

Frieda was reading, and she looked up as he entered the living room, her eyes full of love.

She laid her book down and got up, and was in his arms in a second.

I love your strong arms around me, she thought, *and your soft lips against mine, and oh, your touch, and when we make love it's—*

"There's just one thing wrong," she said, with that light in her eyes that he knew so well.

"And what's that, my love?"

"We've got too many clothes on!"

"Well, we know what to do about that!"

He followed her upstairs, watching her hips sway.

That is a lovely arse…

Some time later, he said quietly, "You have no idea how I longed for you when I was away in the war."

"Even before we were married?"

"Oh, yes. I always wanted you, from the first moment I saw you. Love took a little longer, though."

She giggled softly. "So it was pure lust at first!"

"Oh, yes. Your eyes, and that lovely arse of yours, and the way your skirt swings. I used to think about you a lot."

"So when did you fall in love with me?"

"Summer '16, when I was in the barracks after Verdun. You remember, we started going out."

"And you wanted me to go to bed with you."

"But you wouldn't drop your knickers until we were married."

"And then you were passed fit, and they were about to send you to the Somme, and I didn't think you'd come back."

"And you *still* wouldn't drop them!"

"Until our wedding night."

"Mmm. Quite a night that was… and it's got better and better."

His hands moved slowly along her body, and her lips met his again.

"I suppose," he said in the morning, "I'd better get out of bed and go to work."

Her arms tightened round him.

"You can't get out of bed without giving me another kiss," she murmured.

"Top lips or lower ones?"

The bedroom door burst open and the boys ran in.

"You can answer that later," he said.

"Can we go and see Prince?" Peter asked.

"Can we? Can we?" Ernst leapt onto the bed.

Max laughed. "Yes, all right! Frieda, do we have any carrots?"

"I expect so."

The boys ran ahead into the stable yard.

"Prince! Prince!"

A long black face, a familiar whinny, a pair of liquid brown eyes. Whiskers tickling his neck.

I'm glad I brought you home.

Frieda saw the mutual affection.

I'm glad you bought him, she thought. *He might help you get better.*

"He's been as good as gold, sir," Jeismann said. "No trouble at all."

"I'll go for a ride at lunchtime," said Max.

"You could ride first thing in the mornings," said Frieda.

He looked at her and raised his eyebrows, and she blushed.

There are better things to do then, he didn't need to say.

When he got to the office, Horstmann and Kurowski looked at him enquiringly.

"How was your trip?" asked Horstmann.

Max hesitated.

"Interesting," he said after a while.

The other two looked at each other. Kurowski opened his mouth.

Oberst Geissler walked in, and they stood up.

"Good morning, sir."

"Good morning, gentlemen. Schelling, I'll be very interested in your comments on Fort Vaux, and on the rest of it as well, of course."

"I'll give you my report on the Fort in a couple of hours, sir – just want to read it through once more."

"Of course… What's this about you walking around with a horse following you, like a dog?"

"A friend I made on my trip, sir. It seemed wrong to leave him behind."

"Indeed?"

"He's in the barracks stables, sir. His name's Prince and he used to belong to a French colonel."

"Well, maybe we should have a look at him at lunchtime."

"I did plan to ride then, sir."

"Splendid. You fellows coming?"

"Definitely, sir," said Horstmann.

"Count me in too, sir," said Kurowski.

"Well, carry on."

"Sir."

The door closed behind him. Horstmann and Kurowski looked at Max.

He shrugged. "It's just as I said. I hired him to get about on, and – well, he – you'll see."

The other two looked at each other again, but said nothing.

Max took the report in to Geissler just before lunch.

"Thank you, Schelling – were there many errors?"

"Enough to make the trip worthwhile, sir."

"Good…" Geissler paused, as if wondering whether to say the next words. "Would you – I realise you might not want to do this, so it's a request and please feel free to refuse – but would you be prepared to write a personal account of your involvement in the battle? Those accounts are so valuable, really bring the fighting alive for the readers."

Do they want it brought alive? I suppose they must.

"Take some time to think about it." Geissler looked at his watch. "Shall we go and see this horse of yours?"

Max smiled. "Yes, sir."

"So what did your lovely wife say when you arrived home with a horse?" Horstmann asked on the way to the stables.

"Oh, you know Frieda – nothing ever worries her."

"No, nor Susanne."

"Stop being so bloody smug, you two," said Kurowski. "I'm staying a happy bachelor!"

Prince whinnied when he saw Max, and nudged his neck.

"You're a bloody fine judge of horseflesh, Schelling," said Geissler, running a hand over Prince's neck and shoulders. "Splendid animal. Wouldn't consider selling him, I suppose?"

"No, sir."

"No, of course not. Well, off you go. Don't let me hold you up."

"He is bloody lovely," Horstmann said in the afternoon.

"Bet he goes well," said Kurowski.

"Yes, he does."

They looked at Max and then at each other.

Max left the room a while later.

"Curious," said Kurowski.

"Doubt we'll hear the full story," said Horstmann. "But then it's not our business."